THE

VIEW

FROM

HALF DOME

A NOVEL

JILL CAUGHERTY

Black Rose Writing | Texas

The author grants the final approval for this literary material.

First printing

This is a work of fiction. Names, characters, businesses, places, events, and incidents are either the products of the author's imagination or used in a fictitious manner. Any resemblance to actual persons, living or dead, or actual events is purely coincidental.

ISBN: 978-1-68513-180-7
PUBLISHED BY BLACK ROSE WRITING
www.blackrosewriting.com

Printed in the United States of America
Suggested Retail Price (SRP) $21.95

The View from Half Dome is printed in Book Antiqua

*As a planet-friendly publisher, Black Rose Writing does its best to eliminate unnecessary waste to reduce paper usage and energy costs, while never compromising the reading experience. As a result, the final word count vs. page count may not meet common expectations.

Praise for
THE VIEW FROM HALF DOME

"Well-developed characters, careful attention to
historical detail, a gorgeous setting and
a story that will stay with you. 5 Stars!"
–Gail Ward Olmsted, author of *Miranda Writes*

"A touching coming of age tale set against the
towering beauty of Yosemite National Park,
where a young woman's dreams reach as high
as its tallest peaks."
–Jean Roberts, author of *The Frowning Madonna*

"Open this book to enjoy the scenes in Yosemite, and stay for
well-drawn characters that include the park's first female
ranger-naturalist, Enid Michael. Highly recommended."
–Linda Ulleseit, author of *Under the Almond Trees*

"Isabel will steal your heart with her hopeful spirit."
–Kerry Chaput, author of *Daughter of the King*

"Historical fiction at its very best: a wonderful story that
immerses the reader in a distant era. Readers of Sue Monk
Kidd and Kim Michele Richardson will enjoy
Caugherty's deeply touching story."
–David Rabin, author of *In Danger of Judgment*

"The breezy, conversational prose is engaging, capturing the
despair of the Depression and the frustration of women
struggling for equality. Isabel is a sturdy, compelling
protagonist, but it's quirky Enid who will linger in readers'
minds. A gentle, poignant tale with nicely developed real and
fictional characters." **–*Kirkus Reviews***

For Lara, who always blazes her own path.

THE

VIEW

FROM

HALF DOME

"Everybody needs beauty as well as bread, places to play in and pray in, where nature may heal and give strength to body and soul."
–John Muir

CHAPTER ONE

May 1934

When the trolley bell clanged, Isabel nudged her younger sister and stepped after her into the street. A foot away, a man in a fedora slouched beneath the awning of the dry goods store, blowing smoke rings. His eyes roved over Isabel in a leer. She seized Audrey's hand and whirled down the sidewalk. Wind gusted through her cardigan.

"Izzie, we're going too fast!"

Isabel gave her sister's palm an encouraging squeeze. Because of the rumored gangs and muggings at knifepoint, she didn't linger on her way home, but she didn't want to frighten Audrey. When Mother first described their new place, Isabel had thought it would be near Union Square and the elegant department stores, but it was actually on the fringes of the Tenderloin, a neighborhood of bars, flophouses, brothels, and gambling lofts.

She slowed when they reached the horizon of gray and clay-white row houses, partitioned into low-rent apartments. They edged around a group of children playing marbles and scrambled up the stairs to their stoop. Fog had blanketed her high school by the wharf, but here the sky wasn't hazy enough to conceal the building's blemishes, including the sagging roof and dented door.

From the neighboring stoop, a boy jeered, "Hurry-scurry. Bet you're scared you'll catch a whupping."

Isabel ignored him and turned the key in the lock. The trip home took over forty-five minutes, but at least they could remain in their old schools.

"Do your homework," she said to Audrey, searching the cupboard for something to fry with the chicken gizzards Mother had brought from the hotel.

"Aw. You're not doing yours."

"I have to make supper before Mother comes home."

Audrey leaped over a box of Dad's books they didn't have the space to unpack. The flat was dim and compact—a one-bedroom ground-level unit with kitchenette and mildewed privy. The tiny parlor had a water-stained ceiling and a sofa that had doubled as a bed for their older brother, James, until he quit the docks and joined the CCC at Yosemite.

Arms raised high above her head, Audrey twirled across the floor. Impulsively, Isabel caught her waist and tickled her ribs.

"Stop," her sister said, giggling.

"Little scamp! Start your homework."

Audrey made a face but removed a notebook from her satchel.

Isabel found a partly moldy onion, sliced away the black parts, and dumped it into a pan with the gizzards. As she stirred, her elbow bumped against the icebox. Swiveling, she banged her hip on the counter and swore under her breath. She had a sudden, sharp longing to be outdoors, in fresh air—anywhere but here. James, at least, had the luck of working in a beautiful park. When she shoved up the window over the sink, the stench of rotted food drifted in from the alley. The front window overlooking Turk wouldn't budge. Down the street, a horn blared, and tires skidded.

The doorknob rattled, and Mother shuffled inside and removed her overcoat. She still looked small and unfamiliar in her black and white maid uniform. Dad's brogans, which she stuffed with cotton balls and newspaper, swallowed her feet. In the last few months, her face had grown waxy and angular. Strands of once-shiny dark hair slithered from her bun, and creases cut across her cheeks, spiraling toward her chin.

Audrey flew to her, and Mother cupped her head. Then, shaking her loose, she let out a long sigh.

"Are you all right?" Isabel said. Maybe her boss at the Sir Francis Drake had dressed her down, as he had last week, when he'd accused her of leaving a room untidy, though she'd sworn she had cleaned until it sparkled, insisting she'd never do a half-assed job.

She yanked off Dad's shoes and flopped into a chair. "It's my head again. And back. Sore as the devil. Must be getting old."

"You're not old. Just tired."

"I'm the other side of young. Everything goes downhill after forty. Aches and pains are just the beginning." Her eyes sharpened to a flinty gray as she extended her swollen legs. From the adjoining flat, a baby bawled, and a man barked at someone to make the noise stop.

Isabel imitated Mother's soothing tone from years ago. "Anyone would be sore after cleaning nine hours straight."

Audrey hovered by her side, feet tapping. "Milly asked if I can go to her house tomorrow after school. Can I, Mother, please?"

"We'll see. Stop waltzing around. I've got a splitting head." She pressed her fingers to her temples. "Staff scurried around like rats today for some Hollywood bigwig."

"Who was it?" Isabel asked.

Audrey mimed a rapid series of tap moves. "Did you get to see, Mother? Were there reporters?"

"I told you to stop that and sit down." An exasperated cluck. "Rumor was he's Myrna Loy's agent. Didn't see hide nor hair of him. He held court in his suite, demanding one thing after

3

another." The corners of her mouth turned down. "Whiskey, ice, towels. Then for supper, hors d'oeuvres, prime rib, creamed potatoes, crème brulée, the works. That's how the highfalutin eat."

Isabel carried the fried gizzards, beans, and a handful of week-old rolls to the table. Steam rose from the platter as she spooned stew onto each plate.

Mother said, "Any mail?"

"Only bills," Isabel told her. They all hoped for news from James. After arriving at the CCC Cascades camp last month, he had sent them a note and twenty-five dollars. Last spring, when he turned eighteen, he had joined Dad on the docks as a longshoreman. Mother had pleaded with him to find something safer and steadier. A year later, he finally had.

As they finished eating, a faint scuttling sounded from behind the wall.

"What in blazes?" Mother began. The scuttling stopped, then resumed, a low-pitched scratching. "Oh sweet Jesus, don't tell me we have mice." She rose and pressed her ear against the wall, and the scuttling moved a foot away, as though miniature feet had scampered ahead on a journey. "Blast! This place is a pigsty. We'll have to clean every last inch." Storming to the counter, she slid out drawers, flung open cupboards.

A shiver ran down Isabel's arms and legs. She watched dumbly as Mother hurled silverware to the floor, dragged down canisters of flour and sugar, pitched cans. Audrey remained frozen at the table, her jaw hanging open.

Mother pinned Isabel with a glare. "Don't just stand there. Give me a hand."

Instinct warned Isabel not to speak. She dampened a dishrag and stood on tiptoes to wipe inside the cupboards.

Mother grabbed the broom and jabbed it against the floor. "Look at those crumbs. That's what's tempting them."

Isabel stopped wiping and followed Mother's gaze. She wondered whether the crumbs were from the rolls they had eaten at supper but didn't dare suggest it. Mother prodded the broom behind the garbage can and shrieked. Isabel hurried over, and together they stared at tiny black clumps.

Mother's voice rose to a roar. "We're going to sweep and scrub till the floor's clean enough to eat on. *Understand*?" She shoved the broom into Isabel's hands.

Isabel's chest went clammy. She turned long enough to catch Audrey's eyes, popped wide with fright, then swept the droppings and crumbs onto a newspaper and carried it to the alley. Skirt tucked between her knees, she scoured the linoleum, pausing only to wring out the dishcloth. As she crouched in the weak light, her face crushed to the floor, she couldn't help but feel like a rodent herself. When Audrey knelt beside her with a rag, she attempted a reassuring smile. After a while, Audrey's head sagged. Isabel took the rag from her and pushed her gently toward the table. She and Mother worked in tense silence, punctuated by swishes and the bang of drawers.

Isabel's neck and shoulders throbbed when she finally stood. "All clean."

Mother tossed her rag onto the counter and peered at the linoleum. "Where there are droppings, you can be sure there's a nest. We'll need to set out traps."

Isabel shuddered. At the sink, Mother wrung out the rags. Her mouth was hard, her face leached of color.

"Mother, go to bed," Isabel urged.

Mother's eyes flickered as if she meant to object, but she shambled down the short length of raggedy carpet behind the parlor.

When the bedroom door snapped shut, Isabel released a breath. It wasn't like Mother to lose her cool, but in the past four months, she'd suffered hardships that would chip away at anyone's strength. Only a year ago, she had been vivacious, flush with plans. Last summer, she had organized a picnic at Golden Gate Park. While Isabel and James had tossed rings, Dad had chased Audrey in a game of tag. Mother had hopped up and down, cheering for Audrey to race away. After Dad had captured her, Audrey had fallen, giggling, onto the sand.

"No harm done, Ellie," Dad had told Mother with a wink. "See, she's fine. All bones intact." At first Mother had pretended to scold, but then she had gulped with laughter, clutching her sides.

"Izzie?" Audrey said in a small voice, "I wish Mother wasn't so upset. I'd do anything to cheer her up."

"I know, honey. She's just tired is all. And a little shocked. She'll feel better after a good night's sleep."

"You always say she'll feel better in the morning. But then she hardly *ever* does." Audrey's voice wavered, and without warning, she slid onto the floor and wept. Her cinnamon hair spilled over her face, and the bony swell of her ribs jutted through her hand-me-down dress, which swamped her ankles.

Isabel dropped beside her and bolstered her sister's head against her chest. The scuttling in the walls resumed in a new place, behind the stove. The mice must have tunneled behind the flimsy insulation. Isabel felt sick.

"Hush," she whispered, stroking Audrey's hair. "It's all right."

"I don't want to live with mice." Audrey's breath snagged in sharp gasps.

Isabel drew her arms around her sister and rocked. "Shh, honey, don't cry." She felt Audrey's heart thrashing like a trapped bird.

"I want to go back to Rainbow Lane," Audrey wailed. It was her nickname for their old street with houses painted in vivid gold, turquoise, cotton candy pink, lime green.

Isabel thought of their apartment in the blue Victorian with its rounded tower, the fireplace with carved mantel, porcelain dishes and figurines, garden of night-blooming jasmine. She admired the original owners' optimism in choosing bold, unconventional colors to rebuild their street after the '06 earthquake and fires.

"I'd like that, too, but this is home now."

"There's nothing here but ch… chores and mice. Milly gets to play in her own backyard."

"We can play here, too. We've just got to use our imaginations." It was something Dad had done with her when she was younger than Audrey—propped her on his lap and pretended they were traveling together to an exotic place: the cold, glowing ridges of the moon; a circus sideshow with clowns and elephants; a magical forest with fairy inhabitants.

Digging a crumpled handkerchief from her skirt pocket, Isabel dabbed around Audrey's swollen eyes. After several minutes, her sister's tears subsided.

Audrey sniffled. "Let's play now."

Isabel started to say it was time for bed, but her sister had endured far more than a nine-year-old should handle and deserved a break. "For a little while."

"Let's pretend we're mermaids. That's what Milly and Frances and I do at recess. I make up stories for us to act out."

"In this game, we'll travel to a faraway land. We can invent it together. But you've got to concentrate until you feel you're really there." Isabel grasped Audrey's hand and guided her under the table. They sat cross-legged, knees touching. "Close your eyes. We're floating on a sea. Feel that wave?"

"No, silly, it's a purple dolphin who wants to give us a ride! He almost knocked me over."

"A dolphin, truly? Gee, I'm drenched!" Isabel pretended to shake water from her hair, and mirth crept around Audrey's lips. "Tell me where we're going. What's it like?"

"Big and beautiful and magical. It's an island by the ocean." Audrey's voice grew spirited. "With mountains and trees and flowers. And animals that talk and play!"

"It sounds lovely. Look, you can see it way out there. Those green and white patches are trees surrounded by cliffs."

Audrey jiggled her knees. "After we land, let's go exploring!"

Taking turns, they described their arrival on the isle's white sand beach—the brilliant-colored flowers, rabbits and dogs and ponies, the castle-like rim of mountains, plus all the fruit and fish they could eat. They were heroines, rescuing turtles, diving for shells, searching for treasure. On this island, time passed in the blink of an eye, so no one would know they'd gone. It was their secret; neither could tell a soul.

"Let's stay a week," Audrey said.

Slipping a hand around her sister's neck, Isabel told her yes, of course. How glorious it would be to have nothing to do, nowhere to be. As they gorged themselves on tropical fruit, she tasted juice, sank into a warm, soft quilt of sand.

Suddenly, wind battered against the windows, and they jumped. From the bedroom, mattress coils creaked, and Mother let out a groan. Isabel gathered Audrey back into her arms, but the spell was broken. When Audrey's eyelids drooped, she led her to the mattress they shared at the foot of Mother's bed. Audrey didn't protest as Isabel slipped a nightgown over her head. Isabel had a deadline—editing a student essay for the school paper—but the energy she'd mustered in the last few hours had spiraled out of her. She would have to finish it first thing tomorrow and type it over lunch in the secretary's office.

Audrey fell asleep instantly, drawing deep, steady breaths. Isabel undressed and crawled beside her. Tears she hadn't realized she'd been holding trailed down her cheeks. She perceived, dimly, they were an accumulation of many things: the void left by Dad and James, the dump of a flat, Mother's moods, the grind of chores and school, her nickel-and-dime job. No spare time.

She longed for James to grip her hands, listen in solidarity as she spilled her fears. She had few friends, had always confided in her older brother. She would tell him: *Now we're down by two, just the females left, and I can't hold it all together.* Their family was a tatty sweater losing shape as strands of yarn snaked away. A deadening torpor crept over her. She closed her eyes and waited for the reprieve of sleep.

Instead, an image of James popped into her head. She pictured him squatting around a campfire under the stars with other CCC recruits, mountains in the distance. Her brother and his crew were doubtless working hard, building dams and clearing trees for new trails and campgrounds. Yet she envied him his freedom—all that invigorating space to roam. Boys could escape and explore, while girls were stuck at home.

Bit by bit, a bitter yearning bubbled up her gut. If not for Mother and Audrey, she would break free from San Francisco and go somewhere warm and wild and pretty. She imagined fleeing the grime and gloom, rambling among trees, breathing pure air. But immediately she banished the thought. Leaving would be selfish, not to mention impossible, since she had no means. Nothing but a self-indulgent fantasy.

She laid a hand on Audrey's arm and listened to the soft rise and fall of her sister's breath. Maybe, at least, she could snatch a small sliver of time for herself, away from obligations. As she considered the possibilities, an idea wriggled into her head. She weighed it from different angles. No denying, it made her nervous. But it might be the most interesting thing she had done in months. She decided to give it a try, providing she could find the right opportunity.

CHAPTER TWO

"I'm going out for a smoke." Mother's eyes were sunken and glassy, as though she had already thrust her daughters from her mind and bolted down the street with her cigarettes. A draft billowed through the room, and Isabel shivered. With the oven turned off, the San Francisco damp had seeped into the flat.

"Since when did you smoke?" Isabel wanted to ask, but she knew. Since James left, since the hotel job had begun wearing her down. Mother rolled her own cigarettes, but tobacco was an expensive habit. They should save every penny for rent and food.

"Let me come with you." Audrey reached for Mother's arm, but Mother plucked away her fingers.

"No, honey. Stay here. I won't be but a minute." She gave Isabel a look that meant she was to watch Audrey.

Isabel tried to hide her resentment. "Come on, Audrey, let's eat supper."

"I'm not hungry. You eat, Izz, and I'll keep Mother company."

Mother snapped, "Can't I get just ten minutes of peace and quiet?"

Audrey took a jerky step backward. Mother wriggled into her coat, patted her pockets. The door banged shut behind her.

Isabel set out two bowls of fish chowder. "Eat up, honey," she said, when Audrey stirred her spoon dejectedly. "We can't afford to waste food."

"Mother didn't eat."

"We'll save her some."

"I don't want any. She can have mine."

"You're a growing girl. You've got to eat." She worried Audrey was becoming too thin. "Go on, take a bite."

"*You're* not my mother. You can't tell me what to do."

Isabel narrowed her eyes. "While Mother's away, I'm in charge. You know that."

"But she's *not* away, she's just around the corner with her smokes."

Isabel made to rise, a storm brewing in her chest. "Audrey, stop your back-talk this instant and mind me." Even to herself, she sounded eerily like Mother.

Audrey stared back in defiance. "All *right*. You don't have to shout."

"We can listen to a program while we eat, then play a game of cards," Isabel suggested, hoping to distract her sister. Mother had wanted to sell the radio, but they had wheedled her into keeping it, promising they would only turn it on once or twice a week to conserve batteries.

Isabel turned a knob, and after a burst of static, the melancholy strain of violins stuttered through the room. She would have preferred *The Romance of Helen Trent* or *Jack Armstrong, All-American Boy*, and Audrey's favorite program was *Little Orphan Annie*. But bit by bit, the music enfolded her in a velvet-smooth cocoon and buoyed her until she imagined her body floating high above the city.

Mr. Whiskers, the big orange cat Audrey had rescued from the alley last week after they discovered the mice, rubbed against Isabel's legs, and she reached down to stroke him. Mother had agreed to keep him on the condition that he purge all the rodents. So far he had proven his worth by snaring a mouse in the kitchen and tossing it like a toy until, bored, he had snapped his jaws around its neck and flung its limp body into a corner. Isabel and Audrey adored his soft mews and fluffy fur, his habit of curling onto their laps and purring.

"Remember how Dad used to let us stay up late and listen to programs?" Audrey frowned at her bowl. "Sometimes I can't remember his face anymore."

"It happens to me, too. But it'll come back to you over time." Isabel wasn't certain this was true. If she concentrated, she could almost glimpse Dad's dark hair and eyes, his muscular arms. Something struck her lungs like the beating of wings—a quick thrust of pain.

When the announcer came on at the bottom of the hour, she realized it had been over thirty minutes since Mother left with her smokes. "Put on your nightgown while I check on Mother."

"It's not even late. I'll go, too."

"Listen, if you're ready for bed by the time I get back, we'll play something more fun than cards. We'll explore the parts of the isle we haven't seen." She lowered her voice. "We might even see *fairies*." For the past week, whenever they were alone, they joined hands beneath the wobbly table and traveled there, capering through gardens of enormous pink camellias and white bunnies, over squishy sand where wild horses galloped. On their island, no one met harm. You could eat and drink as much as you wanted, sleep beneath a canopy of stars, never go hungry or fall ill.

Audrey nodded, her face brightening. "Since it's our very own, we should name it... isle of something..."

Isabel thought for a moment. "How about Isle of Castaways?" She had concocted the name on a whim, but she liked it instantly—a secret haven where, like shipwreck survivors, they had improbably swept ashore.

"Mysterious and perfect!" Audrey made moon eyes.

Isabel slid on her jacket and removed her key from the hook on the door. Outside, the city hummed with Friday night noise: raucous hoots from the corner bar; automobiles rumbling up Turk; waitresses and chefs hustling to their jobs; sirens wailing; glass shattering onto the street from an apartment a few doors down; a man's shout. A light rain fell, and she squinted through the mist.

She found Mother a block from the flat, standing in the lee of a building opposite the bar, a cigarette cupped behind her hand. She glanced up with a trace of unease, and Isabel understood she hadn't wanted company.

"I wanted to check on you."

Mother puffed smoke from the corner of her mouth. "Something happened today."

Isabel felt a sudden chill. "What is it?"

"Hotel's cutting my hours starting next week."

"But why? I thought they were ramping up for tourists. Surely they need more help over summer, when people go on vacation?"

Mother snorted. "Who goes on vacation anymore, except the very rich?" She leaned toward Isabel. "Anyways, I'll bet they're giving some snooty kid the chance to earn spending cash over summer break. That's how these people are. They don't give a damn about folks who need work." She tapped ashes onto the sidewalk.

Isabel couldn't bring herself to ask whether this would ruin their budget. An automobile screeched around the block, its horn blaring.

"James will send twenty-five dollars every month, so that will tide us over," Mother said, as if reading her mind. "And I can sell my pearls. They'll fetch a little."

"But Dad gave you…"

Mother shook her head. "Doesn't matter. He's gone."

Something slimy slid down Isabel's throat. In January, after Dad died on the docks of a heart attack, the foreman had shoved in another fellow without missing a beat. And now Dad would be forsaken a second time—this time by his own wife. It hadn't been five months, and already she was exorcising him from their lives. "Dad wouldn't have pawned our valuables," Isabel muttered.

"Because he was a romantic, God love him. Never could face the truth. Thought he could change things by writing under a pen name in that commie paper, when the shipowners always had the upper hand."

Isabel gaped at Mother, stunned she would dismiss him as a Don Quixote who had thrown himself at a hopeless task. She wanted to shout that he had been an optimist who had fought for something bigger than himself. But when she opened her mouth, nothing came out.

For years, Dad had penned articles in a clandestine rag about the atrocious waterfront conditions he'd experienced firsthand. Longshoremen toiled in skeleton crews for measly pay, regularly suffered injuries or lost their lives. In hindsight, she wondered whether Dad had foreseen his own end.

Once, after explaining why he was fighting for better conditions, he had said, *Someday you'll blaze your own path, too, Izz. You have a strong will and a sharp mind.* She grimaced. With her voice caught in her throat and her chances of leaving the city next to nil, she only felt incapable and helpless.

"Anyways, what other choice do we have? Apply for relief? Become hoboes? At least you've got the part-time gig at McGilligan's."

"Yes." Isabel's voice was barely above a whisper. It was ludicrous to hope her earnings at the grocer's could sustain them. Before leaving for Yosemite, James had told Isabel that Mr. McGilligan needed a helper for a few hours a week. No doubt a charity offer, since Dad and Mr. McGilligan had been fishing buddies. Later, she understood the job was James' parting gift to her. He must have known she'd need something to take her mind elsewhere while he was away.

Mother drew on the cigarette, puffing smoke into a spiraling plume above their heads. "How I hate cleaning up after rich slobs with their high hats. The lot of 'em throw a dozen towels on the floor and don't bother to flush the toilets. They leave whole trays of food in their rooms—caviar and wine and God knows what else. Dirty underwear stuffed in beds, crumbs in the sheets. The country might be in ruins, but you'd never know it from the waste in those swanky suites."

"What animals."

"Not all." Mother's face turned wistful. "Yesterday, some fellow left two quarters on the dresser with a note for the housekeeper."

"That was thoughtful." Mother must receive precious little encouragement at work. Unconsciously, Isabel scratched the bright eczema stains on her neck until she caught herself and dropped her hands. The rain accelerated from a persistent drip to angry dashes.

"Go back inside and get dry," Mother said.

Isabel touched Mother's shoulder, then dodged across the street. A blustery wind whipped against the blisters on her cheeks, raw and biting. Above the bar, neon lights flashed, and a woman in high heels tumbled out with a man. They teetered together on the sidewalk. Before Isabel let herself into the flat, she turned to gaze back at the corner. Mother cut a small, shadowy-looking figure, her cigarette smoke mingling with the fog that cloaked her.

·   ·   ·

At the end of fifth period, Isabel sneaked a look at the back of the classroom. She had decided to try her idea—not so much for the fun it might bring, because that seemed unlikely, but for the chance to do something after school besides chores or her two-bit job. Stolen time to herself without Mother or Audrey. But first she had to work up her nerve.

Claude DeVille, a boy in her geometry class, had asked her several times to study with him after school, and she had always told him she was too busy. He towered over her by a foot, had skinny arms and legs, and wore wire-rimmed spectacles. She wasn't sure why he wanted her for his study partner, since he always had the right answers in class and volunteered to work through proofs at the blackboard. Once she had wondered whether he might have a romantic interest in her, then quickly dismissed the idea. She was quiet, and except for her wavy chestnut hair, she considered herself plain: just five feet tall, crooked teeth, broad nose, small breasts, scarlet splotches of eczema on her cheeks, throat, and elbows. To hide the rashes, she wore long sleeves and unfashionably high necklines.

When the bell rang, she waited for Claude outside the classroom and tentatively called his name. He turned.

"I was wondering… " She swallowed. *Spit it out.* "Since the geometry final's next week, would you like to study together?"

Surprise bloomed across his face. Maybe he thought her too forward. She blushed as his gaze traveled down her outfit: a middy blouse with high collar, long dark skirt and ankle socks. The blouse had been Mother's from over a decade ago, and Isabel had taken in the seams and shortened the long sailor ribbon. Now she saw it made her look outdated. And her hair, though long and thick, was also old-fashioned, wound in coils around her head. She held her breath, preparing to spin away.

"Sure. Where and when you have in mind?"

Isabel looked down, ashamed for not having thought it through. "Here, tomorrow?"

He pursed his lips, thinking. "There's a café down the road. Owner's a family friend, so we can sit at a booth before the supper crowd arrives. I'll take you there after school." She sent him a smile and hurried down the hall. Claude would be *her* secret; she wouldn't breathe a word to a soul.

CHAPTER THREE

The next day after school, Isabel followed Claude down the stone staircase onto the sidewalk. Although she had worried they would run out of things to say, he chatted with her like a longtime friend, and she could picture growing almost as comfortable with him as she was with James. His favorite class, he told her, was chemistry. His voice grew animated as he described the experiments he had tried at home: triggering iron to rust in thermite reactions; making polymer bouncy balls; tinkering with sugar and sulfuric acid. He mimed mixing chemicals in beakers.

Watching his eyes light up, like sunshine glancing the depths of a murky pool, Isabel couldn't help but admire his curiosity. When he asked about her family, she spoke briefly of Dad's death, then Mother, James, Audrey, and Mr. Whiskers.

He gave her an appraising look. "You must be made of strong stuff."

"My brother's the strong one. He's with the CCC at Yosemite."

"That's a beautiful park. My family camped there when I was nine or ten. Everywhere you look are trees and wildflowers. Bears go right up to the campgrounds. Foxes and deer, too." Isabel filed away these tidbits with other mental photographs of James to sort through later.

The Warm Comforts Café was tucked between a barber shop and shoeshine place. Except for the graying proprietor, it was empty.

"This is Isabel, my friend from school," Claude told Mr. Carmelo, who wiped his hands on his apron as he hobbled over. "All right if we study?"

With a wink, Mr. Carmelo gestured at the unoccupied tables, and Isabel followed Claude to a booth with a red-checked oilcloth. After he helped her with several proofs she hadn't understood, he turned a steady gaze on her.

"Since you edit the school paper, you must be a whiz at English. I could sure use your help studying for the final. I didn't finish reading *Moby Dick*."

Isabel had devoured the novel every opportunity she found. She loved how books let you steal inside other people's minds while whisking you to different times and places. Though Dad hadn't left behind anything of material value, he had bequeathed her his love of words. He had been a voracious reader, too, though he hadn't finished school; he'd had to leave at sixteen to work. And like Isabel, he had admired Emily Dickinson's poetry, joking she was a distant relation, since they shared surnames.

As Isabel explained the theme, Claude's eyes glinted with a kind of awe. When a strand of her hair drooped along the table near his hand, his fingers danced toward it, as if daring to stroke it, and Isabel swelled with a surprising, sensual power. *Claude saw her as bright and attractive.* For a moment, she was speechless.

A man in an old suit and bowler hat entered the café, and Mr. Carmelo showed him to a table. Soon a mouth-watering smell of meat and potatoes sizzled from the kitchen. With faint alarm, Isabel rose and told Claude she had to go. It had to be past five, well past the time she worked at the grocery. Audrey would be home alone. Worse, Mother might have returned and would wonder where in the world she was.

As they walked to the streetcar stop, shadows dangled onto the sidewalk. "What are your plans for summer?" Claude asked.

"Keep working at Mr. McGilligan's, so long as he'll let me. And watch my sister while my mother's at the Sir Francis Drake. And..." Isabel hesitated. "My sister wants to visit our brother at Yosemite." Audrey often spoke wistfully about traveling to see James. "But I don't know how we'd get there, short of hopping the rails." She gave a wry laugh.

"Huh. If you're serious about going, maybe I could borrow a car and drive you there partway."

"You know how to drive?"

"The basics, anyhow."

"It's kind of you to offer, but it's just a pipe dream. I don't even know how far it is."

"I'd have to figure things out first. If you decide to go, let me know."

She thanked him, surprised he would even consider it.

"Say, can you meet next Thursday after finals?" Claude asked when they reached the trolley stop. "We can celebrate the end of school." He named a park in the Western Addition. Then, to Isabel's astonishment, he leaned down and grazed his lips against her cheek. Not a kiss, but the promise of one. A tingle shimmied down her belly. Maybe he was presumptuous, but she decided she didn't mind. She smiled in reply, a flush crawling up her throat.

On the trolley, she felt an unexpected ray of joy, as if every inch of her skin had burst alive. Over and over, she examined the look Claude had given her in the café — something resembling admiration — and recalled the smooth feel of his lips. The stolen time away had given her the heady sensation of gliding toward a place as magical and unreal as the Isle of Castaways. When she disembarked at Market, automobiles thundered by in both directions. She warned herself to pay attention; it was dangerous to lose your head here. To make up for lost time, she cut down an alley littered with shards of glass. As she ran, the sole of her left shoe flapped. She dashed up the stairs to their stoop, then paused at the door, panting. Mother was hurling a torrent of words, one atop another. Isabel's throat went dry, and she stuffed down the urge to pivot and race back down the street.

Inside, smoke curled from the stove, billowing out the window over the sink, and an acrid stench like burned toast wafted through the room. Isabel stood motionless, trying to grasp what had happened. Audrey was crouched beside the stove, her knees mashed to her chest. Her face was pinned beneath her hands, and her breath was coming fast and jagged.

Mother scowled down at her. "Any minute the fire marshal will bang on our door."

In dismay, Isabel slid beside Audrey. Her sister slumped against her, tears streaming down her cheeks.

"Audrey, honey, what's wrong? What happened?"

Audrey's sobs lurched out, long and shattered. "I was baking cookies, but they burned something awful. And now Mr. Whiskers has run away!" A strand of gooseflesh popped onto Isabel's arms.

Mother sent Isabel a withering look. "Where the devil have you been, young lady? You don't work Thursdays."

Isabel clambered up from the floor, searching for an excuse. "Sorry I'm late. I stayed after school and lost track of time." That morning, she had told Audrey to go home alone, the same as she did on the days when Isabel worked at Mr. McGilligan's. When Audrey had asked why, she had explained she needed to finish something at school.

"What were you doing?" Mother said suspiciously. "School ended over three hours ago."

Isabel lowered her head and improvised, "Studying for finals... with Elaine." She refused to say Claude's name; it was her right to keep him a secret.

Mother towered over her. "You're lying! You didn't meet any girl, did you." In a sudden fluid motion, she reared back an arm and walloped the side of Isabel's face. Isabel yelped and ducked, cupping her cheek.

"How could you be so selfish and thoughtless! You left your sister alone for *hours*." She stomped over and booted Isabel against the shins.

Isabel's knees buckled, and she tumbled to the floor. Her lunch of chowder soup flooded her mouth, and she felt queasy. Audrey's wet howls catapulted through the flat.

"You should be ashamed! Here I was counting on you, yet you stayed away so long that Audrey almost burned down the flat! The whole building could have gone up in flames!"

"I'm sorry, truly." The fiery splotches on Isabel's cheeks and neck stung. She clawed at them with her fingernails, wanting to scrub them raw.

Mother pointed at the sink. "Clean that up, then start supper."

Shakily, Isabel struggled up and peered at the cookie pan. Large black globs smeared its surface. She ran water and scraped at the burned batter. Mother's footsteps clomped down the hall, and the bedroom door slammed.

Audrey's shoulders quivered as she wept. "I didn't mean to burn them. They were supposed to be a surprise for Mother."

Isabel knelt and stroked her sister's back. "It's all right, honey. It's not your fault."

"I used up the last of the flour and sugar," Audrey choked out between sobs.

Isabel embraced her, wanting to bring them both a little comfort. She didn't realize she was also crying, until she touched her cheeks, and the pads of her fingers were damp. Rivulets streaked down her throat.

"Izzie, you're hurt!"

Isabel shook her head and wiped her eyes. "I'm all right."

"Mother says I'm not old enough to cook." Her sister's face was pinched, like an adult's. "She says I shouldn't even try."

"I know you meant well. It's the thought that counts. Mother's not herself these days."

"She never is."

She started to object, but Audrey was right. If you saw Mother from afar, you'd guess she was in her prime with promises ahead — husband, home, children. You wouldn't guess she was convinced her best days were over. Just last December, she had joked, baked, presided over card games. If only she would pull herself together and dredge up a little hope. Surely she could have praised Audrey's good intentions instead of lashing out in panic. But as Isabel grew indignant, she reminded herself that she alone deserved the blame for the near fire. *Her* fault for coming home so late.

"Let's check the front stoop to see if Mr. Whiskers has come back." She helped Audrey to her feet, and they opened the door and crooned for the cat. When he didn't appear, Audrey's disappointment was sharp and immediate. She sucked in her cheeks, and her face turned rigid.

"Right before he ran away, he flattened his ears and raised his hackles," her sister said dully.

"He'll be back," Isabel said, attempting a confident tone. "He's probably hiding until the smoke clears." She leaned toward Audrey. "Listen, after supper, when Mother's in bed, we'll visit the Isle of Castaways." She envisioned a puff of sea air fluttering against her cheeks.

Her sister nodded, and maybe despite herself, her eyes brightened. Neither of them would ever tell Mother about their lush, magical island. Nor would Isabel stop meeting Claude. She promised herself to be more careful next time.

CHAPTER FOUR

"You're home early," Isabel said, keeping her voice casual, as she and Audrey entered the flat. Mother was stirring a pot of soup at the stove. The back of her chocolate-brown hair, thrust into a bun, sprouted gray threads. She hadn't spoken to Isabel since last night's cookie fiasco.

"Management moved us to the summer schedule today." When Mother turned from the stove, her face was sour. "La di da, they've cut my hours."

"I forgot," Isabel said helplessly, setting down her satchel. Audrey skipped to the kitchen and wrapped her arms around Mother's waist. Mother gave her a tired smile that didn't reach her eyes.

"Let me do that." Isabel took the spoon from Mother and stepped in front of the stove.

"Mother, may I listen to *Little Orphan Annie*?" Audrey said.

After several moments, Mother gave a sharp squeak. "What on *earth*?"

Isabel glanced behind her shoulder. Mother was spreading strands of Audrey's hair between her fingers and peering at her scalp.

"Mother, you're hurting me. Please, may I listen?"

With a look of revulsion, Mother pinched her index finger and thumb together and whipped her hand from Audrey's head. "Yes, go." She dropped into a chair at the table.

In the parlor, Audrey turned on the radio and squatted on the rug, knees hugged to her chest. As Mr. Whiskers brushed against her skirt, she stroked his fur and sang, "Who's that little chatter box? The one with pretty auburn locks? Whom do you see? It's Little Orphan Annie!"

"What's wrong?" Isabel asked in a low voice.

"They say bad things come in threes. I don't know if this counts as the second or third, but your sister has lice. Just spotted a few crawling through her scalp. Might be that cat, for all I know."

Isabel set down the spoon and glanced at Audrey. "I'm sure it's not Mr. Whiskers' fault."

"What's not Mr. Whisker's fault?" Audrey called from the rug, her eyes darting up in alarm. She lifted the tabby and snuggled him against her chest. "He's been ever so good. And he's killed all the mice." As far as Isabel could tell, Audrey was right; Mr. Whiskers had rid the flat of the dark bleating things.

"Or it's this filth we're living in. After supper, I'll have to wash and cut both your hair and use a fine-toothed comb on Audrey. The less hair they've got to hide under, the better. And then we'll wash the linens."

"Mine, too?" Isabel reached for her hair, remembering how Claude had wished to touch it. "I'm sure I don't have lice."

"You might not think so, but you and Audrey sleep on the same mattress. And this isn't the last of it. They're stubborn hangers-on."

"There's no need. I can manage it myself." She tried not to sound desperate.

"Cutting's the only thing that will help."

"I'll wash and comb it first. Let me try."

Mother harrumphed and shook her head. "Waste of time." After a short silence, she said, "Tell me, who's this boy you dropped everything to meet yesterday?"

Isabel turned off the stove. "What do you mean?"

"Don't be coy. I know you didn't meet a girl."

Isabel considered making something up, but in the end, she flushed and muttered Claude's name, adding that they had only been studying for next week's finals.

"I see." Mother gave Isabel a shrewd look.

While they ate supper, Isabel racked her brain for ways to forestall Mother's plans. If she had to, she would flat out refuse. Maybe Mother would get distracted and forget. But immediately after they washed the dishes, she commanded Audrey to sit at a chair, then wedged the trashcan against the back of the chair legs. In the wan light, she withdrew a heavy pair of silver scissors from her sewing box and leaned over Audrey's head, snipping. Long locks fell in heaps into the can. Mother continued cutting until Audrey's hair hung just below her ears.

"Now you've got a bob," she said, handing Audrey a small mirror.

Audrey wrinkled her nose. "I look like a boy."

"You look cute," Mother said firmly. She pulled the chair to the sink and instructed Audrey to kneel on it. As Audrey hung her head over the faucet, Mother scrubbed her scalp with a combination of lye soap and petroleum jelly. "Pat it down as good as you can," she instructed, wrapping a towel around Audrey's head. "Once it's dry, I'll go through it with a comb."

She pointed at Isabel. "Your turn." She had hauled the chair back beneath the lightbulb. The scissors gleamed in her hand, and Isabel shuddered.

"No. I don't want it cut."

"This isn't your choice. I'm going to cut mine, too."

"Mother, don't make me."

"Don't be a ninny. Come here."

"No!" Isabel yelled, grabbing a hank of her hair. "I want to keep it long."

"Oh, for the love of God. It'll grow back."

"No, I won't do it." In an instant, she seized her hair with both hands and yanked her fists behind her head. From the table, Audrey gaped.

Mother narrowed her eyes. "If this is because of that boy, I can tell you he'll like your hair even less if varmints are skittering through it. Now come here before I lose my patience."

Isabel recoiled, and her mouth went dry. "No," she choked. To her horror, tears rolled down her face.

"For shame," Mother whisper-hissed. "Audrey didn't cry. Feeling sorry for yourself won't do a lick of good."

A fever flared over Isabel's throat and cheeks until she wanted to claw them. Mother was right; she was setting a terrible example. Like a Frankenstein, she lurched to the chair and slumped down, sniffling back tears. Inside her head, she screamed at herself to run, *now*, but her legs were inert, leaden. The scissors meted out a metallic rhythm, sneaking up and glancing her scalp with cold precision. She imagined her hair falling in dark piles behind her, like small animals curling against each other for consolation. A thin whimper rose from her throat.

Mother gripped Isabel's head to straighten it. "There are more important things in life than hair and gallivanting around with boys." Isabel's neck prickled; it was uncanny how Mother had read her mind. "Wash your hair while I comb Audrey's." Mother pointed her at the sink.

Isabel stumbled toward it, not daring to look in the hand mirror on the table. As she scrubbed her scalp, she discovered she could barely run her fingers through it. She already knew it was dreadful and short—her one fine trait, ruined. When Mother ordered her to strip the linens for the wash, she grumbled under her breath, filling with a mutinous rage. As soon as Mother turned, she bared her lips and raised a fist, longing to scream until her lungs exploded. But when she glimpsed Audrey's bulging eyes, she dropped her gaze and pivoted away. In truth, it was herself she hated: her shorn hair, rashes, idiotic acquiescence, and stupid, useless vanity. But beneath that stirred a deeper regret, as if something inside her own soul had been hacked off and discarded.

•　　　•　　　•

"Where shall we travel today?" Isabel said, clasping Audrey's hand beneath the table after Mother went to bed. The window sash was pushed up, letting in dank air and the stench of decaying fish. "Paris? A circus? The Alps?" She was teasing; she knew how her sister would answer.

"The Isle of Castaways!"

"The Isle of Castaways it is. Shall we go by sea?"

"No, by plane, like Miss Earhart."

"Then we must concentrate." They dropped their chins. "Hear the engines roar. We're about to take off."

A smile tugged at Audrey's lips. "We're lifting so fast I've lost my hat! It fell all the way down. See, it's just a tiny speck!"

"It's calm and peaceful up here." Isabel tilted her face into the breeze. "Say, did you know that people who stay on the isle for good never grow old?"

Audrey frowned. "If they stay for good, they'll get awful lonely."

"No one's lonely or sad on the isle. They… forget what they left behind."

"I don't want to forget anything I've left. Not Mother or Mr. Whiskers or *The Velveteen Rabbit*." It was her favorite book. "So I'm sorry, Izz, I can't stay for good."

Isabel glanced at her sister in surprise. "All right, then we won't."

Audrey patted her belly. "I'm hungry. Let's eat as soon as we land."

"Sure. We'll catch fish and gather all the mangoes and peaches and coconuts we can find until our bellies are so stuffed we can't move."

Audrey giggled. "Don't forget buttered rolls and chocolate milk."

"Look, we're close." Way below, a ring of cliffs encircled a verdant valley.

Audrey squinted out of an eye and squeezed Isabel's hand. "We can walk barefoot in the sand." She sighed, and sunshine enveloped them like a baby's blanket, tucking itself around their toes and sparkling in their hair.

"Hold on tight, we're coming down."

"Gee, my stomach's all aflutter."

"Now up! We've done it!" Isabel leaned forward, palms bracing knees.

"Izz, after we eat, let's search for buried treasure! Then we'll be rich, and we can move back to Rainbow Lane." The sisters scrambled onto the sand and splashed each other at the edge of the shore. As a wave slapped their faces, they whooped, and Audrey clung to Isabel's arm.

• • •

After Audrey fell asleep, Isabel writhed on the mattress. She couldn't bear to touch her hair; the jagged bob revolted her. Anyhow, she had decided that what Mother did no longer mattered. She could beat her oldest daughter, even send her packing. Isabel would continue meeting Claude, so long as he didn't give up on her. She had already plotted how to enjoy a smidgen of privacy with him at the park next week. Better yet, she could do it without leaving Audrey alone in the flat.

CHAPTER FIVE

While Isabel and Audrey waited for the trolley bound for Fillmore, a light rain fell, and fog from the Bay lingered over the street. Isabel pulled the hood of Audrey's pea coat over her head. Her sister jerked away, protesting she wasn't a baby. But on the streetcar, she scooted close to Isabel and grasped her arm.

"Now that school's out, let's visit James!" Her mouth hovered over Isabel's ear. "We'll have such an adventure, Izz!"

"Yosemite's far, and we have no way of getting there." To avoid getting her sister's hopes up, she didn't mention Claude's offer. Besides, leaving the city suddenly felt less urgent, now that she and Claude had arranged a tryst. A tiny thrill whizzed down her vertebrae. Last week, after Mother snipped her hair, Isabel had worried that her uneven boy's mane would squash his interest. But when he caught up with her after class and gently asked why she'd cut it, she had confided about Audrey and the lice, Mother's knee-jerk reaction. To her relief, he had declared her eyes were even prettier and stood out more. She said to Audrey, "Anyhow, we'll see James in a few more months when he gets leave to come home."

"That's *ages* from now." Audrey's voice grew fierce. "If *you* won't go, I'll go by myself."

Isabel touched her sister's shoulder, intending to say something conciliatory, but Audrey twisted away and swung her face to the window.

They disembarked below Sacramento and walked uphill through a neighborhood of hamburger joints, antique shops and theaters. When the rain intensified, they broke into a trot, heads tucked in their hoods. Isabel had told Audrey she was meeting a friend at a park, and she could play on the swings while Isabel and her friend took a short walk.

"Which friend?" Audrey had asked. When Isabel had blushed, she had cried, "A boy, I bet!"

Lafayette Square Park had sloping green hills, crisscrossed with gravel paths and hedges. Two flights of a grand stone staircase rose from the street, flanked by shrubs and flowering bushes. The rain swirled, crisp and cool, as they climbed past eucalyptus, cypress, and palm trees. Near the crest of the hill, they stopped at a playground with a stone bench and fountain, where Isabel had agreed to rendezvous with Claude. As she bounced from foot to foot, she could almost feel her blood whooshing, warm and light, through her body.

Queen Anne Victorians squeezed together on the street below. In the distance, a sliver of the San Francisco Bay sparkled blue, despite the fog. When Isabel saw Claude emerge from the fog and charge toward her, she hopped on her toes and waved. Funny how she'd half feared he wouldn't show. He approached her with a grin, carrying a long navy umbrella.

"This is my sister," Isabel said, glowing. "She'll stay here while we go on a walk." When she explained that Mother wouldn't let Audrey stay by herself at home for long, her sister scowled.

Claude extended his palm, and Audrey returned his handshake shyly.

"Will you be all right in the playground for a little while?" Isabel said. She was determined to be home before Mother returned and had a chance to ask questions.

Audrey tossed her head. "Course."

"Do you want to borrow my umbrella?" Claude asked her. She eyed it indifferently.

"We won't be long," Isabel said.

Audrey gazed at the empty swings. "I wish there was someone to play with."

"I know. I'm sorry the weather isn't cooperating. Remember how you used to love hunting for stones?" Isabel's voice skipped up an octave. "Maybe you can search for interesting ones to paint and decorate. They'll make great props for later." *For our trips to the Isle of Castaways*, she didn't say, hoping Audrey would understand.

Audrey met her eyes with a thin glimmer of hope. Afterwards, Isabel recognized that look as the anticipation of traveling together to the Isle while Mother lay abed and they sat beneath the table—the knowledge that in a few breaths, they would leave the flat and tunnel into another land.

She said, "Don't wander far. If you look for stones, stay on the path and don't leave the park, promise?"

"Here," Claude thrust the umbrella into her hands and winked. "In case you need it while you're rock hunting." Audrey's lips turned up in a faint smile as she popped the shade open and closed. Isabel followed Claude out of the playground. When she glanced back, her sister was pirouetting, the umbrella balanced high above her head.

At first, as Isabel rambled with Claude up the wet path, she felt a dip of giddiness, as if by claiming a bit of freedom for themselves they had pulled off a miraculous stunt. She couldn't help but marvel at how easy it had been to orchestrate this escape.

"There's a grove of trees ahead," Claude said. "Where we can *talk*." He took Isabel's hand, twining his fingers through hers, and a frisson coursed from the heat of his palm up her arm as she grasped his meaning. *This* was what she'd hoped for.

As they strolled, Claude described his part-time job as a paper boy, adding that in his spare time, when he wasn't tinkering with experiments, he'd begun making a chair for his mother.

"It must be swell to build things," Isabel said. "I don't have that knack."

"You're good at many other things. English, for one."

She was grateful he hadn't suggested sewing or cooking. "I've always loved reading, same as my father. Also editing the paper." *Wordsmithing*, Dad had called it, *polishing ideas*. His involvement with the secret longshoremen's rag had inspired her. Editing was a way of connecting with her classmates without the awkwardness of face-to-face encounters. More than that, it temporarily allowed her to forget the wretched things she didn't want to remember. She shrugged. "Must be I like tinkering with words."

Claude squeezed her hand. "Know something? I'm not only glad school's out, I'm glad I've gotten to know you. You're different from most girls. You care about things that matter." She welled with unexpected pleasure.

Glimpsing the battered white siding of a rambling house, she said, "Does anyone live there?"

"Nope. Holladay mansion and grounds are abandoned. City's tried for years to convince the owners to sell, but they won't budge."

Isabel spied flowering jasmine and honeysuckle bushes, a footpath, outbuilding and lawn, now overgrown with weeds and moss. Portions of the mansion materialized in the fog: dusty-white clapboards, darkened with mold and rot, a pile of boards in a corner, broken windows above a side portico. "It's creepy."

"I'll protect you, my dear," Claude said in a British accent. She giggled as he guided her off the path into the grove.

As soon as they were concealed by the eucalyptus trees, which formed a little tent from the rain, Claude moved toward her. She held her breath when his lips caressed hers — a sweet burst of warmth like hot fudge. He smelled of sandalwood soap mingled with a tinge of sweat. Her stomach teetered — a cart on a ferris wheel.

He leaned back and stared into her eyes. "Practice makes perfect." When he removed her hood and stroked her hair, Isabel felt like a favored pet, captured but oddly glad for it. "Not that we're bad," he said. "But it's ever so fun getting better." She opened her mouth to speak, but he pulled her toward him and grasped her shoulders. This time it was a longer kiss, his lips seeking hers and resting there, moist and warm. She started to draw away, worried she was being fast, letting him do too much too soon. But then she decided it was romantic and inevitable.

Claude petted her cheeks in small delicate motions. "I'd like to take you on a proper date sometime, to supper and a picture." His hand lingered over her throat, and she gently shook it off.

She wondered how she would explain a date to Mother. "Maybe soon, without Audrey." As she said Audrey's name aloud, it occurred to her that many minutes had lapsed, and they should see about her sister. *Just a little longer.* Inside this grove with Claude was a precious space and time she wanted to imprint into her memory and examine later. After they kissed a third time, Isabel stepped away and said they should fetch Audrey. Her back turned, she patted down her hair and lips.

"Ready, Madame?" he said with a wink and flourish. Offering her the crook of his arm, he led her out of the grove and down the path toward the playground.

They had descended over half the distance to the playground when a terrible shriek, like squealing tires or brakes, echoed up the hill. It might have come from the street at the base of the park. A foreboding passed over Isabel, a kind of blind animal panic she couldn't explain. Shivering, she looked up at Claude.

"Let's go a little faster," she said, clutching his arm tighter.

The path was slick with rain, but they accelerated their pace, picking their way rapidly down to the playground. From further below rose shouts and commotion. With dawning apprehension, Isabel understood something awful had happened. At the playground, she scanned the slides and sandbox, but Audrey wasn't there. Blood pounded between her ears. She and Claude exchanged a dark look, and she knew they both feared the same thing: somehow, inexplicably, Audrey was connected to the chaos and noise below.

"She's not here," she said stupidly, her voice tinged with dread. "I've got to find her."

"We will. Let's keep going. She's probably around the next bend, looking for stones."

As they continued down the path, Isabel clinging to Claude's arm and stumbling over the wet gravel, she made out a small knot of people in the mist. They seemed to be gathered at the top of the stone stairs leading from the park to Sacramento Street.

"Oh, dear God." Isabel was panting now, sick with fear, furious at herself for leaving Audrey alone.

A woman with a terrier suddenly appeared, stepping toward them on the path. Isabel cried, "Do you know what happened? We heard shouts."

The woman paused, and the dog strained forward on its leash. Her face arranged itself into a guarded look, one meant to convey bad news. "There's been an accident. A young girl was hit by an automobile. They're waiting for the ambulance and police."

Isabel didn't wait to hear more. The blood drained from her head, and she felt faint. Letting go of Claude's arm, she began running down the path, staggering and tripping, desperate to reach the scene, even if it meant sliding down face first.

As she neared the stairs, she saw a semicircle of three or four men, a young mother holding a toddler by the hand, and an older woman. They were facing the edge of Sacramento Avenue. Isabel stopped and leaned over, bracing her hands against her knees, panting hard and intermittently gasping for air. Claude caught up with her and said something, but she ignored him and lunged toward the crowd. They snagged glances at her wild, panicked eyes and moved aside as she shoved past. Her eyes skimmed the wet concrete road and the slumped doll-body, not making sense of it. When a cry hurtled up her throat, she stuffed both hands against her mouth.

What happened next occurred in slow motion, like moving picture frames crawling onto the screen one at a time. Much later, she rewound the reel again and again, always returning to the moment at the playground before she left Audrey.

First, she recognized the jagged, broken spines of Claude's navy umbrella scattered in the middle of the street. Heart thundering, she sank to her knees and forced herself to look at the body lying crumpled like a discarded sack of potatoes on the side of the road. A man in a raincoat and dark breeches hovered over it, pressing with both hands. From somewhere in the recesses of her brain, she grasped that he was attempting resuscitation.

The body belonged to a small girl strewn atop a gray pea coat. Her legs splayed apart at an unnatural angle like a broken china doll's, white and bony. Her dress was hitched above her knees, her feet concealed by ankle socks within an impractical pair of Mary Janes. Dark blood pooled around her head and shoulders. A flattened lock of auburn hair lay smeared against the pavement, but her face was obscured by the man who leaned over her on his knees, pumping her chest. A few yards away, a black automobile was parked haphazardly across the road, blocking traffic.

At first, Isabel decided it was another girl, a stranger, someone who happened to look like Audrey from behind. A mistake, no doubt. *Someone else's tragedy. Someone else's sister and daughter. Audrey must be elsewhere in the park, still searching for stones.* This had to be the case, even as nausea swelled up Isabel's intestines, crushing her stomach. Rain pelted onto her head, face, coat, legs, seeping into her clothes. The man shouted for people to stand back, and she blinked and stared again at the grisly scene.

Now there was no mistaking the pea coat, the bobbed cinnamon hair, Claude's umbrella; and in a staggering rush, the world converged inside her brain, smacking her ears, narrowing, suffocating, until she couldn't breathe. Someone screamed, over and over, a long, keening wail as the man continued pressing her sister's chest and the crowd moved back, transfixed by the unfolding horror.

When the noise stopped, she leaned over the curb, retched for several seconds, then vomited. Her mouth filled with a rancid, putrid taste. She dropped to her knees in a daze. Someone laid a hand on her arm—maybe Claude—but she shook him off.

At the periphery of her consciousness, as if at the other end of a tunnel, she heard someone say, "That's the girl's sister. Give her some space, will you!" then "Here comes the ambulance." Sirens shrieked; lights flashed; brakes squealed as the vehicle skidded up behind the parked automobile.

Delirious, Isabel struggled upright and yelled hoarsely, "Audrey! Let me see her. *Please! Audrey!*" Someone slipped an arm around her waist, and she recognized the elderly woman, who helped her to her feet.

"Stand back, stand back!" a medic shouted, and two men carried a stretcher to the limp body, hoisted it into the maw of the waiting ambulance.

"Let me go, let me go, too," Isabel sobbed. The man who had been attempting resuscitation conferred briefly with one of the medics, and they stared at her.

"Please, take me with you!"

The older woman escorted her toward the medics, supporting her with an arm around her waist, and Claude took her other side. Her head lolled back helplessly. If Audrey didn't survive, she prayed she wouldn't, either.

"Miss, are you the sister?" a medic said.

She might have nodded, but her knees gave out, and Claude and the woman steadied her by gripping beneath her arms. Her body sagged like a corpse, suspended on either side. The medics scribbled something onto a pad that Claude said. He may have spoken to Isabel, too, but a giant gust of wind blasted through her ears, and she couldn't hear him or anyone else, couldn't speak, either.

The men hauled her into the ambulance and pushed her onto a jump seat beside the stretcher. The ambulance jerked forward, maneuvering around the blocked intersection, then zoomed ahead, red lights winking, though she could no longer hear the siren.

At first she was relieved to leave the scene of the disaster, but when a medic leaned over the stretcher with a stethoscope, she screamed, terrified. The other medic frowned and approached her, his face grim. Seizing her arm, he yanked up her coat and dress sleeve. She screeched and tried to fight him off, but he held her arm with a steel-like grip and plunged a stinging needle into her flesh. At last it no longer mattered, because he dropped her arm and moved away, as though repulsed, and everything went mercifully black.

CHAPTER SIX

Isabel woke on a cot in a sterile white room, partitioned into two halves by a crudely strung-up bedsheet. Behind the sheet, she glimpsed another bed on wheels, and next to it a machine that hummed and whirred. It took her a few seconds to remember where she was, but when she did, she let loose a sob, as it was exactly like waking from a nightmare only to discover it was a real horror she didn't know whether she could bear.

A nurse in a crisp white uniform and Red Cross hat bustled into the room and pulled aside the sheet. "You're awake," she said.

"Where's my sister?" Isabel said in rising desperation. "Audrey Dickinson?"

"You've had quite a shock. Are you feeling well enough to stand? We really shouldn't use a bed for someone who's not sick, but they had to sedate you in the ambulance ride over. It's not hospital policy to keep anyone who..."

"Where's Audrey? Please, ma'am."

"Can you stand?" the nurse repeated.

Isabel struggled to a sitting position and swung her legs over the narrow bed. Her dress was damp and muddy. Her shoes lay on the floor, and she shoved her feet into them.

"Please, can you take me to my sister?" If it would help, she would beg, genuflect.

"Follow me," the nurse said briskly. Isabel tripped after her, lightheaded, listing to the side. She chided herself for wasting precious moments unconscious when she should have been at Audrey's bedside, providing comfort. The nurse led her into a small waiting room and pointed to a chair. "Wait right here."

Isabel gaped at her, aghast. "I have to see Audrey. Please, ma'am, won't you take me to her?"

A middle-aged woman on the other side of the room laid down her magazine and peered at Isabel from behind her spectacles.

The nurse turned to her with a pitying gaze. "Wait here, and the doctor will be with you shortly. But first give me your telephone number, and we'll contact your family."

Isabel started to weep. "My father's dead, and Mother..."

"Yes?" the nurse leaned toward her. A tinny sob escaped Isabel's throat. She hiccupped out Mother's name and address. "We don't have a telephone."

"Someone else, then, who might?"

A sudden chill seized Isabel, followed by a wave of dizziness. She croaked the name of their building's superintendent and Mr. McGilligan's grocery. "Which hospital is this?"

"Lane on Webster Street," the nurse said, not unkindly, and left.

Bewildered mothers, a bereft older couple, a belligerent man and his wife, and families with wailing children wandered into the waiting room. Isabel couldn't bear to sit while Audrey was in pain, doubtless wondering why she'd been abandoned in a strange hospital. She straightened when the nurse returned with a paper cup of water and handkerchief.

"Thought you might be thirsty. Also, I reached your super. He'll go to your flat and tell your mother to come directly."

"Where's the doctor who's to see me?"

The nurse patted her arm. "Once your mother arrives, he'll speak to you both."

"But Audrey... how is she?"

The nurse looked away. "The doctor will explain everything. Just rest till your mother arrives. The rain and traffic might delay her." Before Isabel could speak, she dashed out.

Briefly, Isabel wondered about Claude. But in the end, she didn't care. She could never forgive either herself or him. And Mother... she dreaded seeing her face after she heard the news. She held onto a measure of hope: Audrey was asleep, and they would go to her bedside, soothe her, nurse her back to health. The empty paper cup lay at Isabel's feet. Her throat was numb and cracked, but she dared not search for a water fountain. Twilight shadows from the double windows fanned across the room, and she shut her eyes.

Suddenly, strong hands seized her shoulders. A gravelly voice demanded, "Dear God, what happened? The receptionist told me to wait here while they fetch the doctor."

Isabel blinked at the gray, lined face bending over her in a man's coat and brogans. It took her a few seconds to register it was Mother. Her hands were rough with calluses, and the dark creases under her eyes made her look a decade older. Mother shook her again.

"An automobile hit Audrey," she choked out, "At Lafayette Square. We went there this afternoon. It was raining, and she ran straight into the street to look for stones before I could stop her." Her throat constricted with the bald-faced lie. She stiffened, wondering whether Mother suspected her culpability.

Mother sank into a chair beside her. "Where the devil is Lafayette Square? And why..."

The nurse hurried toward them. "Mrs. Dickinson? Follow me, please."

"Where's my daughter?" Mother cried.

"Please, ma'am, this way."

Mother's eyes flared with panic. The nurse led them to an office off the main hall, where a doctor in white coat and stethoscope stood beside a pair of metal chairs. He threw them an uneasy glance and jiggled a hand inside his pocket. Ice settled in Isabel's fingers and toes.

"This is Audrey Dickinson's mother and sister," the nurse said, closing the door.

"Tell me quick. Where's my daughter? Is she all right?"

"Won't you please sit down?" the doctor said in a gentle voice. "I advise it, Mrs. Dickinson."

Mother remained standing. Isabel hovered just behind, her heart slamming against her ribcage. She already knew the doctor would deliver dreadful news, the very worst.

He folded his hands together. "Mrs. Dickinson, I'm terribly sorry, but your daughter died just after four this afternoon. The impact of the automobile was too much. We did everything we could to save her, but I'm afraid it was too late." He mumbled something about a fractured spine, but Isabel couldn't make sense of his words.

"No, no, no, dear God, no," Mother keened, her wails ricocheting through the room. Her limbs began to convulse, and she swayed.

"Please have a seat," the doctor urged. The nurse held Mother's shoulders as her legs gave, and she collapsed into a chair and moaned.

Isabel blinked, and the doctor was gone. A relentless black ocean churned inside her head. As the floor spun, she stumbled into a chair, groping for Mother's hand. The nurse offered Mother a cup of water, but she pushed it away with a howl, and it splashed on the floor.

A strangled sound wrenched from Isabel's mouth. As the nurse held her head, she gagged the remaining contents of her stomach onto the floor. The nurse swiped her lips with a cloth and left. Later still, someone guided them out the door, down the whitewashed hallway, as Isabel clung fast to Mother's arm.

In front of the hospital, they were handed into a taxi. It rumbled down the street, depositing them at the nearest trolley stop.

"So this is it," Mother said as they staggered like a pair of drunks to wait for the streetcar. "They've washed their hands of us."

On the streetcar, Mother sagged forward, head in her hands. Her back and shoulders trembled. When they reached the flat, she slumped against the counter, still in her coat and brogans, and lit a cigarette. It was the first time she had smoked indoors. Her face was rigid, warning Isabel not to speak. Neither of them fixed supper. Isabel had no appetite. Besides, she knew she didn't deserve to eat.

She burrowed onto the mattress she'd shared with Audrey and caressed the small shape her sister had made. Inconceivable she'd burst with life hours ago, and now she'd been dumped like a shell while the ocean writhed away, vast and indifferent. If only it would drag her away, too. Smothering a cry, she bargained silently with God: she'd renounce boys forever if only he'd return Audrey. Later, she prayed for her thoughts to be erased, though she knew that wish wouldn't be granted, either.

Through the wee hours of the morning, she thrashed under the sheets, waiting for Mother, who didn't come to bed. Although Mother hadn't spoken since the streetcar stop, Isabel heard her silent accusation: as the older sister, she had failed. Utterly. She wanted Mother to scream the words out loud, whip and punish her as she surely deserved. If she learned the full story, she would never forgive her, and that, too, was fair.

CHAPTER SEVEN

Isabel hunched over the table, sipping stale coffee. A gray slant of light dribbled through the kitchen blinds. She couldn't tell and didn't care whether it was morning or afternoon. Mother had left to ring the hotel and make funeral arrangements, but Isabel couldn't summon the energy to sweep and clean, let alone wash the dishes.

When Mother finally hobbled through the door, her face was white and stunned. She drooped against the sofa and lit a cigarette.

Isabel chanced, "Did you reach the hotel?"

"They told me if I don't go back to work right after the funeral, I'll lose my job for good."

"But… they can't do that."

"Of course they can. I'm poor, and a thousand other people will take my place. That's our sorry lot." Her eyes grew savage as she blew a ring of smoke. "I telegrammed James. Told him not to risk his job by coming here. Anyways, the burial's day after tomorrow. He can't possibly make it home in time."

Isabel bit down hard on her lip. It would be a small solace for all of them to be together. She hoped James would disregard Mother's advice and come, anyhow. Coughing, Mother shuffled into the bedroom, leaving a contrail of smoke. Behind the door, the bed springs groaned.

•   •   •

"So much for the church," Mother said as they walked home after the funeral reception. Clouds scudded across the sky, and fog shrouded the storefronts. "Nothing makes a whit of difference when we're damned with one disaster after another. As far as I care, there isn't a God, because he doesn't look after the poor people. For the likes of us, life is senseless and short."

Isabel stiffened and shot a look behind in case any parishioners had overheard. She thought of James receiving Mother's telegram, his anguish after realizing he wouldn't see Audrey again, even in death. The pavement beneath her feet felt squishy. In the kitchen, the bouquet of lilies from the super secreted a sweet, cloying fragrance that turned her stomach.

•   •   •

Two days later, she walked to Mr. McGilligan's grocery. It was a long trek uptown, over forty-five minutes, which she normally shortened by taking the trolley partway, but she needed motion, distraction. She wasn't even sure she still had her job, but she had nothing to lose by going.

Mr. McGilligan hurried toward her, tugging his suspenders. "You poor child."

Isabel blinked back tears. He was a tall, gaunt man in his forties with graying sideburns, stubbled chin, and a penchant for jazz. He had a corny sense of humor, but Isabel didn't mind; he was familiar and solid and didn't take guff. Better yet, he had been good friends with Dad, had told her more than once that her father had helped folks see things for what they were and how they could be better.

He laid a hand on her arm. "I'm right sorry about your sister. Saved a little something for you and your mother." He withdrew a brown paper package from behind the counter. "It's not much, just some coffee, sugar, and canned peas you might use."

Isabel felt a wisp of warmth. "Can you give me something to do, please? Anything. I want to keep busy." Her voice wobbled as she gazed, desperate, around the shop. She would work without pay if she had to.

To her relief, he nodded. "You can straighten the shelves on the last aisle and clear out some space. We've got cans in back you can set out there."

"Yes, sir." Isabel reached for the apron he kept behind the counter.

"But take it slow. Whatever you can manage." She was grateful when he turned on the radio: a hiss of static, then a saxophone's bright melody.

Before Isabel left, Mr. McGilligan told her the longshoremen had begun striking, standing up to the shipowners for the same reasons Dad had exposed in the secret paper: risking their lives for lousy pay to haul enormous cargo loads from ships, operate pulleys and winches, drive jitneys. Even scoring a day's work was a roll of the dice, since they were at the mercy of the hiring boss. Dad would have been glad of the strike, Isabel was sure. Only now the thing he had fought for had sprung into motion without him.

Outside, a dense fog had rolled in from the Bay. Fragments sprang from the mist: a woman's high heel inches ahead; a sliver of a green store awning. At Market, the crowd thickened, and the city's breadwinners stampeded and shoved Isabel aside without pardon. She didn't blame them; she was small and inconsequential, nobody on whom an entire family could depend. Chancing a shortcut, she dodged past the shambles of a building rumored to house an opium den. Suddenly, a shadow fell into her path, and she sensed movement from a window overhead. *Was this where a man was murdered? Robbed blind and left for dead?* She skittered out of the alley, her heart clobbering.

When she entered the flat, Mother was gone, and Mr. Whiskers didn't emerge from the alley. The night they returned from the hospital, he had skulked into the alley, as if by instinct he'd known the flat had been flung into chaos with the little girl gone. When Isabel crooned his name from the stoop, she heard a rustle as a rat scuttled into a garbage can. Shuddering, she shut the door.

She had shoved a chicken thigh into the oven when a rap at the door startled her. Cautiously she opened it a crack. Claude stood on the stoop, his face shadowy and contrite. She stepped back with a kick of revulsion.

He peered at her through the crack. "May I come in?" She narrowed her eyes. She didn't want to speak to him, let alone see him. "Just for a minute?" His mouth contorted, as though he feared she would turn him away.

She stood glaring at him and felt satisfied when his eyes flickered with uncertainty. She said coldly, "I'll come out. But I can't be gone long. Mother…"

"It won't be but a minute."

She didn't take her coat, and as an afterthought she grabbed the key, then slammed and locked the door. The nerve of him to come here. How did he even know how to find her? With a rising brew of anger, she marched down the street. Now he knew where she lived, the hovel and seedy neighborhood. He trotted after her.

"I left the oven on." Her voice was harsh with accusation. "Mother will be home any minute and wonder where I've gone. What do you want?"

Claude touched her arm. For a few seconds, her pulse fluttered with the old thrill, but she caught herself and twisted from him. The stink of rotting food down the alley blew through her nostrils, and the wind blasted her off balance. She pinned her arms against her chest, wanting the cold to whip into her.

"Oh God, Isabel." He started to say something else, then abruptly stopped. A stream of automobiles rumbled past. In a tremulous voice, he said, "I read about it in the paper the next day. It's tragic, what happened. I'm awfully sorry."

"Lot of good sorry does now." As soon as she said it, she regretted it. Mother's words, not hers. A horn blared at the corner, and she turned toward the noise in a daze.

"I wanted to find you at the hospital, but I didn't know where they'd taken you, and I knew I wouldn't be welcome, since they only allow family."

She stole a peek at him. He looked leaner, his cheeks angular, eyes red and mouth ashy, as though he hadn't slept much. "How'd you find me?" She slung the words at him.

"A little detective work. You said once you live west of Market. Then I remembered you work for a grocer named McGilligan."

She drew a sharp intake of air. "You went to see him? You asked him for my *address*?" She felt like an insect he had captured for a science experiment, pinned and pried apart.

"I had to see how you were getting on. I... I couldn't bear it. At first Mr. McGilligan didn't want to tell me where you live. He said he'd need to clear it with you. But he must have seen I was desperate, and I let him know I'm your friend."

"You tricked him into it," she burst out, though she knew she was being unfair.

He looked at her in surprise. "Maybe you don't believe so anymore, but I still think of you as a friend. I couldn't forgive myself if I didn't come by to pay my respects." When the light changed, he followed her around a corner and across a street, past a tobacco shop, pharmacy, and an old speakeasy.

"So now you've paid them," she said. "If that's all you wanted, I need to go home."

"I understand if you blame me. Hell, I understand if you never want to see me again."

"Well." She let this sit between them, thick and reproachful, but that didn't feel right, either. "At the end of the day, it was my fault." Her voice cracked, and to her horror, her eyes clotted with tears. She pressed a palm against her face.

"Don't ever think so." Claude dug a hanky from his pocket and handed it to her. "It's not your fault, Izz. It was a terrible accident that could've happened to anyone."

"No." The words rang out, cold and shrill. "It didn't have to happen. It *wouldn't* have happened if I hadn't met you at the park. Or else if I hadn't left Audrey on her own while..." She sucked in her breath and swung from him. Tears leaking down her cheeks, she stumbled back toward Turk. For all she knew, Mother was at the flat, waiting and wondering.

"Wait a minute, Isabel. Please." His voice was strained. Reluctantly she let him catch up, then thrust the kerchief at him, her hands trembling. "Keep it. I..." he stammered, stopped. "I know nothing I say or do will ever be enough. I'm just... terribly sorry. If I could go back and change things, I'd do it in an instant..." He swallowed, removed a piece of paper from his pocket. "Here. It's my folks' address and telephone number. If there's anything you need, ring me." She took it from him uncertainly. His family must be well off if they could afford a telephone. "I'm serious. I want to help you and your family any way I can. If you've got chores to be done or anything else, give me a call. Please."

Isabel crumpled the paper into her dress pocket and edged away. She wanted to be rid of him and hole back up in the flat. "Thanks," she said stiffly.

He gazed at her with a helpless longing, and she turned and bolted down the street, feeling his eyes on her back. A wonder she'd ever been attracted to him. Now she felt nothing but disgust and shame for agreeing to their rendezvous. If anyone knew, they would rightly brand her a girl of poor judgment and loose morals. She stamped across the street before the light changed, half wishing a lorry truck would swerve into her path and end it all right there.

When she let herself into the flat, Mother whirled from the stove. "Dammit all, you left the oven on! Were you trying to burn down the flat on top of everything else?"

"I'm sorry." It seemed it was all she said to Mother these days. Inadequate, hopelessly empty words. "I was looking for Mr. Whiskers." The lie slipped from her lips.

Mother tutted. "Burn the place to a crisp for a miserable cat."

Isabel hung her head. "Audrey loved him." She recalled how her sister had clutched him close like a baby, nuzzling her cheek against his fur.

"Don't." Mother looked as though she'd been slapped. Her eyes grew hooded, and Isabel glimpsed a trace of a young child's sorrow in her face. It was odd to think of the girl her mother had once been, concealed behind her hard, gray irises. But it was no use; Audrey's presence lingered in the flat: barrettes and ribbons she had woven through her hair, the faint impression of her skull upon the pillow, her earthy smell on the unwashed bedsheets, her gingham dress hanging in the closet, the dog-eared copy of *The Velveteen Rabbit*, which they had read together countless times, Mr. Whiskers' bed of blankets.

Isabel pulled the chicken thigh out of the oven. It was barely warm, but she divided the meat in two and slid each half onto a pair of plates. Mother ate several bites, then frowned and pushed away her plate. Clearing her throat, she announced she had a telegram from James. The camp sergeant had given him leave to come home, though he needed to scrape together cash and find a ride.

Isabel leaned forward, her pulse leaping. "When?"

Mother shook her head and touched her lips, as though they were bruised and tender. "We can't afford for him to come home before his stint ends."

"We could go to him." But as soon as she said it, Isabel realized it wouldn't work. "Why shouldn't he come home for a few days?"

Mother lobbed her an incredulous look. "Do you know how much that would cost? It's better for him to stay where he is. He'll be home in another few months, anyhow." Isabel fought down a wave of hysteria. She needed James; he alone would understand.

"Anyways, what good would it do? Audrey's buried. And I can't take time off work." Isabel's eyes turned watery. She ducked her head, not wanting Mother to see her tears. "It's best to stay busy. Regretting the past won't do a lick of good," Mother said, not unkindly. "This is the hand we've been dealt. The sooner you accept it, the better." Isabel tried to speak, but her voice was bottled, and she couldn't force out the words. With a shiver, she lurched to the sink. She was relieved when Mother grabbed her smokes and muttered she was going out to telegram James. Clearly she preferred being alone, too. There was nothing to say or share, just the guilt that sat between them like a heavy cargo sack.

That night on the mattress, she bunched her knees to her chest. Their family had unwound, just as she'd feared. It was clear Mr. Whiskers wasn't coming back, either. He must have run away for good this time. Her stomach knotted, and she shifted to her side to ease the quick stab of pain. All of a sudden, she sat up as a thought took hold. If Mother wouldn't let James come home, she could go to him at Yosemite — the trip Audrey always wanted to make. Besides, there was nothing holding her in San Francisco any longer. If she could find a job in or near the park, she might even stay for good. For several minutes, she puzzled over how she would get there, since she didn't have money for train fare. Then she remembered Claude and his offer.

CHAPTER EIGHT

In the telephone booth on the corner, Isabel lifted the receiver before she lost her nerve. Fumbling in her purse for a coin, she rasped out Claude's number to the operator. The phone bleated six times before a woman answered. Swallowing, Isabel asked for Claude.

"Who is this?"

"A friend from school," she mumbled, then said reluctantly, "Isabel Dickinson." Muffled voices in the background, a clatter as the phone was laid down.

When Claude picked up, Isabel blurted, "I have a favor to ask."

"Go ahead. I'm listening."

"Do you... can you get an automobile? I need to go to Yosemite."

There was a silence. "I can try to borrow one. When do you need to go?"

"As soon as possible." She knew she sounded desperate.

"Give me a few days to see what I can do. I'll come find you when I have news."

"All right." She swayed in the booth, suddenly winded.

Isabel had finished washing dishes and was reading a book when a knock sounded at the door. She jumped up and hurried over, though Mother lay on the sofa listening to Jack Benny and gave no sign of moving. Claude hung in the doorframe, his cheeks ruddy from the wind, a dark scarf wound around his neck. Isabel watched him, hopeful.

"Who is it?" Mother called sharply.

"A friend from school. I'm going out for a minute. I won't be long."

They moved toward the street corner, not speaking. Isabel darted a look back at the flat, but the door remained closed. She turned the corner, and Claude followed.

He twisted his head toward her. "I can borrow a truck day after tomorrow, but I've got to have it back by Monday with a full tank. It's my buddy's uncle's truck, and Sunday's his day off."

A brief spark of hope charged through her like an electric current, a dangerous thing. She gripped her elbows.

"So we'd need to leave before dawn, 'cause it takes all day to get there. Dirt roads and lots of traffic. And afterwards, I'll have to turn around and drive right back."

She made rapid calculations: she'd need to get ready tomorrow, pack a bag and hide it.

"Can you be ready by four on Sunday morning?" Claude was saying.

"Yes, sure I can." Her voice floated out bright, eager.

"Say, where will you stay while you're there?"

"With my brother. But there wasn't time to let him know..."

Claude raised a brow. "Sure you'll be allowed to stay? The CCC doesn't take girls."

Isabel frowned. She hadn't thought of this, but she didn't want to reveal her ignorance. "They'll make room for me. There's bound to be a sleeping bag I can borrow, off by myself."

Claude looked skeptical. "I'll pull up in front of your apartment Sunday."

"Who was at the door?" Mother demanded when she returned.

"Elaine from school." She fumbled for an excuse. "She invited me to lunch tomorrow, but I told her I was too busy."

Mother snorted. "She came all this way to ask you that?" But to Isabel's relief, she closed her eyes.

In the morning, Mother winced and pressed her lower back, then handed Isabel a list of groceries to buy. After she left for the hotel, Isabel leaned against the counter, dizzy with the thought of all the things she had to do. She decided to tackle them one at a time. First, she packed a knapsack with basic clothes: a dress, two skirts and blouses, underwear and toiletries. From the back of the closet, where Audrey's few belongings were stacked, she withdrew *The Velveteen Rabbit* and stuffed it into the bottom of the knapsack. It was a fitting memento of Audrey; when she was feeling blue, she would read passages.

After a moment's deliberation, she withdrew three dollars from the jam jar in the back of the cupboard, rationalizing that at least part of it was her own savings. All the same, she was racked by a flurry of guilt. But she simply couldn't risk going on such a long trip without cash; she would need to pay Claude for gas and other expenses. She resolved to earn back the money and repay Mother as soon as possible.

After scrubbing down the flat and washing and hanging out clothes, she scrawled a few lines to Mother, explaining she had gone to see James. She slipped the note into her pocket. Then, her mind racing, she set out for the store to buy staples for Mother, along with bread, cheese, and fish paste she would use to make sandwiches for the road.

For over an hour that night, she counted sheep. Even after Mother's snores snuffled from the bed, she counted for several more minutes before tiptoeing to the closet. Once, when

Mother's snores abruptly stopped, Isabel froze until they resumed. Cautiously she groped in the closet for the knapsack. In the darkened parlor, she yanked on her dress and stuffed her nightgown, canteen, and sandwiches into the pack. She must have dozed on the sofa, because she jerked upright to the sound of a bleating horn.

A truck idled in front, headlights blazing. Her pulse sped up. She dashed a look at the bedroom door, worried Mother would wake. Swiftly she wriggled into her coat and placed Mother's note on the table where she would be sure to find it. Then she eased outside, carefully shutting the door behind her. The truck's passenger door clicked open, and she scrambled over the running board into the cab, settling the knapsack at her feet. In an urgent tone, she told Claude to go. Even now, Mother might swarm outside, demanding what in hell Isabel was doing at this ungodly hour.

As the truck lurched ahead with a belch, Isabel's heart gave an erratic kick, and she clutched the edge of the seat. She was doing it: leaving Mother, the flat, the San Francisco cold. At long last she was traveling to a beautiful, wondrous place. That James waited at the end of the journey was icing on the cake.

CHAPTER NINE

In the shuttered stillness of pre-dawn, they bumped down Turk. It was deserted, save for a few lorries and scattered lights. On the corner of Market, a pair of shadows staggered in front of a dance hall.

Isabel was feverish with excitement; her pulse tapped an unsteady rhythm. The cab reeked of stale cigarettes and sour body odor. She cranked open the passenger window.

"It'll be awhile before we're out of the city," Claude said, squinting at the road.

"You drive real well." An olive branch of sorts.

"Nah. I get by. A pal taught me the basics. But I don't have a license. If we get stopped by a copper…"

"Just drive careful."

"There's a map in the glove box under your seat. Take a look, will you? Fellow I borrowed the truck from said we'll follow Highway 99 through Tracy then onto Modesto. When we get to Merced, we switch to Highway 140, and that'll take us to Yosemite."

Isabel fumbled under the seat and withdrew a folded map. "It's too dark to read."

"Sun'll be up in over an hour. We might not be far from Tracy by then."

She compressed her lips and stared out the window, determined not to let the conversation get too friendly. Funny how once she had feelings for this boy, and now he might as well have been a distant acquaintance. She would have to squash any romantic notions he still harbored.

"Say, does your mother know you're going to Yosemite?"

Isabel swiveled toward Claude, stumbling to form a response. "She... I left her a note." He said nothing, perhaps passing silent judgment. She wondered what Mr. McGilligan would think when he also learned she'd left. At least he could easily replace her. She wasn't fool enough to think she was special. He would likely do better with someone bigger and stronger, anyway.

They rolled east out of the city onto an unpaved two-lane highway. Dust and gravel rumbled around the wheels. Groggy from her fitful night, Isabel slumped against the seat. The truck jerked and thumped over rocks and ditches. But because dozing was difficult and unfair to Claude besides, she forced her eyes open.

"Looks like we're in Tracy," she said, studying the map as they approached a small agricultural town. Smears of gold and scarlet light tipped over the edge of the sky. Railroad lines crisscrossed the highway outside town, and on the main street, they passed the Central Pacific Railroad depot and squat storefronts with striped green awnings.

"Let's stop for a bite," Claude said. "I could use a cup of coffee." He pulled up in front of a diner. Through the glass, Isabel saw a pair of old men slouched in a booth. Claude held the door for her and touched her shoulder, but she wrenched away. She didn't want to stoke his hopes and give him ideas.

They slid onto stools at the counter. The waitress, a stern woman with a mop of blonde hair and a painted red mouth, swung her gaze from Claude to Isabel suspiciously. "Mighty early for teenagers."

Isabel's face went hot, and she leaned away from Claude. Maybe she could pretend she was his sister. Claude paid five cents for coffee and cream. When Isabel asked for water, the waitress gave her a scornful look, then filled a glass from the tap and banged it down in front of her.

"These stools are for paying customers, so you kids better hurry it up and move on. No loitering."

"I paid for the coffee," Claude muttered, but the waitress turned her back to them.

Beneath the counter, Isabel slipped a sandwich to Claude, and they took furtive bites. It occurred to her that Mother was awake and had probably read the note. Would she curse? Tear the paper to shreds, relieved to be rid of a wayward daughter who had caused her nothing but trouble? She ran her tongue over her teeth. Her throat was caked with dust. The waitress stood behind the counter, glaring, until they gathered the rest of the sandwiches and left.

"Jeez, she was a pill," Claude grumbled as he started the engine.

On Highway 99, they drove past dairy farms, pastures with grazing cows, farmers on tractors, almond and orange groves and corn fields. Every few miles, Isabel saw colorful, stylized billboards with snippets from Burma-Shave ads. She read the lines to Claude, and they grinned after stringing the series together. "Bachelor's quarters, Dog on the rug, Whiskers to blame, No one to hug, Burma-Shave."

"How you doing?" Claude said after a while.

Isabel blinked at him in surprise. With nothing to do except gaze out the window, she had to struggle not to think of the dead. Dad and Audrey sat beside her like ghosts, glassy-eyed with regret for unfulfilled dreams. This trip was as much Audrey's wish as hers. She shivered and rubbed her arms, though the sun was hot, and the sky gleamed a deep blue.

She kept her voice even. "All right. How about you? You're the one driving."

"Tank's about halfway full. I'll fill up in Merced. There's an oilcan in the truck bed." He moved his hand toward hers, and she wrenched her fingers away as though she had touched a hot stove. He muttered, "Sorry. Stupid reflex."

Frowning, she faced the window. Highway 140, a three lane unpaved road, ran north and east to Yosemite, sloping uphill through fruit and olive orchards and the wide green expanse of the San Joaquin Valley. Traffic had increased. Now that they were closer, she felt a tremor of unease about how James would receive her. What if Claude were right, and she couldn't stay at the camp? A lump formed inside her throat.

The morning James had left for the CCC, Isabel had said without thinking, "Easy for you to leave us in this dump while you go somewhere pretty." Her brother had recoiled as though she had slugged him, and instantly she'd regretted her words. She knew he had applied to the CCC gig because Mother had begged him to find something steady and safe, away from the docks. Though Isabel had spluttered an apology, she worried he had taken her careless words to heart.

When the snow-lined contours of the Sierra Nevada Mountain Range emerged, shimmering in a bath of golden light, she gasped softly. Glorious liquid greens of fir and spruce trees, blues of ridges. She took a deep breath, her lungs expanding. But before long, the bumpiness and steep ascent of the dirt road made her nauseous, and she closed her eyes and gripped her stomach.

"Carsick?" Claude said.

"A little. I'll get over it. It's just..." Another swell of nausea spilled up her throat, and she turned her face.

"Let me know if you want to stop."

A breeze from the open window punched her cheeks." Keep going." She palmed her forehead, gulping air.

In Mariposa, they puttered down Main Street past antique gold mining signs and a billboard advertising an inn for Yosemite tourists. Claude parked in front of a cafe, where they hoped to refill their water jugs. Inside, Isabel clutched the canteens against her chest, trying not to look nervous. A waitress pointed her to the washroom.

When she emerged, the waitress was standing by the door, arms folded beneath her ample bosom. She pierced Isabel with a slow gaze. "You a tourist on your way to Yosemite?"

"No. Yes. I mean, not exactly. I'm visiting my brother. He's at a CCC camp there."

A mocking smile gathered around the woman's lips. "Your brother, huh?"

Isabel flushed. "Yes. He's been gone awhile and..."

"Traveling alone?"

"A... a friend is driving me."

"That so?" The woman smirked, and Isabel's face heated. She saw Claude pacing in front of the diner and beelined toward the door. The woman sniggered, "That your friend?" She broke into a long cackle.

Mortified, Isabel fled outside and begged Claude to go, now. He took one look at her and started the truck. She was grateful he didn't ask why the big hurry.

After an hour, they stopped behind a long, unmoving stream of automobiles. Claude swore under his breath and craned his head out the window. "Excuse me, sir, what's going on?"

A man in the roadster ahead of them frowned. "It's the control road up to El Portal. Authorities open it every hour in the opposite direction. Too dangerous to do it any other way."

"How much longer you figure before it opens this way?"

"Anyone's guess. Half an hour, forty-five minutes? Say, be careful when we start going. Folks' radiators are like to boil over on account of the steep grade. Hang onto your water. You might need it for your motor."

"We've been drinking a lot of the water," Isabel said, worried.

When the caravan of automobiles began moving in fits and starts, Claude cranked the engine, shifted gears, and eased forward. Progress was painstakingly slow as they inched up the incline. They passed a few automobiles on the shoulder, hoods open and steaming. To Isabel's dismay, the truck sputtered and belched smoke. She steeled herself as the engine idled then died. Behind them, automobiles honked.

Someone yelled, "Dagnammit, shift it to neutral and slide it off the road. You can't block the whole bum line!"

Claude clambered out, his shirt soaked with sweat. "Can you help me coast it over there?" he asked Isabel. When she stared at him, dumbfounded, he assured her, "When it's in neutral, it's more like a loaded wheelbarrow. Just take it easy and hang onto the rear bumper."

She was amazed when they succeeded in moving the truck onto the shoulder. Claude peered into the engine and asked for a towel, which he wrapped around the pump. After pouring water onto the tubing, he rocked onto his heels. "Let's give 'er a try."

Isabel sagged with relief when the truck grumbled and roared to life. They shifted back onto the road, cutting off a red-faced man in a Chevy, who blasted his horn and shook a fist.

Claude touched her arm, and she jumped.

She thrust his fingers aside. "Don't."

"Sorry. It's just… I wish…"

"What?" she said sharply, her face clouding.

"I wish we could go back to that day and do things differently."

"Stop! I'll leave this truck. I swear I'll do it." She pressed the door handle.

"No, wait! I'm sorry, Izz! I never meant to upset you."

Tears sprang to her eyes, and she fumbled for her kerchief, snapping her head away.

"I promise I won't say another word about it." His voice was low, repentant.

The Sierra Nevada Range climbed toward the tips of the clouds. Firs and distant snowy peaks glistened in the sunlight, and the air was instantly thinner, brisker. Isabel leaned out the window and filled her lungs. When she saw a sign for the Yosemite Arch Rock Entrance, her pulse quickened, and she let out a little cheer. Claude glanced at her with a grin. They edged forward a few feet behind a queue of automobiles.

He said, "I suppose they'll charge us to get in."

She hadn't thought of this. Her temples throbbed, whether from the excitement of being so close to James and the park or from having to wait longer, she wasn't sure. She hadn't brought aspirin tablets, hadn't even considered she might need them. As the engine belched gasoline fumes, she pinched her forehead.

When they reached the guard station, a park ranger said, "Welcome to Yosemite. Two dollars admission. Any dogs, cats, or firearms?"

"No, sir," Claude said.

"Here." Isabel thrust two bills at Claude. It was a steep price for what she had assumed was a free national park—almost all the cash she'd brought. Thank goodness she had enough. "Sir, can you tell us how to get to the CCC Cascades camp?" she asked as the ranger handed them a receipt with a folded map.

"It's down near Tamarack Creek and the Merced River. Keep following El Portal Road for about three miles. You'll see the camp off to the right." His eyes glided over her. "Camp supervisor's awful strict. You on government business?"

"My brother's there," Isabel said in a small voice.

"They don't take visitors." He waved them on, and the truck jettied ahead with a stutter.

Isabel swallowed hard at the prospect of riding back to the city with Claude. He must have thought of it, too, because he said, "I'll wait to make sure you can stay. But I won't have much time to spare." She didn't reply.

On either side of the narrow dirt road, two enormous granite boulders rose and joined twenty or thirty feet overhead, forming the arch entrance into the park. Leaves of gnarled oak trees and manzanita bordered the cave-like tunnel. As they passed beneath the mossy rocks, Isabel gave a low whoop. Hanging out the window, she tasted the air, which was crisp and dry, so different from San Francisco.

She sipped the heady smell of pine and cedar and whispered, "I'm here, Audrey. I made it." A white-tailed deer pranced across the road and disappeared into the shrubs. She spied a thin column of smoke circling above a clearing, where wooden barracks and army tents clustered together in the makings of a Wild West Outpost, surrounded by a forest. She counted seven wooden-planked shelters and between them neat rows of squat tents.

"Looks like a little town." She wanted to leap out of the truck, run breathless toward the men and find James, though she knew it would be more complicated.

Claude swung the truck onto a rutted set of tracks leading to the camp. Young men in high laced boots, khaki hats and trousers sawed timber, scrubbed clothes on washboards, hauled tin buckets to the barracks, unloaded logs from trailers attached to trucks, and whittled vegetables on planked tables.

Isabel shaded her eyes, scanning for James. Smoke spiraled from a campfire in a central open-air building. She whiffed smoked meat, and her stomach rumbled. A few yards from the cluster of buildings, Claude braked and turned off the engine.

Nervously, Isabel touched her throat, feeling the eczema's flame. She had gripped the door handle when a broad-shouldered man in khaki uniform approached the driver's side.

His face was pocked, and a thin scar ran down the crease of his forehead. Isabel guessed he was in his late forties.

"Help you?"

"Yes, sir. We're here to see this young lady's brother."

"James Dickinson," Isabel said, leaning toward the window. "He works at Cascades. Can you please let us know where to find him?"

The man frowned and crossed his arms. "Cascades has over two hundred men, and we run it like an army camp. Only recruits are allowed on premise."

"Please, sir. We've driven all the way from San Francisco. Can I see him for just a moment?" Isabel's voice trembled. With sinking certainty, she understood he would turn her away, and she would be forced to return to the city with Claude. Willing herself not to cry, she bit her lip.

"The government owns this camp. I don't make the rules. What you're asking is awful unusual."

"It would only be for a minute or two." Claude glanced at Isabel, who slumped in her seat, wringing her hands.

"This some family emergency?" The man jerked his chin toward the burlap tents, then leveled a gaze on Isabel.

She faltered, "Yes, sir. It's awfully important."

He gave her a long, probing look. "Then I reckon for a minute. Might have a helluva time finding him, though you're lucky on a couple counts. It's almost supper on a Sunday, so most of the recruits are here." He strode toward the center of the clearing, near the campfire and barracks. Isabel and Claude scrabbled out of the truck and trotted to catch up.

"What did you say his name was?" the man called behind to Isabel. Darting close to his heels, she told him, and he mumbled something she couldn't hear.

"Yes, sir, Mr. Mayhall," a boy around twenty sang after the older man spoke into his ear. The boy sprinted toward one of the makeshift structures. Clearly, Mr. Mayhall commanded respect.

He nodded at Isabel and Claude. "They're going to try and find his section."

"Thank you, sir," Isabel croaked, bowing her head and twining her fingers together. She didn't dare look at Claude, sure he was thinking they would have to head straight back to San Francisco. An utter waste of a trip. But after all, he had offered, despite the fact that nothing either of them did could ever be penance for that terrible, fateful afternoon.

Mr. Mayhall vanished into a fenced off area that might have been private quarters. Wrung-out trousers and shirts, socks and underwear dangled on clotheslines between trees. A pair of bare-chested men sat on army cots inside one of the open-air tents, scraping potatoes with pocket knives. Groups of recruits milled among the buildings. One boy ground to a halt and stared at Isabel. Maybe she was one of the few females he had seen in weeks or months. Embarrassed, she averted her gaze. Then, with mounting concern, she raked her eyes over the barracks, still not seeing James.

While Claude paced back and forth, she sank onto the ground, certain they would wait a long time. She peered at the cerulean blue of the sky, so unlike the gray clouds and fog of San Francisco. Instantly she experienced a jolt of recognition. *The Isle of Castaways* – an oasis lush with trees, flowers, and animals, encircled by cliffs. She half expected to see a glittering kingdom rising in the distance. Closing her eyes, she could sense Audrey beside her, humming, bouncing.

"Isabel! Good God!"

Her eyes flew open, and to her relief, she saw James jogging toward her. His hair was trimmed short; his arms were lean and tanned; he wore army trousers and a short-sleeved denim shirt. Isabel leaped up and staggered toward him. Tumbling into his arms and pressing her face against his chest, she dissolved into sobs.

CHAPTER TEN

Outside the Cascades Camp mess hall, Isabel sat on a stool, facing James. Minutes earlier, after a tense conversation with the senior leader of his section and Commander Mayhall, her brother had convinced both men to permit Isabel and Claude to stay for supper on the condition they didn't receive extra meals; the recruits' food portions were strictly allotted.

"There's no need to share," Isabel had protested. "I've brought enough for us all."

But James would hear none of it. So the three of them had divided his serving of boiled chicken, roasted potatoes, canned peas and a roll, plus a fish paste sandwich and cheese slices that Isabel had packed. Isabel reserved the last sandwich, raisins, and orange slices for Claude to eat on the way back to the city. She would do without, especially since the long trip for this short visit had been entirely her fault.

To allow Isabel and James privacy, Claude had taken his portion onto a fallen log a few yards away. The din of men's voices, guffaws, and clattering utensils sailed out of the open-air mess hall. Opposite was a crude blacksmith and tool shop, and James pointed out the lavatory and showers, administrative offices, rec hall, medical dispensary, and motor garages.

"I can't believe you came all this way, Izz," he said, balancing a tin plate on his knees. He forced a smile, but it slipped. In profile, he resembled their father: high forehead and regal nose; shock of dark hair; smattering of whiskers on his cheeks; lean torso; long, muscular limbs.

"It was unbearable without you. I had to see you."

"I *wanted* to come. They gave me leave. It felt wrong not being at Audrey's service." Before she could reassure him, a shadow crossed his face. "Can't for the life of me understand how an auto..." He gritted his teeth, and Isabel heard his unspoken question. *How had an automobile killed their sister?*

Her hands trembled as she lifted a morsel of chicken to her mouth. Fighting back tears, she said, "She was collecting rocks at a park, and it was raining and foggy. And ... before I knew it, she ran into the street. I... I didn't stop her in time. It was my fault for not paying closer attention."

She couldn't bear to spell the awful truth, what Mother could never know: how she had left Audrey alone as she strolled with her sweetheart elsewhere in the park. She waited nervously for James to draw his own conclusions and acknowledge her culpability. It would give her some relief to shoo it out into the open, her irresponsibility as the older sister.

But he shook his head, his eyes widening. "Don't say that. You're not to blame."

"But I am. Truly. There's no getting around it."

"You mustn't think that way. It's horribly sad and tragic, but it was an accident." He reached over, squeezed her hand.

She made an inaudible grunt, wishing her brother hadn't repeated Claude's words. Her eyes prickled with tears.

"Say, does Mother know you're here?"

"I left a note."

"A *note*? She'll be frantic. Especially after everything that's happened."

"I don't think so. She'd rather I stay out of her way."

"She's grieving, Izz. It's a lot of tragedy to take in a few short months."

She bit her lip savagely, tasting blood. "Yes, but it was more than that. After a while, she couldn't stand the sight of me. Almost like she blamed..."

"Audrey was old enough to know not to run into the street. And you didn't leave her alone!" The tendons on his neck stood up like guy wires.

But she was alone. Isabel's stomach clenched, and she blinked back tears. "You know how her mind was always floating off to other things. And she was only nine. It was my job to take care of her. I should've been better prepared."

James shook his head at his plate. "There's nothing you or anyone else could have done, short of keeping her on a leash. You can't think that way."

She picked listlessly at her food, her appetite gone. It was far worse than she had led him to believe. If her brother knew that even more than irresponsibility, her self-centered lust had triggered the accident, he would be horrified, would rightfully never forgive her. She sneaked a look at Claude, squatting on the log and chewing his food. The pine trees surrounding the camp swayed, emitting a waft of incense.

James followed her gaze and swallowed a slug of water from a tin cup at his feet. "Listen, Izz, it's a damn awful thing. Terribly unfortunate, too, that it happened to poor Audrey." He brushed at his eyes. "But no one's to blame. Maybe this was God's plan, all along. Our cross to bear."

She stared at him, her mouth widening in disbelief, ears ringing.

He took a bite of his roll. "That's what I've told myself, anyhow. We had her for a few precious years. There's nothing anyone could have done to keep her longer than God wanted."

Isabel struggled to contain her tears, but they rushed down her cheeks. "If that's true, when will he stop? First Dad, then moving to a crummy place and you leaving, and now Audrey. Why does he keep punishing us so?" She bowed her head, trying to suppress the shriek rising from her throat. The last thing she wanted was to make a scene in front of all these men, who in minutes would finish their meals and troop out of the mess hall.

James leaned over and stroked her arm. "Shh. I meant that as a comfort. Dad and Audrey are in a better place."

"A better place for them would be *here*, with *us!*" She dropped her hands to her lap, remembering Mother's remark that there might as well not be a God, since he didn't look after the poor people like them. An inexplicable fury mounted inside her. A God who didn't allow her sister to grow up and took Dad in his prime was a terrible God, indifferent at best. Fighting an urge to spew bitter, hurtful words, she studied James' tense jaw, dark eyes and hair, so like Dad's. But it would be wrong to dash the comfort he sought.

They finished their meal in silence. From the mess hall, plates clinked as they were deposited into washboards, chairs scraped on the plank floor, boots scuffled, voices boomed.

James darted a look toward the hall, and Isabel touched his arm in alarm. "You have to go?"

"Soon. I have cleaning duty, but I traded my shift tonight. I've got another twenty, thirty minutes. You heading straight back to the city?" He glanced at Claude, who had risen and stuffed his hands in his pockets.

Isabel swallowed, her eyes welling. Without thinking, she blurted, "I can't. I can't bear to go back yet. Please, can I stay, just for a little while?"

"This is an all-men's camp, Izz. Government owned, too. Commander Wild Bill's an old logger, and he runs it strict. Even if I said you could stay, there's not a chance he'd let you." James' face was sympathetic.

She nodded at the futility of it. It had been a childish, foolhardy plan, coming here, she saw that now. With sinking spirits, she shot out last minute suggestions, anyway, aware they sounded crazy. "I could camp nearby. You could loan me a blanket?"

"How would you eat? What about..." James nodded at Claude.

"He would go back without me," she said quickly, her cheeks suffusing with heat as she noted the impropriety.

"And then how would you get back to the city? If it were up to me, of course, I'd find somewhere for you to bunk down. But Cascades is like an army corps. I'm sorry, Izzie, it's impossible."

He was right, but she wasn't ready to admit defeat. A queer feeling overtook her, as though she had spied a menacing man in the shadows, someone who meant her harm.

"James," she tried, choking back tears. "I..." Her hands fluttered to her temples, where a stinging throb had begun. Without warning, she was nauseous, the drumming in her ears obliterating her thoughts. She cradled her head with both hands.

"Izz, are you all right?"

Dimly she was aware of James peering over her, but she couldn't focus. "I feel sick," she whispered. "A terrible bad headache." It had struck in an instant, the worst she'd experienced, punching the wind out of her lungs and buckling her knees. She slumped over. Claude's voice joined with James' as they bent over her, conferring. The pain in her head was splintering, and any little movement sent a sudden lurch of nausea up her gullet.

"A migraine," Claude murmured. "My mother gets them. They can come on a sudden from nerves."

James wormed a tin cup of water to her lips. "Drink this," he urged.

She managed a sip, but water dribbled down her chin, and she jerked away. "Can't." She chanced opening an eye but immediately closed it when a flash of light assaulted her. Bile shot up her throat. "I'm going to be sick." She doubled over, retching, her forehead slick and hot. When she was done, she sank onto the ground, limp and spent, her mouth sour with vomit, her head spinning. Inside her eyelids, she saw shimmering spots. A heavy numbness crept up her arms. Someone wiped her face and pressed a cool rag against her forehead.

James hovered in the periphery, a blurry silhouette. "Stay right here, Izzie. I'm fetching the medic." She tried to find her voice to protest, but the words failed her, and she lay listlessly. Noises buzzed above her—feet tramping, men coughing, talking, marching, a painful flurry of sound and bright darts of light.

Someone large and unfamiliar knelt beside her, touching her shoulder. "Here, now. Lift your head." James' voice mingled with Claude's, rattling details of her sudden headache and nausea, while a stranger volleyed questions. A cold stethoscope plunged against her chest, and a meaty hand gripped her wrist, feeling for her pulse.

"Easy does it," the stranger said. "Swallow this." A bitter, chalky tablet slid under her tongue, and a tiny cup of vile liquid thrust toward her lips. She took a quick swallow then sank back, retching from the sudden movement and the yelping hot pain in her head.

She must have briefly lost consciousness, because the next thing she knew she was lying face-up on a narrow stretcher as marching legs swung her forward. Nausea from the jerky movement, amplified noise of boots crunching against gravel, branches crackling underfoot, and swimming dots in her eyes overtook her; and her body heaved, expending itself of the last remnants of food she had consumed since breakfast.

CHAPTER ELEVEN

Distant murmurs drifted from a fog: first a woman's soprano, then the counterpoint of a tenor. Isabel blinked in confusion, trying to make sense of the voices as they gathered strength. Sunlight dappled across a bare floor, where a wooden chair was shoved into a corner beside a blue and white painted desk. A blanket was tucked beneath her chin. She caught a faint whiff of lavender.

Then it came back to her in a rush: her arrival at the CCC camp after the long drive; supper with James; his explanation she couldn't stay; her distress and the terrible headache. Surely she wasn't at Yosemite or the camp. She must have slept for hours, since the sunlight penetrating the room was bright and all-consuming.

Shifting onto an elbow, she uncurled her legs onto a short, squeaky brown sofa. With a frisson of alarm, she scanned the strange surroundings. The room was tiny, barely larger than a water closet. A pot of wildflowers perched in the sill beneath a single square pane of glass. On the desk sat an old typewriter, a sheaf of paper and jar of ink, and on the floor beneath the window sprawled a stack of cardboard boxes. Peeking inside the blanket, Isabel was relieved to discover she was still wearing the same blouse and skirt. Her old, dirty stockings and shoes, along with her crumpled knapsack, lay stacked at the foot of the sofa.

She struggled to hear the voices, but they had paused, and she realized they belonged to people just outside the wall. The thought made her swing her feet onto the floor and pull herself upright, her heart pounding. As she slipped on her stockings and shoes, a gentle rap at the door sent all fibers of her body on edge.

"Is it safe to enter?" called a woman's lilting, flute-like voice.

Isabel squeaked a yes.

The door swung open, and a tall, middle-aged woman with striking, inquisitive eyes, the color of a blue jay, crossed to the sofa and perched beside Isabel. Her sandy brown hair, streaked with silver, was pinned in a bun, and she wore a long dark skirt and a crumpled, button-down man's shirt. Fine wrinkles gathered at her throat and corners of her eyes. As she peered at Isabel, a vertical groove popped between her brows.

"You look a mite bit better. How're you feeling?"

Isabel grazed her fingers along her temples. "My head doesn't hurt so much, but it's still..." She groped for the right word. "Foggy."

The woman nodded. "That's not surprising. The camp medic gave you a draught of laudanum for the pain."

"Where am I?"

"In my apartment above the post office. My husband's the assistant postmaster." She frowned. "You must have fainted last night, else the laudanum put you to sleep. Some of the Cascades boys help me with my wildflower garden, and a couple of them drove you here yesterday evening."

"I'm still at Yosemite?"

"Yes. Yes, you are."

A fireplace coziness gathered inside Isabel. "Thank you for keeping me, ma'am."

"Just my husband and I live here, though we don't have much space." A wary look crossed her face. "You can stay a tad longer, least till you're well and arrangements are made for you to go home." She nodded at the desk. "This is a storage room we use for typing. Last night we dragged the sofa in so you could sleep in peace. It was a tight squeeze, but it fit. Just."

Isabel heard a note of reproach in her voice, so she uttered another hurried thanks. Undoubtedly, the woman and her husband would like to be rid of her as soon as possible.

"You're Isabel?"

"Yes, ma'am."

"I'm Enid Michael." She gave Isabel a scrutinizing look. "Your brother rode over with the boys who dropped you here last night. He said he'd be round later today to check on you."

"Oh, I'm awfully glad." She hadn't expected the luck of seeing James again so soon. Briefly she wondered about Claude and concluded he must have left last night to return the truck. She worried he hadn't had enough cash for gas or food.

"Would you like something to eat? The kettle's on, and I've set out biscuits and jam."

Immediately Isabel grew aware of a sharp hunger pang. "Yes, please. Thank you."

"Come out when you're ready. Privy's next door."

In the lavatory, she slapped water over her face, glanced in the mirror above the sink. The eczema spots had faded slightly, and her complexion was pasty, drained. At least the cold water helped snap her mind to attention.

On the opposite side of the privy, another door led to a bedroom. Closest to the storage room where Isabel had slept, the hallway opened to a tiny kitchen with a small table and two straight-backed chairs. A white cupboard, sink, stove, and icebox stood against the wall opposite the table. Above the sink, a window was propped open, and a chorus of birds twittered among the stinging breath of pines. Sketches of flowers hung on the whitewashed walls. A small sitting area, crammed with a wooden bookshelf, table and phonograph, pair of chairs, rocker, and watercolor paintings, adjoined the kitchen.

Mrs. Michael stood at the counter, arranging biscuits on a plate next to a pot of bright red jam. "Have a seat." She waved at the table, and Isabel slid into a chair.

"Is your stomach upset?"

"A touch."

"I have a concoction that will help: tea of mint and yarrow, straight from my garden." She poured steaming water from a kettle into a chipped green ceramic mug, steeped with herbs, and set it on a woven placemat before Isabel.

"Since it's just my husband and me, we only have two of everything." Mrs. Michael sat opposite Isabel. "I'm afraid you've caught us flat-footed."

"I'm sorry for causing you trouble."

Mrs. Michael flapped a hand. "I only mean we're not used to company, except for our wild friends the birds, deer, and bears."

Isabel detected another faint rebuke in Mrs. Michael's words, but her curiosity got the better of her. "Bears? Truly?"

"Yosemite's full of them. But they're like most creatures. If you don't disturb them, they tend not to disturb you. It's when tourists tempt them by leaving out food that they go exploring and become nuisances. We hold daily feedings so they're not as liable to go after the campers' suppers."

Isabel's stomach lurched at the thought. She leaned toward the open window to inhale fresh air. A clutch of pines wobbled in the breeze. Just beyond climbed a mammoth ridge of striated gray and white rock, brightened at the base by dark green conifers. They must be in the center of the valley. The minty tea helped settle her stomach. When she sampled a buttered biscuit with jam, her mouth burst with the tangy sweet flavor.

"Jam's delicious," she said to Mrs. Michael.

"I made it yesterday with strawberries picked straight from my garden."

This was the second time Mrs. Michael had mentioned her garden. How on earth had she enlisted the CCC boys to help her with it? But when the older woman didn't make further conversation, Isabel thought about what she would say to James, how she would manage a ride back to the city. A familiar weariness overtook her. With a sigh, she finished her biscuit.

Mrs. Michael took a sip from a brown ceramic mug, which didn't match Isabel's green, then straightened. "The Cascades boys said you came all the way from San Francisco."

Isabel nodded. She caught a trace of suspicion in Mrs. Michael's eyes.

"I admire your gumption for making such a long trip, especially since the CCC doesn't allow visitors."

Isabel debated whether to reveal her ignorance about the camp rules. "I had to see my brother," she said finally.

"Must have been awfully important." After a beat, she said, "I don't mean to pry."

Isabel hesitated, but she saw only curiosity, not judgment, in the older woman's face. Besides, Mrs. Michael had shared her home with a stranger. Still, intuition warned her to keep her explanation about the trip as brief as possible. Taking a breath, she summarized Dad's heart attack and the move, omitting details of the Tenderloin and their flat. Her voice quavered as she spoke of James' departure for the CCC. When she mentioned Audrey, her eyes pooled. She couldn't possibly brave the subject of her death. Horrified that she might cry before a stranger, she bowed her head, fighting to fence in her tears. Mrs. Michael pressed a handkerchief into her palm.

Isabel dabbed at her eyes. "I'm sorry."

"For someone so young, you've been through a lot in a short time." Mrs. Michael reached over to pat Isabel's arm, then rapidly withdrew her hand as though Isabel were a wild animal who might bite. Probably her explanation hadn't made sense.

Isabel took a few shaky breaths and clarified, "I... I couldn't bear to be in the flat any longer. I wanted to be with James, in the open air and mountains..." She stopped, not saying it was Audrey who had wanted to come.

Mrs. Michael's eyes sparked, and her face softened, as if a younger, vivacious woman had slipped into her place. "I know just what you mean. I grew up in Gilroy and Los Angeles, but I moved here years ago, after my husband and I married, and now Yosemite is home." She licked her lips and angled her head toward the window. "There's something pure about living in Nature and waking to mountain air."

Isabel leaned forward, longing to cast her depressing story behind and fill up every nook and cranny inside her head with the captivating tale she was sure Mrs. Michael would tell.

The older woman met Isabel's eyes. Maybe she understood that Isabel wanted nothing more than to listen. "We first arrived here fifteen years ago, before employees were given rooms above the post office. So Charles and I set up house in a tent on a sandbar." She smiled. "Some say I'm crazy, but I preferred living in that tent to anywhere indoors. We camped on Roe Island on the Merced River and had marvelous views of Half Dome and Yosemite Falls. At dawn we'd step outside to watch the sun reflecting off the water." Her face grew wistful. "I had precious little housekeeping. We didn't have a privy, just a pit toilet. So I scrubbed our clothes on a washboard, and we bathed in the Merced. Had plenty of visitors, too—chipmunks and deer and dippers. Back then, Yosemite wasn't as jammed with tourists and automobiles."

Isabel brushed a stray tear from beneath her eye. "It sounds wonderful."

"It was. I loved how simply we lived! You don't realize what a burden modern things can be until you no longer have them. Some folks would say it was terribly spartan, but I didn't mind a bit. Fact, I'd trade all the conveniences in the world to live there again. The funny thing is, I hadn't done anything so unusual until then, and I was almost forty."

Isabel performed a quick mental calculation and determined Mrs. Michael was in her fifties. "You must have the chance to do many unusual things here." She peered at the pale outline of the mountains.

"And more than most. I'm a ranger-naturalist, so I'm outdoors every day, even in fall and winter. Truth is, I've loved being around plants and animals my whole life, but it took me a long time to get here."

Isabel didn't know whether she meant a long time before she had arrived at Yosemite, or a long time before she had become a ranger. Maybe both. "You're a ranger?" she said with a touch of awe. She hadn't known it was possible for a woman.

Her hostess bobbed her head. "I do the usual things like leading hikes and nature walks, but I also oversee the public wildflower garden. And I know the backcountry inside out, better than anyone, though some won't admit it. You see, I'm the only female naturalist on Yosemite's staff." Her voice rippled like a bell, but her jaw had hardened.

She glanced at her watch and thinned her lips. "Usually by now I've taken a walk and checked on my garden." As if to emphasize the implication, she paused. "Now that you've eaten, I'd like to head over there."

"Of course." Isabel swallowed, weighing a possibility. "If it's all right with you, may I join you?" She added quickly, "I promise not to get in your way." It might be her only chance to see any part of Yosemite.

"If you're feeling well enough, you're welcome to take a gander. But if you're any bit unsure, then stay and rest until your brother gets here."

"I *do* feel rested. I'd love to see the garden." She allowed herself a small surge of excitement. If she were lucky, she might get one or two more days at Yosemite. She tried not to think of what would come next and resolved to make the most of her short time at the park, if only for Audrey's sake.

Mrs. Michael's cheeks pinkened. "I must admit I enjoy showing off my lovelies. After all, they're meant for the public eye." She began clearing Isabel's dishes, but Isabel took them from her, insisting she didn't want her to go to any more trouble.

While Isabel washed the plates and mugs, Mrs. Michael propped a white brimmed hat onto her head and stuffed a wax packet from the icebox into her skirt pocket. As Isabel turned from the sink, her hostess gestured for her to follow her out the door. She had begun descending the stairs when Isabel called tentatively, "Did you forget to lock up?"

Mrs. Michael continued rapidly down the staircase. "I never bother locking up. There's nothing here for the taking, and not a soul in the park would try to enter." She craned a look back at Isabel, her eyes twinkling. "No people, at least. And if an animal barged in and tried to make himself at home, I wouldn't mind a bit. After all, they never bear any malice."

Isabel decided Mrs. Michael meant that only humans, not animals, would possibly harbor ill intentions. She couldn't help but agree.

CHAPTER TWELVE

Mrs. Michael rounded the corner of the stone facade, and Isabel hurried after her. A breeze stirred through the pines, and a squirrel scampered across the path into the woods. Dark rafters from the post office's upper story sheltered three separate glass-paned double doors, trimmed in white and evenly spaced between stone layers. Like all the buildings in the New Village, Mrs. Michael explained, the post office was made from the park's granite and timber, designed to blend in with the natural surroundings.

She nodded at the center door, which displayed a magnified photo of a one-cent stamp featuring a cliff flanked by evergreens. "The 1934 stamps are coming out in July. They'll commemorate the national parks, and the very first will honor Yosemite."

Isabel inspected the photo. "It's lovely."

"Also deadly. That's El Capitan—three thousand feet of vertical rock, a real challenge for climbers. Charles and I have scaled a small part of it to collect rare flowers."

"You climb rocks?

Mrs. Michael's eyes sparkled with a faint victory, like a mischievous child who has jumped on a bed without getting caught. "Yes, but not the traditional way with ropes."

"Then how?"

"Just our hands and grip shoes. I tease other climbers that ropes insult the mountains."

Isabel was speechless. A woman, climbing mountains with nothing but bare hands? But before she could ask more questions, Mrs. Michael pressed her forehead to the pane. Through the glass, Isabel saw clerks sorting bundles of mail.

"There's my husband." She fluttered her fingers at the glass and swiveled away.

They strolled around the corner into a plaza encircled by conifers, where Mrs. Michael pointed out Best's Art Studio. "The father of my friend Virginia owns that studio. He lives in rooms right above it." She turned to Isabel. "You've heard of Virginia's husband, the photographer Ansel Adams?"

"His name sounds familiar."

"He's becoming famous for his photos of Yosemite. Several are on display inside. And he's from San Francisco, like you." She gave Isabel a sharp glance. "The Adams spend their summers here in the park." They had stopped in the center of the plaza, and Mrs. Michael indicated a semicircle of stone buildings with weathered roofs and rustic wooden upper stories, trimmed with logs: the Visitor's Center, Rangers' Club, administration building and museum, where a dozen automobiles were parked. The Sierra Nevada cliffs, faintly lined by what Mrs. Michael called the Ledge Trail, swelled around them in majestic ridges.

She held a palm against a sudden gust of wind, explaining they were at an elevation of four thousand feet. "You might not feel it now, but at night it cools way down. Ideal hunting weather for ring-tailed cats."

Isabel wanted to ask about the cats, but Mrs. Michael moved to a different topic, and Isabel was a trifle bewildered by how effortlessly she buzzed through ideas. Just as one took hold, she released it for another while Isabel scrambled to catch up. Maybe as a ranger she was accustomed to efficiently dispensing her knowledge in bite-sized chunks.

Mrs. Michael gestured at the administration building. "I used to keep a wildflower exhibit in front, but my garden behind the museum is a much better experience for visitors." Her voice rang with a note of pride. "Come." Isabel turned after her down a sandy path through a creaky wrought-iron gate that swept into a dazzling field of flowers.

She stood still, catching her breath at the fiery blur of red, pink, green, blue, yellow and purple blooms. Long stems sprang toward the sun; paths crisscrossed through the maze. Isabel recognized Indian paintbrushes, geraniums, marigolds, sunflowers, strawberries. Vivid midnight larkspurs receded to misty forget-me-nots then transitioned into soft yellow and pink buds. In the center of the field ran a little stream. Around them towered the snow-capped Sierras. A florid fragrance flooded Isabel's nostrils, and she clasped her hands and lifted her chin.

Mrs. Michael spread her arms as though greeting a friend, then bounded, unabashed, across the flagstones. She knelt by individual plants, murmuring and cupping them like babies' cheeks. From behind, as she lifted her skirts and bustled forward, her spry gait resembled a much younger woman's.

Tourists in sun hats strolled down the paths. Isabel spun in all directions, gazing at the bursts of tiny shoots. Her heart gave a kick as she considered their beauty was ephemeral, surely gone by fall.

Grasping the brim of her hat, Mrs. Michael whirled toward Isabel, as if just remembering her. "Meet my lovelies. They're all natives I picked on my climbs with Charles. Some are from elevations between eight and thirteen thousand feet." She waved at the plots. "I've organized them by life zones according to where we found them. Over there are blue bugles and monkeyflowers, and beyond are asters and goldenrods. Alpine columbine, shooting stars, and white violets are to your left, and my lilies, lady-slippers and phantom orchids are on your right."

Suddenly she stooped beside an orchid and gazed at it admiringly, like a proud parent. "Ah, Cora, you're getting so tall!" To Isabel, she said, "I've always thought the lady's slipper looks like a Victorian lady with her ivory cheeks, pink mouth, and auburn curls. Do you see?"

Isabel inclined her head, then pointed to a spray of feathery purple flowers, where a butterfly flitted. "Is that lavender?"

Mrs. Michael glanced at the plant. "Lessingia, though a lot of folks confuse her with lavender and say she'd make a nice bouquet. Behind are buckwheat and Sierra Nevada lotus." She motioned toward a veil of gray-green and gold sprinkled buds. "The Sierra lupine in back are even a deeper purple, see? You've come at the perfect time. Most of the flowers peak in late June and July."

"This is beautiful." Isabel sought the right word. "Breathtaking."

Mrs. Michael's eyes gleamed. "The boys from Cascades have helped tremendously. They laid down these paths and fenced in the back of the garden bordering the Indian Canyon." Isabel followed her gaze. Four or five straw teepees clustered at the far wall tens of yards away, where a Native American woman wove a basket while a small group watched. "They even brought the ancient spring in the center there to life. Tourists love it, and we use it to water the plants. Next, they'll add hoses to irrigate the garden year round."

Isabel's lips opened and closed as a sudden energy thrummed inside her. The garden appeared boundless, breathing color, unrestrained. "I've never seen anything like this. Not even the Golden Gate Park comes close."

"That's how I felt when I first arrived at Yosemite, and I expect it's how a lot of folks feel here. Overcome with wonder." Mrs. Michael recited, "Hope is the thing with feathers that perches in the soul, and sings the tune without the words and never stops at all. And sweetest in the gale is heard, and sore must be the storm, that could abash the little bird that kept so many warm."

Crinkling her eyes at the lines by her favorite poet, Isabel finished, "I've heard it in the chilliest land, and on the strangest sea, yet never in Extremity it asked a thing of me."

"Ah, you like Miss Dickinson's poetry, too."

"Ever since I was little. We share the same last name." Though Miss Dickinson's poems were from a different century, they spoke to Isabel like a childhood friend, making her blink in recognition.

"Is that so? They must have told me your surname yesterday when they brought you to the apartment, but I'd plumb forgotten. I've never met anyone else who'd remember that line."

A quiet thrill sparked through Isabel's chest.

Mrs. Michael murmured, "Perhaps you'd like to buy a flower? But I could never sell. If you would like to borrow, until the daffodil unties her yellow bonnet..."

Isabel was mesmerized by her sing-song voice and the pleasure radiating across her face.

"Emily was also a botanist and gardener, and she described exactly how I feel about my garden. Every flower is precious and divine."

Isabel nodded slowly.

"I'm not a churchgoer, but wandering through the garden or trails at the park is the closest I'll get to a spiritual experience." Mrs. Michael colored, as though she had said too much. She indicated a bench a few yards away. "Let's sit."

Isabel accompanied her to a granite seat in the shade of a sycamore tree and manzanita bushes, and Mrs. Michael withdrew the packet from her pocket and handed her a cookie. "I grabbed some gingerbread before we left."

As they ate, Mrs. Michael said, "This is the perfect spot for seeing, hearing, and smelling everything in the garden."

"It's peaceful."

"A family of hummingbirds live just behind. We also get goldfinches, woodpeckers, robins, and tanagers, over by the coffeeberry bush, where I've left feeding tables."

Isabel turned, astounded, to see a picnic table covered with crumbs, where a flock of birds hovered, delicately picking and swooping away morsels. "That's all for the birds?" She couldn't help but think it was a terrible waste of food when so many folks were hungry.

"It's leftover hotcake and bread from the Government Mess."

"But surely there are people…"

"I know what you're thinking, but believe me, the kitchen makes so much they couldn't possibly feed everyone with it. Besides, especially in winter, birds have a hard time finding food."

Isabel disagreed but stayed silent. Obviously Mrs. Michael hadn't seen the slums in San Francisco, bums trawling through garbage cans for scraps to eat. Wasn't it immoral to waste food on birds when people were starving? From the corner of her eye, she studied Mrs. Michael. Maybe she didn't understand what lay beyond the park.

"Miss Marjorie Montgomery Ward is the lady behind the garden," Mrs. Michael was saying. "Three years ago, she made a generous donation to start it, and I was lucky to be chosen to oversee it."

An older couple promenaded past. The white-haired lady wore a sun bonnet and ankle-length gown. "Oh do look at this, Henry! Can you believe how darling?"

"She's the bitter root known as Yosemite lewisia," Mrs. Michael called, and the couple turned in surprise.

Mrs. Michael patted down her skirts and strode toward them. "You see her rose colored petals and golden anthers? I found this variety on the south ridge of Half Dome in early June last year. There's also the Kellogg's lewisia of the same family, but they're white with spatula shaped leaves, kind of like water lilies made of tissue. That variety blooms on El Capitan and the sandy ridges toward Eagle Peak."

"My. Aren't they lovely!"

"I hold a flower and tree walk from Camp Curry every Tuesday morning. Tomorrow, if you're interested."

The woman glanced at her husband and nodded. "Yes, indeed."

"Mrs. Enid Michael, Ranger-Naturalist." Mrs. Michael extended a hand. The woman grasped it.

"We're Mr. and Mrs. Lyman. This is our first visit to the park in ten years."

"Welcome back. I hope to see you at the nature walk. And if you have time, come back here some evening, when the primroses pop open. They have a beautiful yellow bloom. Plus you can see the stars without obstruction. The Yosemite sky at night is more brilliant than any carnival big top."

After the couple strolled away, Mrs. Michael returned to the bench and watched small groups of visitors, ready to leap up to answer their questions. And, she told Isabel sotto voce, to make sure they didn't trample over any of her precious plants.

It occurred to Isabel that Audrey would have loved the garden and the view of the mountains. She felt a deep pang and pressed her hand against her chest. This was far better than any isle of their imagination, because here you could touch the strawberries, smell the flowers, feel the breeze on your cheeks, gaze at the giant stone mountains standing guard. She understood what Mrs. Michael meant by a spiritual experience; there was no need to fill the solitude with words. You had only to soak it up, let it stir something inside you to life.

When Mrs. Michael noted it was past lunchtime, Isabel sprang to her feet, remembering James' visit, and they wound back to the plaza and the apartment above the post office.

As Mrs. Michael warmed vegetable broth over the stove, Isabel thanked her for the trip to the garden. "I never imagined there would be so many flowers." All thriving, wild, alive.

"Like people. Each one's unique. It's much better to meet plants and animals in their own habitat. I used to dry wildflowers and press them under glass, and for a while I displayed cut flowers. But watching them cycle through their stages makes all the difference."

Isabel set a plate of bread on the table. "I suppose that's possible if you live here year round." She glanced at Mrs. Michael with a touch of envy.

"It's one of the reasons I wanted to be a ranger. Many years ago, I was a third grade teacher in Pasadena, but I could never interest my students the way I can outdoors with the visitors. Being cooped up inside with books and chalkboards just doesn't compare."

Isabel felt the tension in her muscles uncoil. Though the apartment was about the same size as their flat in the Tenderloin, it was cheerier and less cramped. Mrs. Michael had propped open the kitchen window, and a bird chittered. Pure air, mingled with pine and light woodsmoke, floated across Isabel's face. Here you were a stone's throw away from a garden of Eden, a copse of silver firs, and a bubbling stream. But she reminded herself not to get cozy. As soon as they confirmed she was well again, they would send her right back to the city and its reek of garbage and automobiles, where opening the window brought you inches from shanties and people down on their luck.

As if guessing her thoughts, Mrs. Michael said, "How's your headache? Did the yarrow do its trick?"

Isabel pressed a palm against her forehead. "It's better, sure enough."

"Yarrow and mint are good cures for aches and gastro upset. Of course, the sleep you had must have helped, too."

"I'm still a little tired." It wasn't exactly a fib, despite the many hours she must have slept the previous evening. But the immediacy of her new surroundings—the apartment, garden, Yosemite itself—had overwhelmed her.

"Why don't you take a nap. Your brother said he'd visit later this afternoon, so there's time."

Isabel didn't protest. After washing the dishes, which she insisted on doing alone, she crawled onto the little couch in the spare room and cocooned her knees to her chest. It was the first room she had ever claimed as her own, albeit temporarily. Having a place to sleep and dress in private was an unexpected luxury, but she had an instant, deep longing to share it with Audrey.

CHAPTER THIRTEEN

When James' sonorous laugh pealed from the other room, Isabel shot upright and slid on her shoes. She'd worn the same outfit for nearly thirty-six hours, but it was too late to do anything about it.

As she flew into the sitting room, her brother jumped to his feet, beaming. "Izzie!" He wrapped her in a bear hug, and she nuzzled her head against the shoulder of his khaki uniform.

He leaned back to study her. "How you feeling?"

"Much better than yesterday."

"You look better. Last night after supper, you fainted. When you came to, the medic gave you a draught of something that made you sleep. I was awful worried."

"I can't remember any of it."

Mrs. Michael rose. "Here, sit down. I'm going out for a quick stroll so you two can catch up. Be back in another fifteen, twenty minutes." She donned her white hat and disappeared out the door.

Isabel dragged her chair close to James. "What else happened? I truly don't remember a thing."

"We took you to the medical dispensary, but they weren't able to keep you. A fellow who works in Mrs. Michael's garden suggested maybe she could take you overnight. So we laid you in the front seat, and I rode over with a couple of the guys. Last night was the first time I met Mrs. Michael and her husband. They're real nice folks, Izzie."

"I know. I haven't met Mr. Michael yet, but Mrs. Michael fed me and took me on a tour of her garden. She's kind."

"They won't be able to keep you more than another couple of nights," James warned, sweeping his gaze around the apartment. "I hear they're a quiet couple, no kids, and they don't have the space. Also, apparently Mr. Michael has some kind of health condition."

Isabel had known she couldn't stay, but hearing James' flat predicament sent a shudder of trepidation through her. "But I've no way to get home. Not immediately, anyhow."

"I thought of that. Your uh… friend left last night after we arranged to take you to Mrs. Michael's. He said he had to get back to the city. But if the Michaels keep you here for a few more days, I can find you a ride partway with the fellow who delivers supplies to camp each week. He might get you as far as El Portal, maybe Merced."

"That's still far from San Francisco."

"I know. I'll scrape together some cash so you can catch the train from there into the city."

"No, James. I couldn't ask you to do that."

"You can think of it as a loan, if you like, just to get you home safe and sound."

She didn't tell him she already owed Mother money. "I don't want to go home."

James frowned. "There's no other choice. You can't stay here or at Cascades, and you've no way to make it on your own."

"I can get a job. I can support myself."

James knotted his brow, drumming his fingers against the chair arm. "I don't know a soul who's hiring outside the CCC."

"I can clean tables or serve food at the mess hall."

"Nope. I told you, there's nothing here for a girl."

"Then in Merced. Anywhere but San Francisco."

"Same difference. What would you do in Merced? And who would hire a sixteen-year-old girl, anyhow, when grown men are out of work?" His voice rose with uncharacteristic impatience.

The tightness in Isabel's temples began again, and she suppressed a sob. He was right, of course. The only thing she was trained to do was organize cans on a shelf and sweep the floor. And that job had been more out of pity, Mr. McGilligan's favor to James. She knew how to type from editing the school paper, but before she could propose applying for a stenographer position, James cut in.

"Look, it's not the end of the world. School will start in a couple more months. That'll keep you busy. Besides, what's so bad about the city? You've lived there your whole life."

"Mother... she's so unhappy and bitter... she doesn't want me around. And San Francisco's depressing. Nothing's the same anymore."

"You've got to brace yourself and bear up, Izz. Mother needs you. Besides, this isn't forever. In another couple of years, you'll graduate high school."

Isabel shook her head, her eyes blurring. Tears spilled down her cheeks and neck. James drew his arm over her shoulders, and she leaned against his chest.

"I'll come home and visit when I get leave. I promise."

Her arms went cold and numb.

Mrs. Michael opened the door and halted when she noticed Isabel's tear-stained face. "Oh dear. Should I be off again for a few?"

James clambered to his feet. "No, ma'am. I'm sorry. I'm just going. I've got to be back at Cascades for supper crew. I was telling my sister what I told you earlier. I'll arrange a ride for her out of the park at the end of the week. Are you sure it's all right if she stays here for a few more days?"

Mrs. Michael nodded. "A few more days won't be a problem. But after that, we'll need the spare room again." Her eyes grew troubled. "And as I mentioned, my husband's condition requires him to avoid any excitement or disturbances."

James gave Isabel a knowing look, and her heart sank. "I understand, ma'am. I'll pay you for your trouble. And if it's too much of a bother, I'll find a ride for her sooner."

Mrs. Michael spread her palm. "No, that's unnecessary. We can keep her through Saturday morning. I'll talk with Mr. Michael tonight."

"Thank you. But if you change your mind or your husband objects, please send word through Arnold when he does his shift in the garden, and I'll be back to collect Izz."

"Yes, all right."

"We're awfully grateful, Mrs. Michael."

James looked at Isabel, and she gave a quick nod and swiped at her eyes.

"Unless I hear otherwise, I'll see you on Saturday morning," James told Isabel. "No later than eight."

She wanted to rush to him and wrap her arms around his neck, but she feared it would send her into a fresh bout of tears. Instead she gazed at him, trying to keep her mouth and chin from trembling. At least she could remain another four days. That was something. She couldn't bear to think of the trip back to San Francisco and the flat, so she shoved it from her mind.

At the last minute, James bent and kissed her forehead.

After he left, Isabel rose shakily. "Can I help you with supper?" She was aware of the catch in her voice, the long wavering slur of the last word.

Mrs. Michael frowned, pursing her lips. "I haven't given it any thought, though I suppose I should. Charlie and I aren't fancy folks."

"Neither am I."

Mrs. Michael peered inside the icebox. "We've got everything we need for soup and bread, plus a salad of berries, tomatoes and greens."

"It sounds perfect. I'll be glad to make it."

"You can make the salad," Mrs. Michael said firmly. She removed a bowl of greens from the icebox and handed Isabel a butter knife. "Go ahead and chop the vegetables and fruit." She gestured to a bowl on the shelf that held a hodgepodge of strawberries and blackberries. Next to it perched a pair of ripe tomatoes and button mushrooms.

Determined to demonstrate her competence, Isabel rapidly diced and arranged the food. She didn't want to give Mrs. Michael any reason to judge her unkindly. Maybe if her hostess formed a positive impression of her, she might allow her to stay a tad longer. Her cheeks burned as she bent over the counter, and she wiped her brow.

Mrs. Michael said, "Not to pry, but do you suffer from eczema?"

Isabel bobbed her head, and her hands flew to her throat.

"Primrose can help. She's one of my garden flowers."

"Is that so?" Isabel murmured, rueful she wouldn't be at Yosemite long enough to try.

Half an hour later, a ruddy-faced man in a tweed cap and knickerbockers entered the apartment. When he saw Isabel, he looked away sheepishly and remained standing by the door. At last he removed his cap, revealing a head of bristly, silver-streaked black hair.

"Charlie, you're home early!" Mrs. Michael said. "Isabel, meet my husband."

He looked so bashful that Isabel regretted presenting him with her hand. He gripped her fingers and quickly released them. Surreptitiously she studied his face for signs of illness, wondering which condition he suffered from.

Mrs. Michael cleared her throat. "Isabel is staying with us a few more days until her brother can arrange a ride for her out of the park."

Mr. Michael blinked, surprised, and a covert message passed between husband and wife. Mrs. Michael put a hand on his arm and murmured into his ear.

Isabel braced herself, suddenly afraid he would object. "Thank you for taking me in last night," she said in a rush. "And for keeping me through the end of the week."

"That's just fine," he mumbled, reddening.

"Of course, we're out of our depths with a young person," Mrs. Michael said, "But I do think it's nice to have a fresh face around." She addressed her husband, but her words sounded forced, as if equally meant to convince herself.

Mr. Michael made no reply, but at Mrs. Michael's request, he brought a chair from the sitting room into the kitchen, and the three of them sat elbow to elbow around the small table. When nobody spoke, Isabel suspected her presence at the table for two had created an unwelcome disruption. She sought a topic that would put them at ease.

To Mrs. Michael, she said, "I heard you tell that couple at the garden that you're leading a nature walk tomorrow."

"Yes. I lead it every Tuesday morning."

Isabel bit her lip, daring herself to voice the question she longed to ask. "Might I join you?" She had the inkling of an idea of how to extend her stay, though the details were fuzzy.

A look of surprise crossed Mrs. Michael's face. "If you'd like."

Mr. Michael darted his eyes at Isabel. "You'll enjoy it. Mrs. Michael is quite the botanist."

"Don't be fooled. I don't have a degree, and I'm not a scholar. Everything I know I've learned from hikes and climbs." She quirked her lips and speared a tomato.

Mr. Michael smiled at his wife.

"And you wouldn't know it because of his day job, but Charlie is an ornithologist. Or rather a bird lover, because ornithologists are the sort who capture and kill birds then stuff them and put them on display, and he'd never dream of doing that. But he knows more about birds than almost anybody at the park."

"Truly?" Isabel sneaked a peek at Mr. Michael, who ducked his head.

"Yes, he does, though he's too modest to admit it. Not much puts Charlie on fire, but he's positively *thrilled* when he sees a rare bird."

Isabel waited for Mrs. Michael to elaborate, but when she didn't, she said to him, "Mrs. Michael said you climb, too. Without ropes." She wondered how he navigated up mountains with a condition that required him to avoid excitement.

Mrs. Michael leveled a gaze at her husband. "He used to. His doctor advised him to stop on account of his heart. But he's still famous around these parts for scaling steep-pitched walls bare-handed." Her voice grew spirited. "He made the first solo ascent of three remote and extremely difficult summits, Devil's Crags and two of the highest Kaweah Peaks. Fact, he taught me how to climb and showed me how to find foot and toeholds along sheer granite. All mountains are alike to him because he doesn't need a trail. He's fearless."

"Mrs. Michael exaggerates. She's my biggest fan."

"Not an exaggeration!" She leaned conspiratorially toward Isabel and recounted an ascent Mr. Michael had led to the Unicorn in Cathedral Peak. "We scaled the rock beneath the Unicorn's saddle, inching hand over hand. It's treacherous, because you have to snag onto a seam and balance there till you're able to grab hold of the next. Often the crevices are too narrow to support more than a finger or toe. Charlie made a course over the rock, and when we reached the saddle, we edged up a gravelly slope onto a comb of solid granite around the peak."

Isabel gave a soft gasp as Mrs. Michael described how they had straddled the gap between the Unicorn and an adjacent summit. Apparently they had hitched around the ragged crest toward the horn, a mass of rock angling from the peak.

"It was a perpendicular twenty-foot drop on either side. We crawled along a narrow ledge to avoid falling rocks. At the end of it, Charles found a handhold and swung up to a granite bench. After he pulled me up, we reached the crest of the horn in a few more steps." She traded a look with her husband.

"The view was stupendous. When we stepped onto the summit, the Sierra peaks leaped around us in a ring, and way below we saw a deep-blue ribbon where the Tuolumne River flows to the foot of the Unicorn. But the descent to the cirque was even trickier. We didn't want to return by the ledge, so we chanced the precipice on the horn's east side." She licked her lips.

"We took two long steps down to a shelf, and then the fun began. All the ledges and toeholds disappeared except for a few shallow seams. So we plastered ourselves against the cliff like starfish and worked our way down the wall for twenty feet until we slid onto an overhang. When we finally reached the cirque, we treated ourselves to a swim in Sapphire Lake."

Isabel let out a shaky breath and unfurled her fingers, which she'd been gripping in a taut, sweaty steeple. "If you'd fallen…"

Mrs. Michael's eyes glinted. "That's part of the thrill. We don't have a safety net, so we can't make any wrong moves. Every step must be flawless."

Isabel stared at her in amazement. She couldn't contemplate climbing with ropes, let alone mastering such a daredevil feat. "Don't you get frightened?"

"Sometimes, but that's never stopped either of us. For years, people have said we're crazy." Mrs. Michael's chin lifted, and

Isabel detected a glimmer of defiance in her eyes. "But since Charlie can no longer go, I don't enjoy the climbs as much, and they seem riskier. I've yet to find another partner as sure-footed and first-rate."

After supper, Mr. Michael slid into the rocking chair and propped on a pair of spectacles to read the paper. Wanting to compensate the Michaels for their hospitality, Isabel washed the dishes. She was glad that instead of objecting, Mrs. Michael joined her husband in the sitting room.

As she hovered over the sink, basking in the fresh air from the window, a snug feeling enveloped her. In an instant, she was back in the Rainbow Lane rooms on an evening before Christmas. The five of them had sat by the fireplace to play cards and sip hot cocoa. Mother had rested a hand on Dad's arm, giggling as he recounted a prank he had pulled as a boy. A fleeting picture postcard.

After putting away the dishes, she gazed at the bookshelf, stuffed with volumes in all shapes and sizes. She longed to read the titles. In the opposite corner of the sitting room, Mrs. Michael perched in a chair beside her husband, a book in her lap. From where she stood, Isabel spied only the black bristles of Mr. Michael's head as he bent over his paper — somehow endearingly familiar. She had the odd sensation she'd caught a last glimpse of Dad. Her breath went shallow, and tears pricked her eyes.

As if Mrs. Michael sensed Isabel's distress, she glanced up, then quickly crossed to the phonograph and located a record from a box on the floor. Clear, soft piano chords rang through the apartment. Mrs. Michael motioned for her to draw up a chair. The song, she said, was Debussy's *Clair De Lune*, French for moonlight. Isabel absorbed the music even as her mind wandered elsewhere. The melody rocked and soothed like a lullaby. Bit by bit, her fingers relaxed their grip; her clutter of thoughts unraveled. She blotted the dampness around her eyes.

Two other pieces followed: *Reverie* and *Arabesque Number One*. Mrs. Michael turned the record over. "*La Mer*. French for the sea. When I close my eyes, I can hear the ripple of waves. See if you can, too."

Isabel obliged her by shutting her lids and was surprised to feel the tranquil eddying of a tide moving back and forth—not a violent black ocean that swallowed flotsam, but waves that supported, cradled. After the song ended, she glanced at Mr. Michael. Maybe the music was meant most of all as a remedy for his condition, because his mouth had gone slack, his lids half closed.

Later that night, Mrs. Michael paused outside the spare room to inquire whether Isabel needed more blankets or sheets. "If you open the window a hair, you'll feel a nice breeze. Perfect sleeping weather."

After she had left, Isabel slipped into her nightdress and propped open the window sash. The moon shone a buttery yellow, and the incense of pines was sharp. Crawling onto the sofa and tucking the blanket over her hips, she recalled Mrs. Michael's comparison between the Yosemite stars and a big top and hoped she could find time to stargaze before she had to leave. The prospect of returning to the city made her stomach twist. Her idea for extending her stay was vague and half-baked; she meant to show the Michaels she could help them. *Hold on a little longer, then a little longer still,* she told herself. A few of the clear, beautiful notes from the French song chimed in her head as she lay in the splatter of moonlight.

Outside swelled a nocturnal symphony of frog croaks, cicada chirps, a quick hoot of an owl. On the other side of the wall, the Michaels chatted in a low, comfortable conversation. How good they had it here—their own private isle, where nothing from the outside could touch them. When Isabel closed her eyes, the faces of those she had lost hovered above her.

The morning Dad had died, they had all eaten breakfast together in the rounded nook of the Victorian on Rainbow Lane. Mother had worried over his plans to meet with the secret group of longshoremen that night.

"Isn't it risky to rub shoulders with those reds?"

Dad had swallowed a forkful of eggs, shaking his head. "The bigger risk is to sit around like stooges while the company pinches every dime. Hell, they're making money hand over fist. Next month at the convention, we're going to overhaul the whole crooked lot." A crease had appeared on her brow, and he had squeezed her shoulder. "Don't fret, Ellie. Come Saturday, I'm taking you out for a night on the town. High time you kicked up your heels."

"Gonna treat me to a steak dinner and show?"

"You bet. Wine, the works. Nothing but the best for my girl."

A slow smile. "Dine like the highfalutin, that'll be a kick."

"Can we go, too, Dad?" Audrey had asked.

"Not this time, kid. Just your mother and me. You'll have to talk Izzie and James into entertaining you. See if they can pull a rabbit out of a sleeve." Isabel had rolled her eyes at James, and they had laughed. The Victorian's octagonal window had glittered their reflections back: a cozy family in communion.

"Remember Saturday," Dad had said, drawing Mother close for a kiss. Tittering, she had thrust two lunch pails into his hands. After he and James had left, Audrey had pressed her face to the window.

"You won't be able to see them," Isabel had told her. "Too dark and foggy." The city mist enshrouded people, made them disappear. From far away, down at the Front, a steamer horn had blasted. That was the last time she saw Dad alive. Her chest heaved.

She had begun drifting to sleep when a voice on the other side of the wall startled her. She sat up, drawing her arms around her waist.

"I caught her crying after supper," Mrs. Michael was saying in a concerned tone. "There's something she's not telling us, but I can't put my finger on it." Isabel strained to listen but couldn't catch Mr. Michael's reply. In a softer voice, Mrs. Michael said, "Could be she ran away."

Isabel clapped a hand over her mouth.

CHAPTER FOURTEEN

Although Isabel's idea about extending her stay was unformed, it galvanized her onto her feet when she heard movement in the apartment. Hastily she pulled on a skirt and blouse. No point in letting the Michaels think she was a lazybones. Based on the snatch of conversation she'd overheard last night, they already suspected her of not telling the whole truth.

Head held high, she entered the kitchen and wished them good morning, hoping to present herself as capable and trustworthy.

"Have some biscuits." Mrs. Michael nodded at a platter on the table. In the sunlight, her eyes blazed a brilliant blue. She wore a long-sleeved white shirt, knee-length khaki trousers, and sturdy boots. "Kettle's on if you want tea."

Isabel crossed to the stove to pour herself a cup, then slipped awkwardly into the vacant chair. As she nibbled a biscuit with jam, she struggled to avoid bumping elbows with Mr. Michael. They ate without speaking until she worried she had intruded on their morning ritual.

When Mrs. Michael said they had to leave in half an hour, Isabel pushed back from the table and clumsily stood. She didn't confess she had never been on a nature walk, wasn't sure what to expect. Mrs. Michael fluttered about the kitchen, filling canteens and wrapping bread in wax paper. To make herself useful, Isabel began carrying dishes to the sink. To her surprise, Mr. Michael took them from her and drew up his sleeves.

"Let me, please," she said, embarrassed. "It's the least I can do." She certainly didn't want to create more work, let alone a disturbance, given his health condition.

He shrugged and stepped aside, and Mrs. Michael said, "On days when I have to be at work earlier, Charlie takes over the dishes. He's not due at the post office till nine."

Sharing duties between husband and wife was the most unusual household arrangement Isabel had heard. But then, Mrs. Michael herself was quirky and unconventional. Before they stepped out the door, Isabel was unable to quell her curiosity and asked her hostess whether she would wear a ranger uniform.

"No, only the male rangers wear them. I just wear this badge." Mrs. Michael's voice echoed with a triumphant note. She reached into a dish on the counter and pinned a shiny National Park Ranger medallion onto her shirt. Propping on her white hat, she appraised Isabel. "The sun will be fierce later on. You'll need a hat, too." She vanished into her bedroom and returned with a wide-brimmed bonnet. After setting it on Isabel's head, she stepped back and nodded, satisfied.

They strode briskly around the New Village post office into the plaza and down a path that cut through the woods. Few visitors were about, and the air was crisp. Sprays of evergreen boughs, glistening with dew, draped overhead. Fingertips of sun arced through the branches, but most of the forest light glowed a luminous green.

Mrs. Michael said that Curry Village Campground, the meeting place for the walk, was only a mile and a half away, but most folks camped in the cheaper public grounds. Curry, she said, was pricey because of its upscale amenities: wooden-floored tents and bungalows for those without their own camping gear, also a grocery, cafeteria, curio shop, even a pool and dance hall.

Suddenly she stopped and lowered her voice. "Look there, behind that oak. A mama deer and her three fawns." A white tail quivered, and a spotted caramel coat scrambled from the underbrush and leaped away. "They're skittish creatures. Some of them, anyway."

"I've never heard of a deer that wasn't skittish," Isabel admitted. She felt a wash of relief that Mrs. Michael was chatting; she had worried her hostess had grown silent because of the suspicion that she had run away.

"About ten years ago, a park employee's wife adopted a fawn as a pet. She called him Jiggs and raised him on a bottle. Fed him mush and milk for breakfast, cake and apple pie for lunch, and greens for supper." Mrs. Michael's voice was bright and practiced, as though she had recited this tale many times to other visitors. Isabel's eyes went wide.

"At night, she gave Jiggs a bottle and blankets. Believe it or not, he followed his mistress to the post office and Rangers' Club. When he was a year old, he developed a pair of antlers and took to napping in empty tents. After a while, he lost one of his spikes. No one knows how. One night he banged against a cottage door, wanting to get in, then knocked a chair beside the door to pieces. Folks knew it was Jiggs because they saw a deer with a single horn flee the scene."

"Is that true?" Isabel burst out, covering her mouth.

"True. At Yosemite, the animals are bolder than elsewhere. Bears, chipmunks, ring-tailed cats, deer, all of them get used to living with humans. We tame some by feeding them."

They arrived at a wide stone bridge with railings. Isabel held her breath, stunned by the sight of the wide flowing river below them and a bluff in the distance.

"The Merced River. And there's Half Dome." Mrs. Michael pointed to the towering giant white shelf of rock to their left. A conifer forest ringed its base like a festive green garland. "Legend says it's a mythical Indian turned to stone. Majestic and brave." Isabel stared in awe, envisioning a sleeping giant that might at any moment roar to life. In a few hours, Mrs. Michael said, visitors would flock to the river with rafts, blankets, and picnic baskets. Isabel leaned over the railing, imagining those families — carefree, on vacation, flush with time. Sadness rose up her chest.

They crossed the river and crunched over pine needles and twigs, following a worn path through the woods. Ahead, a large sign framed in logs hung suspended on two long poles. Tiny lights illuminated its greeting, "Camp Curry, Welcome." Just behind were rows of tents and the Camp Curry Post Office, the official meeting spot for the walk. It was a rustic building trimmed in bark with a hip roof anchored by unpeeled logs.

Within twenty minutes, over two dozen visitors had gathered. Isabel noticed the older couple from the wildflower garden, both in shade hats. Mrs. Michael beckoned families with younger children to come closer. Isabel stood behind her, unsure what to do.

A wiry boy in a ballcap, around five or six, demanded loudly, "Mama, when will we start? I'm bored!" His mother shushed him, but Mrs. Michael sent him an indulgent smile.

Stepping forward and lifting her chin, she introduced herself to the crowd. "The naturalist John Muir wrote something years ago I've always believed: *In every walk with Nature, one receives far more than he seeks.*" Here, more than ever, she said, it was important to stop, observe, and think. The same mantra that would help if ever you found yourself lost in the park.

With Isabel at Mrs. Michael's heels, the group ambled from Camp Curry. Curving her hands around her mouth, Mrs. Michael hollered that they would follow a loop along the Merced to the wildflower garden and back.

As they crossed the bridge and veered onto the river trail, she halted and cupped her ear, and Isabel heard a zinging, witchy-witchy trill.

"The yellow warbler's the most common songbird in the valley. Look, there she goes!"

A plump, tiny mustard-yellow bird with bright black eyes alighted on an azalea twig on the opposite bank. The visitors craned their necks for a better look, but Mrs. Michael waved them on. "Birds are private. We don't need to pry into her business."

"What's her business?" a child near the front asked.

Mrs. Michael turned and knelt. "So many things, just like humans. Feeding her babies, strengthening her house, tending a hurt wing, hunting for food."

The boy gave a satisfied nod.

Further down the trail, Mrs. Michael gestured at a clump of incense cedars. "They're still young, but I love them best in their old age. After their hundredth birthday, they change till you'd hardly know they were once charming little Christmas trees. Their trunk widens, and their branches become sparse, but they look noble and serene, like they want nothing and are ready for whatever comes." Sotto voce, so that only Isabel and a few others could hear, she said, "Just the way I hope to be when I'm old."

A lump gathered in Isabel's throat as she mulled over Mrs. Michael's words. Though it was regrettable that youth was unfairly valued over old age and the decrepit were often overlooked, she was beginning to see the reverse — old age was a blessing and privilege, especially since some never had the chance to grow old. For that matter, she considered, youth and health shouldn't be squandered. She followed Mrs. Michael more closely.

Deeper in the forest, Mrs. Michael introduced them to woodpeckers, violet-green tree swallows, western tanagers, and steller's jays.

"Papa jay hasn't gone far." She indicated a basket-sized nest overhead, where a bird with dark blue feathers and black crown hovered. "Mama's waiting while he guards the neighborhood and brings food back to her. Oh look, there he is!"

Heads swiveled in the direction she pointed, and a larger bird with the same dark blue coloring and black crown flitted toward the first, clenching a squiggly worm-like insect in his beak. Several children jostled each other to see, hopping onto their tiptoes. Papa alighted beside the female and dropped the worm into her open beak.

"Will you look at that!" a woman in the back crooned. "So loving!"

They strolled ahead, pausing to watch the Merced froth in miniature falls. Isabel was roused, the fog in her brain dispelled by a keen curiosity and awareness of a world of tiny creatures she hadn't paid attention to before. She absorbed Mrs. Michael's observations along with the resinous scent of the forest. For the first time in many months, she was astounded to be rooted in this moment alone, no thoughts of past or future. Maybe this was how it felt to be wholly alive.

When Mrs. Michael stopped to describe a bird or point to a deer, half a dozen children hung close by, listening with rapt attention. One little girl began peppering her with questions about the birds and their families. She looked familiar, but at first Isabel couldn't figure out why. Then all at once, she realized that the girl had bouncing auburn curls like Audrey's and was nine or ten.

As they moved ahead, Isabel stole glances, straining to hear her voice and detect other similarities. Was she imagining it, or would Audrey have behaved exactly the same, asked those very questions? She had an odd impulse to snag the girl's hand, whisper that they'd entered an enchanted medieval forest where fairies hid beneath leaves. Pressing her chest, she warned herself to stop foolishness that could swiftly devolve into gloom. With effort, she returned her concentration to the trail, trying to recover the fleeting bliss she'd experienced moments before.

Mrs. Michael beckoned the visitors to circle around a clump of yellow violets blooming above a carpet of pine needles. She held one of the spade-shaped petals, then gently turned it over to reveal a purple wash on the underside. "Isn't she charming?"

"Yes, she is!" shouted the girl who resembled Audrey.

A younger boy shoved her. "Stand back so I can see, Margaret."

Margaret scowled at her brother but let him step forward. As the group continued walking, she bolted ahead, scrambling to keep pace with Mrs. Michael. At the next stop, Mrs. Michael talked about western tanagers and their fondness for eating butter in the campgrounds, which had earned them the nickname of butter bird. After midsummer, she said, they migrated to the cooler woods beyond the rim.

Margaret said, "Do those birds truly eat whole plates of butter? Don't they get sick?"

Mrs. Michael crouched to look her in the eyes. "Yes, they do eat butter, but as far as I know, they don't get sick, because they share. Papa tanager is bold about feeding his family. If he flies away with a stick, he'll share it with everyone. That's why baby tanagers trail after their daddy through the woods, whining. After early spring, Papa's red head and yellow feathers become worn and tattered, 'cause he's been scrambling to feed his young'uns."

Several adults in the group laughed, and Margaret's father boomed, "Sounds awful familiar."

When they emerged from the woods and crossed the plaza, eventually arriving at the gate behind the museum, the tourists erupted into oohs and aahs at the sudden riot of colors.

"Ain't this something!" a woman called out. "All these flowers out of nowhere."

Beaming, Mrs. Michael opened the gate and ushered them through. Margaret and her brother chased each other over the flagstones, giggling, until their mother called them back.

"The whole garden is smiling," Mrs. Michael declared, "now that her children are blooming. In summer, it gets terribly hot from the sun along that north wall, but even so, the mint, figwort, and balsam families thrive." Her voice lilted in its sing-song timbre. The band of children had crowded around her, listening to her anthropomorphic descriptions.

"Ma'am, are the flowers happy?" a tiny girl in a pink frock asked.

"Yes, because they're so well cared for. Even ones from the higher elevations bloom here, sometimes earlier than they would have in the mountains. That's why their heads are high."

One of the men coughed, and another gave a quick roll of his eyes, but the children, captivated, tagged after Mrs. Michael.

"Do they live with their families?" the little girl pressed.

"Sure. That's why they're in the same groups where I found them on my hikes. The alpine flowers grow in high elevations, so I've grouped them together, see." She pointed out cut-leaf daisies, mountain heather, marsh marigold and pussytoes. "But in the garden, they live side by side with plants from other families. Here, the alpine flowers bloom along with plants from the foothills. And those lower elevation plants delay their budding period to bloom in time with plants from the high mountains. Aren't they clever?"

"Clever like birds but in different ways," Margaret piped up, "Since birds don't want to live with anyone except their own families."

Mrs. Michael nodded. "Exactly right. You've heard how birds of a feather flock together? They almost never live with birds from other species. Not the way plants do."

Margaret pondered this. "Maybe birds aren't able to... adapt as well?" She peered up at Mrs. Michael for confirmation, her

107

eyes trusting and intelligent; and Isabel's chest gave a little squeeze. She looked away, trying to steer her thoughts from Audrey.

"That's a wise observation," Mrs. Michael said, "And I see you were listening when I talked about how some animals protect themselves against predators by adapting special traits. Since plants can coexist with other families, they tend to be hardy and resilient, which can be excellent survival traits, too."

Margaret met Mrs. Michael's eyes shyly, pleased. Mrs. Michael turned, then rushed toward a small boy who had begun to pick a flower. "Oh, hello," she said, kneeling beside him, "Won't you please leave Daisy alone? She wants to grow big and tall just like you." After a moment's hesitation, the boy nodded and withdrew his hand.

An hour later, at Camp Curry, Mrs. Michael bid farewell to the visitors, and she and Isabel retraced the path through the woods to the New Village. Mrs. Michael moved with a sprightly gait, hustling over the trail's gentle curves. Without a doubt, she was the most unusual woman Isabel had met. Tramping through Nature was likely the last thing Mother would want, and she wouldn't show a shred of interest in the plants or animals. But as soon as the thought occurred, Isabel chided herself for her disloyalty.

The germ of the idea that had sprung into her mind yesterday struggled to take hold, and she examined it with caution. Could she persuade Mrs. Michael to let her stay the summer in exchange for assisting with the garden? As part of the bargain, she would stay out of Mr. Michael's way, help him maintain peace and quiet. Surely that would be fair? But when she considered how little she could contribute, her face grew hot. She'd likely disrupt Mrs. Michael's routine and slow her down.

Mrs. Michael turned to her, apparently mistaking her rosy cheeks for overheating. "Oh dear, your skin is burning. Fair complexions are prone to sunstroke. You'll need to drink water and rest as soon as we're inside."

Isabel took long, determined strides to keep pace. Neither of them spoke as they wound their way back to the plaza. Since Mrs. Michael seemed to be lost in her own thoughts, she continued pondering her idea. She might know nothing about plants, but there was another way she could help. Furrowing her brow, she wondered how in the world she would find the right opportunity to make her proposal but decided she must.

CHAPTER FIFTEEN

A young man with a buzz cut, wearing the khaki CCC uniform, greeted Mrs. Michael and Isabel at the garden gate. He clutched the handle of a rusted shovel.

"Isabel, this is Arnold," Mrs. Michael said, and the man gave a friendly nod. "I don't know what I'd do without him and the other Cascades boys who tend my lovelies."

Arnold wiped his free palm on his trousers. "Sorry about my filthy paws."

"Isabel's brother is also at Cascades."

Arnold gave Isabel an inquiring look, and she said, "His name is James Dickinson."

Understanding spread across his face. "Sure, I know James. Listen, if the Michaels can't keep you till Saturday, I'm supposed to let him know."

"It's decided. Isabel will stay the week."

"That's swell. I'll tell James." Touching his cap, Arnold strode toward the Indian Canyon in the back of the garden, where he joined another CCC boy.

"They're digging trenches for hoses that will become the garden's irrigation system," Mrs. Michael said.

A dozen yards behind Arnold, Isabel saw a man in a full Indian Chief outfit and headdress dancing among the teepees, surrounded by a group of tourists. "Who's that?"

"Lemee. His name means Rippling Water in Miwok." Mrs. Michael smiled. "But I know him as Chris Brown. He's joined Charlie and me on a few climbs. He and Maggie Howard give demonstrations at that little replica of an Indian village — singing, dancing, basket weaving, baking acorn cakes. The tourists seem to enjoy it. But I wonder whether it's demeaning for him to have to pretend to be an Indian chief for their sake."

She handed Isabel a canteen, spade, gloves, and bag for collecting the weeds. "You can weed through the strawberry patch and across the path, where the weeds are about to strangle the geraniums. If you feel faint, take the canteen and go over to the shade and rest." She pointed to the bench by the brook where they had sat yesterday.

Isabel nodded. At lunch, when Mrs. Michael had said she was heading to the garden, Isabel had begged to join her.

"This is nearly the hottest time of the day, so do be careful."

"I'll be fine." Isabel patted the rim of her bonnet and crouched on a flagstone near the strawberries. "I like being in the sun." With so much wild space, she could indulge herself in a brief taste of freedom. It was exactly what she had wanted during those long months of being closeted in the flat.

"I'll be over there." Mrs. Michael crossed to the other side of the garden.

As she stuffed handfuls of weeds into the bag, Isabel gazed at the glorious blue bowl of sky overhead. Mountains stretched toward its rim. Visitors strolled by, inspecting her work with interest, even approval. On the opposite side of the garden, the tip of Mrs. Michael's white hat bobbed up and down. She felt a spritz of cheer. They were a team, working in tandem. Yanking out weeds and restoring order to the plants took on new importance, for the sake of the garden's beauty and its visitors. In comparison, sweeping floors and shelving cans at the grocery seemed tedious and pointless, though Isabel enjoyed Mr. McGilligan's steady presence and corny jokes.

When she had gathered a full bag of weeds and raked the soil around the plants, Isabel rocked back on her heels and drank from her canteen. Hummingbirds and honeybees dipped among the pink and purple buds. Her insides went still as she grew aware of the brook's gentle whooshing, a breeze fluttering the flower petals, the hum of bees, songbird melodies. It took her a minute to identify the tranquil sensation as peace. It had been weeks since she'd experienced it, not since her last excursion with Audrey to the Isle of Castaways.

In another thirty minutes, her forehead, chest and arms were hot and sweaty, but she had made good progress on the geranium bed. Twisting around, she saw Arnold and another boy bent over their shovels in the canyon. A few feet closer was the bench where she and Mrs. Michael had sat yesterday, and behind it, the table strewn with food. She had the fleeting thought that Mrs. Michael might have more sympathy for the birds than her fellows struggling to make ends meet. But she warned herself it wasn't her business.

After removing most of the remaining weeds, she sat cross-legged in the grass, skirts tucked around her knees, and sipped water. Beneath the brim of her bonnet, she watched Mrs. Michael consulting with Arnold and another CCC recruit. Mrs. Michael glanced up and waved. Determined to demonstrate she was a hard worker who kept her word, Isabel picked up her spade and continued where she had left off.

Mrs. Michael joined her. "My, you've done well."

"I think I plucked out most of the weeds. Except for the last little bit there."

"That's all right. It can wait. You've done more than I expected. In fact, you made up for what I didn't do, since I got caught answering visitors' questions and talking with Arnold and Henry." She squinted. "You're flushed. We better head back." They sauntered to the gate. "How did you like working in the garden?"

Isabel turned to her, surprised. Mrs. Michael was one of the few adults who had ever asked her opinion, let alone about a job. "It was wonderful to be outside."

"I think so, too. You're not hemmed inside a dim space; you're surrounded by Nature. Almost as though the sky and mountains and plants are extensions of your body."

Isabel weighed her curious words and found they rang true. Now was the perfect time to make her proposal. Her heart banged inside her chest.

Wetting her lips, she tried, "Mrs. Michael, I wondered..." The tips of her fingers tingled.

"Yes?" Mrs. Michael fixed Isabel with a probing look, as if she knew exactly what she intended to ask, and Isabel nearly lost her nerve.

Looking at the ground, she blurted, "I know it's a lot to ask, but I wondered if you and Mr. Michael would let me stay with you over the summer? I could earn my keep by cooking and cleaning your apartment, also weeding the garden..." She trailed off. At last she sneaked a peek at Mrs. Michael, certain she had blown her chances. The older woman remained silent, her face wrinkled in thought. Maybe she was recalling her suspicion that Isabel had run away.

Isabel swallowed, wishing belatedly she hadn't phrased it as if she needed a favor. "I mean to say, I can do your chores so you have more time to tend to your ranger duties. And I'd keep to myself so I don't disturb either you or Mr. Michael."

Mrs. Michael sighed and shook her head. "We don't need that kind of help. Besides, our place is only big enough for two people. Mr. Michael's condition makes it trickier, since he requires a lot of peace and quiet. The room where you've been sleeping is meant for storage, but I use it to type up articles about animals in the park and specimens I collect. Then I send them off to the *Yosemite Nature Notes* and *The Stockton Record*."

"I see." Isabel's voice emerged small, defeated.

Mrs. Michael cast her a quick look. "It isn't a problem if you stay for a few days, till the end of the week. But after that, I need the room to type my articles. Charlie sometimes writes pieces about birds for the *Yosemite Nature Notes*, too."

"You could use it anytime. I'd leave and stay out of your way whenever you needed it. And I promise I wouldn't be a burden to you or Mr. Michael."

Mrs. Michael frowned. "I'm sorry, but it won't work. And I'm sure your mother wouldn't want you gone for so long..." Isabel bowed her head, not wanting Mrs. Michael to see the tears welling in her eyes.

During their simple supper, Isabel said little. Mrs. Michael glanced at her occasionally, murmuring to her husband about what a great help in the garden she had been. *Not enough to make a difference*, Isabel thought, then remembered her manners and forced a tiny smile. After supper, she cleared the table and washed the dishes. Though it was now for naught, she wanted the Michaels to see she was a help, not a hindrance, someone who made things simpler without creating a din or disturbance. But disappointment continued to slice through her, and her movements grew slow and lethargic. She blinked hard to keep her eyelids from drooping.

Mrs. Michael waved her into the sitting room, and they drew chairs around the phonograph's fluted silver horn. A scratchy noise burst out, like a long raggedy sigh, then beautiful, triumphant orchestra voices. Mrs. Michael clasped her hands in her lap, a ghost of a smile on her lips. Beside her in the rocker, Mr. Michael read the paper. Bold chords swelled and crashed through the room, like the musical accompaniment to a dramatic picture: invigorating, decisive. A concurrent beat drummed through Isabel's limbs.

When the piece ended, her gaze lingered on a pair of framed watercolors of birds on either side of the bookshelf. "Those pictures are lovely."

Mrs. Michael started, as if emerging from a reverie. Slowly she followed Isabel's gaze. "When I'm out hiking, I sometimes sketch what I see, especially if it's so unusual I won't remember it otherwise. Often I use the sketches as illustrations for my articles in *Yosemite Nature Notes*. Those are a few of my favorites. I painted over the original drawings."

"You capture their likenesses well." Isabel had a sudden thought. "I know how to type... I could type your articles."

"How well do you type?"

"I'm fair." Realizing she had hardly recommended herself, she reddened and added, "I've gotten pretty good this year. We don't have a typewriter at home, but I use the one at my high school to edit our paper."

"Hmm. Is that so?"

Mr. Michael glanced up from his paper.

"Yes, ma'am." Isabel waited, hopeful, as Mrs. Michael pondered this information.

At last she nodded slowly. "I've got to send something to *The Stockton Record* by next Thursday. It's about squirrels at Yosemite." She paused, and Isabel held her breath. "I'll give you my notes on the story, though I have to warn you, it's chicken scratch to the untrained eye. Long ago, the museum secretary gave up trying to figure out my scribbles, which is why I do my own typing. You can try your hand at deciphering it." She gave a rueful chuckle. "Though I'll be amazed if you can make heads or tails of it."

A sudden energy vibrated through Isabel's chest. She should have mentioned her typing skills sooner.

CHAPTER SIXTEEN

In the spare room the next morning, Mrs. Michael rolled a sheet of paper into the typewriter and checked the ribbon roll for ink.

"I've never known anyone who owned a typewriter," Isabel said, impressed. Since her arrival, she had been curious about the Remington, knowing how expensive they were.

"Oh, it's not ours. It's an ancient spare the museum agreed to let me borrow. You see, the ranger-naturalists usually give handwritten pages to the museum secretary to type up for *Yosemite Nature Notes*. But like I told you, she grew frustrated with my long hand and declared it illegible. After a while, she refused to type my articles. This machine was broken beyond repair, or so the museum thought. They agreed to let me borrow it, assuming I could fix it. Charlie replaced half a dozen stuck keys and swapped out the ribbon and repaired the carriage lock. So now it's almost as good as new. Except you'll have to push extra hard on the G, T, and W. Oh, and the J is missing."

Mrs. Michael handed her field notebook to Isabel. It was opened to a page dated May 15, 1934. Isabel scanned the messy scrawl, and Mrs. Michael gave a short, musical laugh. "Looks like a foreign language, doesn't it?"

"I can make it out. Just. Doesn't it begin, 'In the nineteen-thirties, gray squirrels are making a comeback at Yosemite.'"

Mrs. Michael looked surprised. "How'd you manage?"

"I'm used to translating students' handwriting before I edit and type their submissions for the school paper."

"Well, in that case, I'll leave you to it. I've got to head over to the museum for a spell. Please double space all the lines. Makes it easier for the journal to typeset."

For thirty minutes, Isabel scrolled through the article, making corrections to misspelled words, reorganizing several sentences so they flowed better, shortening other sentences. Mrs. Michael hadn't told her she could edit the article, but revising had become a habit, and Isabel hoped she wouldn't mind, providing the changes improved the end result.

She hadn't bothered to focus on the essay, but eventually she realized it was a story about two squirrels "playing a game" over hotcakes and watermelon at the garden feeding table. The ground squirrel raised his hind legs to sniff the tray, where the chickaree squirrel feasted on a morsel. Instantly, the chickaree leaped forward and nipped his rival's nose. Startled, the ground squirrel dropped to the ground, dragging his tail and belly in shame back to his burrow. Mrs. Michael had concluded, "The chickaree proved the champion, though the ground squirrel was twice his size."

Satisfied with the revisions she had made, Isabel typed the article, incorporating her corrections. She had unrolled the paper and set it aside when the apartment door banged open.

A few moments later, Mrs. Michael stood at the threshold of the spare room. "How'd you make out?"

"All right, I think. Here." Nervously Isabel handed her the page.

Mrs. Michael sank onto the sofa to read. Isabel watched her closely, worried she would notice the edits and grow annoyed. Finally, she laid the page on her lap.

"Do you like it? Is it all right?"

Mrs. Michael met her eyes, and Isabel saw with relief that she was smiling. "And how! I thought I was the only one who could

117

translate my bad handwriting. Little did I know you'd improve the way it reads." She stood. "There's a pair of us, don't tell. They'd banish us, you know."

Isabel felt a slight lift at the Emily Dickinson quote, as if a splash of sunlight had warmed her face. "How dreary to be somebody! How public, like a frog. To tell one's name the livelong day to an admiring bog."

Mrs. Michael clapped her hands. "We must be kindred souls."

•

After setting the last of the breakfast dishes to dry beneath the kitchen window, Isabel stole into the sitting room to examine the Michaels' books. A modest collection, but they filled three shelves, crammed together like colorful jigsaw pieces. A volume by Ansel Adams, *Taos Pueblo*, snagged her attention, along with a collection of poems by Emily Dickinson. She also spied titles by Virginia Woolf, Charles Dickens, Henry David Thoreau, Ralph Waldo Emerson, John Muir, F. Scott Fitzgerald, Mark Twain, Jules Verne, Charlotte Brontë, and Walt Whitman. Her heart stirred.

At her elbow, Mrs. Michael recited, "A precious, mouldering pleasure 'tis to meet an antique book in just the dress his century wore."

Isabel turned in surprise. "However have you memorized so many of her lines?"

"As a girl, I read her poems constantly until I learned a few dozen by heart. My mother gave me that blue book on the top shelf for my twelfth birthday. I adored the same things as Emily: gardens, bees, butterflies, birds. And I was also shy. Maybe that's why her poems meant so much to me. She observed an incredible lot from her little corner." Isabel's lips curved up. Mrs.

Michael's reasons for admiring Emily Dickinson's poetry were her own.

A finger of sun from the kitchen window lit up Mrs. Michael's face. "You're welcome to read any of those books."

Isabel touched a leather volume by John Muir, whom she had heard Mrs. Michael mention on the nature walk.

"Muir cofounded the Sierra Club, and his descriptions of Yosemite are phenomenal. Go ahead and borrow it."

Isabel withdrew it from the shelf and flipped through the pages, then slowly replaced it. "I'd better not. There won't be enough time to read it before I have to leave." A needle-like jab pricked the pit of her stomach.

"Charles and I had a long talk last night."

Isabel looked up quickly, searching Mrs. Michael's face for a sign of bad news.

"We know you've been through some terrible trials. And we've decided… if you work for your keep, you can stay with us till the end of August. We don't have much space, but it's enough to take in a girl like you, who doesn't need minding."

Isabel's lips parted in shock.

"Only if your mother agrees, of course. Charles and I are out of our element when it comes to children, but you're not a child. Anyhow, you keep to yourself, and you've adjusted to our routine. And after thinking it over, I realized we can use your help. Fact, it might be just the thing we need. First, weeding the garden. Second, typing the chicken scratch in my notebooks into articles and editing them as you see fit. Also typing and editing Charlie's articles. Third, fixing your splendid meals, doing the dishes and tidying the place. Fourth, leading the groups on the nature walks while I stay a tad behind to point things out and answer questions. And over time, you might help answer questions, too."

119

Isabel gulped. It would take her ages to acquire enough knowledge to answer visitors' questions. "I... I don't know what to say," she stammered. "I've never been so lucky."

Mrs. Michael's eyes twinkled. "It's not luck. You've earned it."

A clasp deep inside her chest swung wide open. She had a wild urge to shout her thanks over and over, like a mantra, but her lips trembled, and her eyes went moist. The rest of the summer. Away from the city, in Yosemite. On impulse, she leaned over and seized Mrs. Michael's hands, surprising them both.

"Thank you, Mrs. Michael. I can't believe it."

"What about your mother? Can she spare you? I'll be glad to write her a note."

Isabel felt Mrs. Michael's eyes on her. "I'll write her," she said quickly. "She won't mind." She dreaded the prospect of explaining her plans to Mother and decided the letter could wait, though Mrs. Michael needn't know. Straightening, she added, "And I promise not to interfere with your routine in any way. You and Mr. Michael will hardly even notice I'm here."

Mrs. Michael flashed Isabel a radiant smile. "Then it's settled."

An hour later, when Isabel ambled alone to the Merced to collect river stones for the garden, she let out a cheer and leaped into the air. She had a crazy desire to do cartwheels along the bank, or if she could, wing herself into the sky. But she reminded herself of the price. If given the chance, she would forsake Yosemite, all of it, to reverse the events that had led her here.

•   •   •

On their way to the garden that afternoon, Mrs. Michael said she would tell Arnold about Isabel's extended stay so he could let

James know. As she left Isabel at the Indian paintbrush patch, she caroled, "Bye for now, butterfly!"

No sooner had Mrs. Michael bid her quaint farewell, than a fairy-like lightness floated over Isabel, even as she dug feverishly at the weeds to loosen their stranglehold from the berries. All at once, she recalled a snippet from an Emily Dickinson poem: "Colors tease; I'm feeling for the air. A power of butterfly must be the aptitude to fly." She lifted her face, and a zing of breeze scampered over her skin—cool and delicious.

When her shoulders and knees began to ache, she stood, stretching, and drank from her canteen. At the back of the garden, Arnold and another CCC boy were digging a trench. Off to her left, a little group had gathered around Mrs. Michael, who gestured at a patch of violets. To the side, a rotund woman held a parasol and fanned herself with her free hand. A gentle gust rippled over the plants, creating a susurrant sound, and an orange butterfly capered over the row of lady slippers.

After Isabel finished weeding another row, she looked up to see Mrs. Michael facing a tall blond man in his mid to late thirties. He wore a ranger hat and olive-green uniform and tie and stood with his boots planted far apart, hands on hips. His face was stern as he stared down at Mrs. Michael, who watched him with clasped hands. Every so often, he flapped a hand dismissively and wrinkled his long, regal nose at her. Isabel was reminded of a schoolgirl receiving a scolding and wondered what in the world this man might have against Mrs. Michael.

As they walked back to the apartment, Mrs. Michael frowned, apparently lost in thought. Several times she began a sentence, only to cut herself off. Isabel considered asking whether she were all right, but cautioned herself not to intrude.

When they neared the post office, Mrs. Michael gave a heavy sigh. At last Isabel ventured, "I saw a man in a ranger uniform in the garden."

"Hmmm. That was my supervisor, Chief Naturalist Harwell. Did you see him speaking to me?"

"Only for a minute or two, I think."

"We don't always see eye to eye."

"Why not?"

"He doesn't approve of what I've done in the garden."

Isabel made a sympathetic murmur. "Whatever for?"

"He disagrees with how I've arranged the plants by life zones—valley floor, trailside, meadow, middle and higher altitudes—instead of by plant communities. Says I should have consulted with him first. And that's just the beginning."

Isabel tossed her head, riled on Mrs. Michael's behalf.

"Maybe I shouldn't say this, but every year he makes it more and more difficult for me to reapply for my position."

"You must apply every year?"

"Yes. I'm only on the payroll during the summer, though I actually work at Yosemite throughout the year; I just don't get paid during the other seasons."

"That's not right."

"That's how it is."

"How does Mr. Harwell make it difficult for you to reapply?"

"He's quick to point out some little fault, which he reports to Superintendent Thomson. Claims I dress slovenly and am stubborn as a mule. But the bigger thing he accused me of is not cooperating with my superiors—meaning him—and coming and going as I please." She harrumphed. "Today he told me I must report to the Museum Secretary when I come and go from work so my hours will be recorded on a time slip." She stopped abruptly, as if deciding she had said too much.

"How terribly unfair!"

"The ironic thing is he was my student in the Field School of Natural History nine or ten summers ago. I used to teach him."

Isabel didn't know what to say. She remembered the man's scowl, his finger wagging in Mrs. Michael's face. What nerve he had.

Mrs. Michael tightened the burlap strap. "It's a given he'll discourage me from applying next summer. And I suspect he'll write a letter to Superintendent Thomson, recommending against my appointment. Every year, it's the same song and dance."

"I'm sorry." It was feeble comfort. Swift anger surged through her. Surely this cocky man didn't deserve Mrs. Michael as his employee. "Does he treat other rangers the same?"

"No, I don't believe so. He's said more than once that the CCC boys would be better supervised by a male naturalist." She looked sideways at Isabel. "If Mr. Harwell were a plant, he'd be a tumbleweed, as dry and rough as they come."

Isabel giggled.

"From my experience, men don't like to be shown up by women, and that's probably how Mr. Harwell sees what I've done with the garden: rubbed his nose in it." Her mouth turned down. "Unfortunately, women have to work twice as hard as men to get half the credit. But Superintendent Thomson appreciates what I've done. He's the one who asked me to oversee the wildflower garden. And there's the rub. Mr. Harwell wants it all for himself. But enough about him!" As though determined to outrun her thoughts of the man, Mrs. Michael quickened her steps, and Isabel matched her pace.

CHAPTER SEVENTEEN

Mr. Michael poked his head through the door, then yanked a foot-and-a-half-long speckled fish from his knapsack and presented it to his surprised wife. With a shy nod at Isabel, he explained he had stolen down to the Merced for the afternoon to catch trout.

Mrs. Michael's cheeks glowed as she planted the trout on the counter. "Isabel will make a feast with it. She's a much better chef than I am." She clapped her hands.

"You should wait until we eat supper before you decide about that," Isabel said, embarrassed.

"Don't worry, we'll enjoy it. You see, whenever we go knapsacking in the mountains, we only bring a little rice, hardtack, and dried fruit—things most folks would consider starvation rations. But we catch as much fish as we can eat, and the trout we cook on those overnight hikes always feels like a treat."

Isabel searched for ingredients to live up to Mrs. Michael's expectations, settling on a pan of muffins, which she baked with corn meal, lard and wildflower honey. She fried the trout in oil and corn meal and garnished it with fresh tomatoes and mushrooms.

As they sat down to supper, Mrs. Michael told her husband with a wink, "You have to admit we're dining unusually well."

He didn't reply. Isabel understood he was taciturn, but she wondered whether news of her extended stay had put a damper on his mood or worse, his health. She hoped not. When Mrs. Michael asked about his day, it was clear they were both far more keen to discuss his stolen afternoon on the river than his hours at the post office.

"Saw an unusual bird," he said to Mrs. Michael.

"Really? Who?" She brightened and turned to Isabel. "Remember I told you Charlie isn't worried about dangerous places like the edges of cliffs? But if he spots a rare bird, watch out!"

"Townsend solitaire. It's been a while since we've seen one."

"Oh my, yes!" To Isabel, she said, "They're like robins but more slender, with tails as long as their bodies. They have gray feathers and a ring around the eye. "

"This one lighted on a juniper above the stream and ate berries. Then he perched on a dead snag in the crown of a Douglas fir and sang for a good fifteen minutes. Some of his friends joined and started a game of tag between the trees. Serenading the whole time."

"Sure wish I'd been there. Isabel and I were in the garden most of the afternoon." Mrs. Michael laid down her fork and described her run-in with Mr. Harwell. "The nerve of him to make me clock my time, when I've put in countless hours during the off season."

Mr. Michael frowned. "His end game is clear."

"Of course. He wants me gone next season, so he can reclaim the garden and redo the landscaping. And then the CCC boys can work under the direction of a male naturalist."

Mr. Michael's cheeks darkened. "It won't happen. Thomson knows you're too knowledgeable, and your tours are among the most popular. He'll never allow it. Besides, this happens every year and you always come out smelling like a rose."

"Don't be so sure, Charlie. Bert Harwell is wily."

"There are ways around him. A little sugar coating won't hurt."

"What, you mean compliment him? Tell him what a wonderful job he's done and bow to his plans?"

"Play to his ego."

"I'll stand firm with my garden, you know that." Her face turned steely. "If pandering to that pompous man will get him off my back, I'll do it in a letter. Tell him I'll boost the number of plants to well over a thousand so he can claim credit for flocks of tourists. Surely that will get his attention." When Mr. Michael didn't reply, she said with indignation, "You think I should promise to do whatever he says is best for the garden, however he sees fit."

Mr. Michael lifted a shoulder. "Can't hurt to let him think you like one or two of his ideas."

Mrs. Michael said to Isabel, "See what I mean about working for men? You have to flatter them constantly and tell them how wise and capable they are. Or else heaven forbid, their egos might shatter. Such bunk."

Isabel considered this. "I sure wouldn't compliment my boss if he didn't deserve it." She was about to add that at least Mr. McGilligan was reasonable, but Mrs. Michael raised an eyebrow; and she broke off, uncertain. "But maybe, if there wasn't any choice…"

"Unfortunately, that's the game I have to play to reach the goal: the means to the end."

"Managing the garden the way you like?"

Mrs. Michael's face grew pensive. "More than that. I want to protect the National Parks, beginning with Yosemite. If folks learn to cherish every creature here, including the plants, they'll keep coming back. The park will be their sanctuary. The garden's a perfect way to inspire them."

Mr. Michael put his hand on his wife's shoulder, and a silent question and answer passed between them. Several quick raps sounded at the door, and they pulled away.

"Who can that be?" Mrs. Michael crossed over and flung open the door.

Isabel caught sight of James' broad shoulders and dark hair. With a yip of delight, she charged to him.

"Hello, Izz! Looks like you won."

"Please come in," Mrs. Michael said.

"No, ma'am, I don't want to intrude. And I've only got a few minutes. Perhaps Izz could go on a short walk with me?"

Isabel looked at Mrs. Michael. "Is it all right with you? I won't be gone long. I'll do the dishes as soon as I get back."

"Go ahead and get a nip of fresh air."

Skirting the corner of the post office into the plaza, Isabel followed James onto the trail that wound to Camp Curry.

"It's like a kingdom of trees out here, isn't it?" James said. "Those giant sequoias and redwoods are majestic, real beauties."

"Mrs. Michael says being outdoors in the park is a spiritual experience."

"Did she now?" He watched her, slantwise.

"Yes, and I think she's right."

She expected him to object in the name of their religion, to bring up the church and its rituals, but he said, "Yeah, almost. John Muir called Yosemite a temple."

Isabel felt an unexpected rush of gratitude for her brother.

He shot her an amused look. "You're awfully lucky the Michaels agreed to let you stay the summer. Sure you won't get in their way? The apartments over the post office are only meant for one or two people, you know. Then there's the expense of food."

"They've got a tiny storage room with a sofa, and that's where I sleep. Anyhow, I don't eat much, and neither do they; we're all content with soups and salads. Plus, I'll earn my keep by cleaning, fixing the meals and weeding in the garden. Even typing up Mrs. Michael's nature articles…"

"This was your idea, wasn't it, Izz? You put them up to it." James wagged a finger. She knew he was teasing, but she colored, anyway, and batted his hand.

"So what if it was? In the end, each of us comes out ahead. Mrs. Michael has more time for her ranger duties and her husband, and I can explore Yosemite."

"Just try to give them space. I hear they're private and even a little eccentric. And you know Mr. Michael isn't in good health."

"I've promised not to get in their way. If anything, I plan to make things easier for them."

"Then I've no doubt you will."

"Mrs. Michael is…" Isabel struggled to find the right word. "She's just a remarkable lady. In every way you can imagine. Did you know she's the only female ranger-naturalist at Yosemite? She knows thousands of interesting facts about plants and animals. And she climbs mountains. Without ropes! Her husband used to climb, too, but because of his heart trouble, she goes alone now. She even writes articles and creates her own illustrations." She peeked at him as he digested this information.

"That's swell. I'm sure she *is* amazing. But listen, Izz, I wanted to talk with you about Mother."

Isabel stiffened, and the tips of her fingers went cold.

"You've got to write to her. You said you left a note, but even so, you ran away, and she's bound to be frantic."

"I *didn't* run away. I told her exactly where I was going. Here. To see you. "

"That's all well and good, but she's your mother, dammit, and you owe her an explanation. Especially if you won't be returning home till the end of summer."

Isabel stared at him, surprised at the anger in his voice.

"I know you suffered a lot after Audrey's death. But think of it from Mother's angle. Now she's lost not just Dad and Audrey, but you and me both! She's utterly alone in that wretched place."

Isabel said nothing.

"You owe her a letter. Besides, you're right over the post office. Should be easy as pie to mail it."

"I'll write her soon." Not immediately, but she kept that to herself, resenting that both her brother and Mrs. Michael had brought up the letter topic, as though she were too young to be trusted with her own decisions. Would they also insist on Mother's permission as a condition for her to stay? She would have to tell Mother her plans were firm, irreversible. She drew her shoulders back.

James tugged her wrist. "That's good. That's for starters. Say, how much do the Michaels know about what happened and why you're here?"

"I told Mrs. Michael about Dad's death and wanting to see you."

"That's all she knows?"

"I don't see how anything else is her business." Isabel freed her wrist and stepped away. Audrey's name hung in the air between them, unspoken.

"All right." James gave a grim nod. "I know you wanted to leave the city and everything that happened, and that's not a bad idea. People rejuvenate at Yosemite. But at some point you have to stop running away."

"Why do you keep saying that?" Her voice rose. "I didn't run away."

He flicked her a look. "Then why didn't you tell Mother goodbye?"

"She was terribly upset. Just being around me was an awful reminder..."

"Of course she was upset, but that doesn't mean she didn't want you around."

"Easy for you to say. You got to escape and come *here*. You weren't alone with Mother and her moods. Even the cat took off..." Her throat clogged as it came rushing back — the drudgery of chores, the dim, suffocating flat, living hand to mouth. With a spark of resentment, she sped up, hustling past thickets of mountain laurel.

James caught up with her. "You're like a deer once you get going."

She made a harsh, rueful laugh.

He touched her arm. "You're right. I wasn't there. I don't envy what you and Mother went through. Can't even begin to imagine how damn awful it must've been. I'm sorry."

"We were stuck in that crummy flat." *While you were here, in this gorgeous park with boundless space.*

"I know." His voice grew low. "I should have been there, too. I wanted to be at Audrey's funeral."

"I told Mother you should come home, but she was worried you'd lose your job and didn't think you should risk..."

"What's done is done. No point rehashing it."

She glimpsed pain in his eyes and knew she couldn't reveal the truth — either about her hand in Audrey's accident or the desperate things they'd endured while he was away. Besides, burdening him wouldn't be fair. He deserved to be spared the details; she could do that much for him.

She slipped her arm through his. They were together now, at least — one small, good thing. "How do you like it here? You haven't told me anything about the camp or the work you're doing." Suddenly she was ashamed that their conversations had revolved almost exclusively around her living situation.

"It's good work. Most of the fellows at camp are from San Francisco, too. They call us junior recruits. We've also got LEMs — Local Experienced Men — like Wild Bill. They have forestry experience, so they're the foremen and supervisors." A spotted fawn plunged across the trail ahead of them. Between each frightened leap, its stomach bounced near the ground.

"During the week, we work hard, like an army corps. In May, I was with a crew that was to rebuild the stairway on the eastern face of Half Dome. We set up a stub camp at the base. Our job was to replace four hundred thirty feet of cable and a few dozen pipe posts with galvanized iron. We had to drill the holes by hand, half a foot deep. To keep from falling, we were tied to the posts."

Isabel gaped at him. "No joke?"

"Dead serious. But boy, it turned dangerous. Almost every afternoon a storm blew in with rain, hail, or snow, and the winds were high."

"In May?"

"Yep. Weather's fickle here. We tore down the stub camp, and Wild Bill said we'll finish later, when there are fewer storms."

"Ooh. I'll worry something awful if you go back."

"Nothing to worry about yet."

"What are you doing now? Not working in Mrs. Michael's garden."

"No. I've been with a crew at Yosemite Village. That's where I was just now. We're installing log benches and planting ferns and shrubs around the administration building and hospital."

"You're truly that close?" She gripped his arm.

"Yep. Next week, we'll move to the museum to add more flagstones around the telescopes in front and clear debris from the road."

"Gee, I hope you'll work in the village for the rest of the summer! Do you have any free time?"

"Not a lot. In the evenings, Sergeant takes roll and holds a bugle call and flag salute. Plus we've got cooking and cleaning duties. Weekend afternoons, we have a little time to relax and play ball."

"Then we can see each other, can't we?"

"Don't see why not. I'll just have to clear it first with the section leader. And if you walk down to the museum, you might catch me on break." He stopped, and they reversed direction down the path. "Listen, Izz, I've got to get back, but I wanted to hear more… about Audrey."

Isabel froze at the catch in her brother's voice.

"Haven't had time to grieve for her." His voice was anguished. He swiped at a smattering of tears around his eyes.

"I'm sorry, James."

"I'd like the two of us to hold our own memorial. Maybe I can find a chaplain… no, scratch that. All I ask is we make time to talk about her some weekend afternoon."

She knew he was waiting for her to agree, but a deep dread had slithered up her torso. "Yes," she heard herself say at last, "Sure we can."

He had no idea, of course, of the role she had played in the tragedy. And, she told herself, he could never know. In the shadows of twilight, she was grateful he couldn't read the horror on her face at the thought of revisiting that day at Lafayette Square.

CHAPTER EIGHTEEN

Over breakfast, Mrs. Michael told Isabel she had duties at the museum, where she was an instructor with Yosemite's Field School for Ranger-Naturalists. "Since I'm on Mr. Harwell's watch list, I need to scoot over there and give a botany lecture. The school's especially important, because most of its graduates become ranger-naturalists themselves, like Mr. Harwell." She met Isabel's eyes. "The men, anyhow. Female graduates aren't considered for positions."

Isabel blew through her teeth. "How can they get away with that?" Scowling, she sipped the primrose tea Mrs. Michael had prepared to help ease her eczema.

"It's a fact of the animal world: males in charge make rules to keep their power. When red stag bucks fight over a doe, they begin by roaring. That way the old bucks can evaluate the size and strength of their opponents before deciding whether to fight. If they started goring right away, the younger bucks would win."

"But you made ranger."

"Through sheer persistence. Years ago, I collected and identified over a thousand plants to prove I knew them inside out. The Yosemite Nature Director finally came around and offered me a summer appointment. The rest of the year, I volunteered and wrote up field reports. By the next summer, he decided he might as well renew my position. Not only am I the only female ranger-naturalist at Yosemite, I'm the only woman on the Field School faculty."

Isabel opened her mouth to protest, but Mrs. Michael said, "I've learned you have to act like what you want to become. Convince yourself first, and others will believe it, too." She swallowed the last of her tea and picked up her burlap sack. "Have fun exploring while I'm away. This afternoon, we'll work in the garden."

In the early morning glow, Isabel sauntered down the wooded trail toward Camp Curry, her breath quickening as she sucked in the piney spice and forest's earthy loam. She watched a buck drinking by the bank of the Merced and recalled Mrs. Michael's observation about those in power setting the rules. At least Mrs. Michael resisted senseless orders, remained irreverent to tradition. She did things, went places other women didn't.

All at once, Isabel remembered the afternoon a month ago when she had impulsively walked to the waterfront after leaving Mr. McGilligan's. She had wanted to catch a glimpse of the strikers. The Embarcadero had been eerily quiet, but a few blocks ahead, near Pier 20, picketers had held signs and marched in an orderly line behind an American flag. Police had swarmed the docks.

Suddenly a stream of police cars with trucks sandwiched between them had exited the piers, and Isabel had heard the picketers' low shouts and jeers. They had hurled what looked like rocks or bottles at the motorcade of scabs. Surely some of those men had known Dad. Rising on tiptoe, she had craned her neck for a closer look. The sun's last embers had flickered across the horizon, all but swallowed by the fog that had blown in.

"This ain't no place for a girl," a voice behind her had snarled.

Isabel had swirled around, too shocked to respond. An old man in torn breeches, pushing a peddler's wagon, had fixed her with a baleful look.

"There's gonna be trouble. Get on home."

She had stepped back, touching the rash on her throat.

"Go on now!" The man had shoved the wagon past her, then turned and glowered.

When he shook a fist, she had fled down Embarcadero, hands clutching her sides. Where *was* a place for a girl, she had wondered, loping past surprised faces of passersby as automobiles and trolleys had hurtled in all directions.

Maybe that place was here. The river smashed against the rocks then lapped with a whoosh; and the breeze, stirring the pine boughs, created an otherworldly music. Mrs. Michael had explained how on Roe Island, she and Mr. Michael had followed the natural rhythms of the land, in harmony with the plants and animals that most folks ignored or took for granted until they needed them.

Animals are so much simpler to understand than people, she had said. *We could all benefit by learning from them. But most folks are oblivious.* Isabel agreed in principle, though it struck her that feeding birds while forgetting foreclosed farmers and the unemployed was another oblivion.

Audrey. She felt a wash of sadness as the Merced rushed over boulders, indifferent to everything in its path. For a long time, she gazed at the river. Finally, she roused herself and drifted back to the apartment.

That afternoon, on the way to the garden, Mrs. Michael pointed to the automobiles lined up around the museum and tutted. "Look how thick the air has gotten from all that smoke and gasoline! Even in this slump, tourists still come in droves. Charles worries the park will lose its peace and quiet with the constant whiz of automobiles and their pollution. And there's no telling how the plants and animals might be affected."

In front of the museum, a crew of CCC boys was clearing brush from a road, and Isabel wondered if James were among them. She suspected the Michaels would view the crew as contributing to the pollution by making it easier for automobiles to zip around. If they thought Yosemite was polluted, they would be absolutely horrified by San Francisco.

Isabel and Mrs. Michael carried hunks of cheese and a tin of berries to a bench by the stream in the wildflower garden. After lunch, they would weed.

"Tell me," Mrs. Michael said. "Are your mother and sister your only relatives in San Francisco?"

Isabel's heart hammered as her face lost its color, but if Mrs. Michael noticed, she didn't say.

"Yes, ma'am. Just the two." She nearly choked on the cheese, ashamed of her lie.

"There's no need to ma'am me, Isabel," Mrs. Michael teased. "I'm not one for formalities. Even being called Mrs. Michael makes me feel stuffy and much too old. Besides, now that you're staying for the summer, you can call me Enid."

It felt wrong to call a lady ten years older than Mother by her first name, but then, Mrs. Michael was utterly unlike Mother.

"Truly," Mrs. Michael insisted. "I don't mind."

"Enid," Isabel said haltingly, and found the word didn't sound as strange, uttered out loud.

"How are your mother and sister?"

Isabel mumbled something about Mother's job at the hotel and said as little as possible about Audrey, except that she was off school for summer break. She didn't meet Mrs. Michael's eyes.

"And I suppose you miss them? Of course they must miss you."

"Ye...es."

"What does your mother think about your being here? Have you written her about staying for the summer?"

Isabel hesitated, twisting a blade of grass through her fingers. "Not yet, but I'm sure she won't mind."

From far away came Mrs. Michael's next questions, gentle but probing. "Does she know you're here?"

Isabel flinched and stared at the grass. She recalled the fragment of conversation she'd overheard, how Mrs. Michael suspected she had run away. "Yes, she knows." This wasn't technically a lie, but it wasn't the whole truth, either.

A trace of alarm wavered across Mrs. Michael's face, and her slate-blue eyes narrowed. "I wondered.... what does she think of your being so far away? I hope she's not terribly worried."

"She knows I came here to visit James. Anyhow, she's... too busy to worry." The words clinked from her lips like ice cubes, cold and brittle. She had no intention of sharing the full story with Mrs. Michael, but concocting a sticky web of lies seemed worse than a sin, a betrayal of her kindness. Frowning, she tugged at her skirt, aware that Mrs. Michael was doubtless preparing to interrogate further. Best to give her a portion of the truth, enough to keep her satisfied. Of course, it was a risk, since she might disapprove and retract her offer for Isabel to stay.

She took a quick breath, and a zip of cold air stung her nose and throat. "My plans came together quickly, so she learned I was leaving at the last minute."

"Did she give her permission?"

"I left her a note."

"Then she didn't find out until after you'd gone?"

"No," Isabel said in a small voice. Mrs. Michael knotted her forehead, clearly perturbed, and she regretted saying so much. She had the terrible thought that the older woman would take matters into her own hands and telegram Mother, arrange for Isabel's immediate return to San Francisco.

Mrs. Michael said slowly, "I've never been a mother, unless you count my birds and flowers. And I do think of them as offspring, just not the human kind. But I'm sure your mother's awfully anxious."

Isabel tilted her head and pinched the grass between her fingers, bracing herself.

"You mustn't let your family worry. No matter what plans you make, you must consider your loved ones." She gave Isabel a penetrating look. "I wouldn't feel right keeping you without your mother's knowledge. Especially if she objects."

Her words conveyed a warning. If that weren't enough, Isabel was already on borrowed time. And no bit of her stay at Yosemite, however gratifying, could ever justify its steep cost. "I mean to write to Mother," she said stiffly. She sneaked a look at Mrs. Michael's face, hoping this would put an end to their conversation.

"I have stationery you can use. After you finish your letter, Charles can stamp and mail it for you."

"Thank you, Mrs. Michael … Enid."

Despite Enid's unfettered smile, Isabel couldn't help but worry that she would watch more closely, now that she knew her suspicions were correct and Isabel had left home in a hurry, without a proper goodbye. She may want to confirm that Mother agreed to let her stay. Worse, she might continue to probe about Audrey. Isabel shut her eyes. Enid was wicked smart and observant, to boot. What if she deduced the truth?

That evening, knowing she had no choice if she wanted to allay Enid's suspicions, Isabel excused herself to write to Mother.

"Let me give you some paper." Enid led the way to the storage room and removed a packet of cream-colored parchment and a pen from the desk. She lingered at the door. "I wanted to tell you: I've planned a hike tomorrow with Ansel and Virginia Adams, the friends from San Francisco who spend their summers in Yosemite. Both of them have served on the Sierra Club's Board of Directors, so they're avid hikers." She lowered her voice, and a pall darkened her face. "It's a shame Charles won't be coming on account of his heart trouble. Are you interested in hiking in his place?"

A little shiver of excitement coursed through Isabel. "Yes, I'd love to."

For many minutes after Enid left, she sat at the desk, pen in hand, completely at a loss about what to write to Mother. Twice she scrawled down a few lines, only to scratch them out and crumple the paper. Finally, not wanting to waste any more of Enid's stationery, she chewed the nib of the pen and began:

Dear Mother,

I'm sorry I left in a hurry. I didn't want to upset you, but that wasn't an excuse for leaving without a proper goodbye. I arrived safely at Yosemite on Sunday evening, and a kind woman, Mrs. Enid Michael, along with her husband, allowed me to stay at their apartment. Mrs. Michael is a ranger-naturalist here, and her husband is the assistant postmaster. She supervises some of the CCC boys from James' camp, which is how I met her.

The Michaels have agreed to let me board with them for the summer, providing I earn my keep. Also, this means I can see James, and he's the reason I came. He's working with a crew in the Yosemite New Village, close to where I'm staying. I'm helping Mrs. Michael with the public wildflower garden she manages. I'm also to type up nature articles for her and help with guided tours. Yosemite is truly a gorgeous park, and I'm lucky to have the opportunity to assist Mrs. Michael for a few months.

Please don't worry about me, as I'm fine. I hope you're doing well, too. Maybe things are easier for you now. If you see Mr. McGilligan, please tell him I'm sorry for not saying goodbye. James sends his love.

Your Daughter,
Isabel

P.S. I'm sorry for taking three dollars from the jam jar. I thought I might need it for the trip to Yosemite, and it turns out, I did. I promise to repay you plus interest as soon as I'm able.

Paying interest on a loan that Mother hadn't granted outright was only fair. The problem was, Isabel wasn't sure when or how she'd earn back the money. She only had one dollar left, and she suspected she would need it to return home when the summer ended. She had also made sure not to ask for Mother's permission, lest she not grant it. Mother had no choice, anyway, now that Isabel was here and the summer was well underway. Satisfied she had kept her promise to James and Enid while assuring Mother of her safety, she sealed the letter. Tomorrow she would ask Mr. Michael to post it.

After dressing for bed, she sifted through the past few days, snapping through them like stills from a movie reel. It had been a blur of motion, too fast to understand while it happened until she picked it apart frame by frame. Buried beneath was the wretched grief threatening to burst through, retribution for her enjoyment of even a minute.

Through the open window, the hum of cicadas swelled to a chatter. When at last her body surrendered to sleep, Isabel entered a vivid dream. She and Audrey skipped along a path at Yosemite, holding hands, as songbirds warbled overhead.

Trembling, she brushed her fingers over Audrey's cheeks and down her curly locks. She had rescued her sister, jettisoned her safe and sound to the Isle of Castaways. Audrey gazed at her with shining eyes, and something hard and taut in Isabel's chest gave way. Breathlessly, she described how they would tend the garden, hike the Sierras, watch for deer, spy bears from afar.

"It's warm here, Audrey," she whispered, "Not damp and chilly like San Francisco. The sun almost always shines."

It was funny how desperate she was to tell Audrey all of it. Her eyes brimmed with tears, and her breath went shallow. Joy and grief must waver together across a thin, blurry line.

"We'll have such fun, Audrey, you'll see. It's the most splendid place we could have landed." She squeezed Audrey's hand down to her sister's delicate finger bones. Their story would have a fairytale ending, just as they'd imagined.

But then Audrey leaped off the path, like a frightened deer, and cantered into the thick of the woods, and Isabel's voice went hoarse calling after her, begging her to wait, come back, come back. Long after her sister had disappeared, Isabel shouted into the terrible silence.

CHAPTER NINETEEN

"Oh, your fair skin!" Enid said, studying Isabel. "Best wear this hat with the wide brim. It's a steep climb to Mount Watkins." They had risen at first light to fill canteens, lace shoes, and pack a rucksack with cheese, bread, chocolate and berries. "It's hard for Charles to have to stay back." Enid heaved a sigh.

Isabel murmured agreement. Surely Dad hadn't had an inkling of his own cardiac troubles; he had never spoken of chest pain or shortness of breath before that fatal day on the docks. Or if he had experienced symptoms, he had stoically kept them to himself, perhaps believing them a byproduct of his job.

The Adams pulled up to the post office in a dusty Dodge. Isabel guessed they were in their early thirties, a good twenty years younger than the Michaels. Virginia's honey-colored hair was twisted into a chignon, and she wore a thin pair of spectacles. Her husband, Ansel, in a Stetson hat and jeans, had dark hair and eyes, a trimmed beard, and a delicate, slightly crooked nose. He called out a lively greeting from the driver's seat.

Isabel climbed after Enid into the back of the automobile. A bulky bag sprawled on the floorboard, which Enid whispered they must be careful not to disturb, as it contained Mr. Adams' camera equipment.

"This is our young guest for the summer, Isabel Dickinson," she told the Adams. "She'll be taking Charlie's place on the hike."

Virginia turned to them, her eyes widening in surprise. "First I've heard you have a guest. You're relations, I imagine? How did..."

"It's a long story. Isabel will earn her room and board by helping me with errands and several important things."

A puzzled look swept over Virginia's face as she extended a hand to Isabel. No doubt she had more questions and would seize the first opportunity to corner Enid in private so she could ask them. Self-conscious, Isabel stared down at her lap.

"You've got some big shoes to fill for Charles," Ansel joked. "Sheer mountain cliffs to scale, to boot. Are you game?"

Knowing he was gaining fame for his photography, Isabel blushed. "I'm ready for hiking, not sure about scaling."

Virginia scolded, "Stop, you. She's young and looks strong, so I wouldn't be surprised if she outpaces us all." She caught Isabel's eyes. "Don't let him scare you. We won't be scaling any cliffs."

"Virginia has lived at Yosemite her whole life," Enid put in. "She knows a thing or two about climbing."

"And if she's in the right mood, she might sing along the way," Ansel said, steering lightly with his left hand.

"Ah yes! Tell Isabel the story of how you two met."

"Funny to say, classical music brought us together. Before Ansel caught the photography bug, he'd planned to become a concert pianist." Virginia gave her husband an affectionate glance. "One year he spent a summer at Yosemite and wanted to practice. After he heard my father kept a Chickering in our rooms above the studio, Ansel called on us, and Papa invited him to come over to play whenever he liked. I was only seventeen and Ansel nineteen."

"Virginia wanted to become a singer, and since I had my heart set on a musical career, we had a lot to talk over. She has a lovely contralto voice, so I persuaded her to sing a Handel aria while I accompanied on piano. We discovered we both had a passion for hiking, too. And now we've abandoned our instruments to scramble over mountains. The woe of it!" He made an exaggerated sigh.

"Of course, photography is Ansel's new passion."

"I've combined two of the things I love for a living."

"His studio is in San Francisco," Enid told Isabel, adding that Isabel was also from the city.

"Whereabouts?" Virginia asked. "When we're not at Yosemite, we live next door to Ansel's parents in the Presidio, though we wish we could stay here all year. It gives us such peace. Where did you say you live?"

Isabel's face flamed, and she grazed the pocks on her throat. "I didn't. Near Market and Turk," she mumbled, not wanting to name the Tenderloin.

"Hmm, I'm not familiar. What brings you here?"

Isabel recounted the story of visiting James.

"What fun you'll have staying with the Michaels! I don't know anyone more knowledgeable about the park than those two. They took me on my first real climb. I'll never forget it."

Isabel waited for her to say more, but Ansel drew the Buick to a creaky stop, and to her amazement, they emerged at a shallow, shimmering lake encircled by evergreens and the shadow of a scarped bank of cliffs.

"That's where Tenaya Creek empties into Mirror Lake. And look, Half Dome," Enid said as they climbed out of the automobile into the respite of cool air. A massive, polished granite formation rose from the opposite bank. Isabel felt a hitch in her chest. This close, it resembled a medieval stone castle. She thought of James and the CCC crew assigned to rebuild the stairway for hikers. A thin patch of snow glistened on its crest.

As Enid grabbed the rucksack from the back seat, Ansel slung the heavy camera bag and a smaller pack over his back and positioned a long wooden tripod over his shoulder.

Enid shaded her eyes at the lake. "I promised Charlie I'd find some interesting birds. And, lo and behold, there's a great blue heron on the opposite shore!" She maneuvered nimbly over a series of large rocks to reach the bank.

Isabel took a few steps closer. To her astonishment, the heron glided into the air with a graceful, leisurely beat, long neck and wings outspread, spindly legs extended behind.

Enid hustled to the woods at the edge of the lake and beckoned them over. "The bee is not afraid of me, I know the butterfly; the pretty people in the woods receive me cordially. The brooks laugh louder…"

"A poem?" Virginia asked.

Isabel met Enid's eyes and smiled. "Emily Dickinson."

They trekked through a dense forest of black oaks and arrived at a trail, mostly bare of trees, that zigzagged in a steep incline up the granite cliff of Mount Watkins.

"It's the beginning of the ascent," Enid said. "We'll go slowly if you'd like. No need to rush when you're not used to the altitude or climb."

After a few paces along the switchback, Isabel panted, her face and throat roasting in the heat. A dozen yards ahead, Ansel and Virginia stepped briskly, disappearing around a bend, and Isabel was impressed that even laden down with heavy equipment, Ansel could easily outpace her. She realized with a stitch of guilt that Enid had hung back out of consideration.

"Stop here a minute," Enid said. In the pin of the path, she unfastened her pack and handed Isabel the canteen. As Isabel sipped, trying not to gulp, Enid pointed out wild lilacs. The sun was blazing onto the trail in full force. "It's usually a hot trek. That's why we wanted to get an early start."

"Let's keep going, then." Isabel returned the canteen.

145

"There's no hurry."

"But it'll only get hotter the longer we stay here. Besides, the Adams will wonder where we are."

"They'll wait."

"I don't want to slow them down."

But as they continued, and sweat dripped down Isabel's throat and chest, she regretted not having drunk more water. At the next switchback, Ansel and Virginia rose together from the shade of a lone oak.

Virginia clucked in sympathy as she ran her eyes across Isabel's flushed face. "Come to the shade," she ordered, steering Isabel by the shoulder to the spot she had vacated. Enid took a swig from the canteen before thrusting it into Isabel's hands.

Ansel said, "Mind if I walk ahead and find some pictures?" Although the Stetson shielded his face and he had rolled up his shirt sleeves and pant legs, beads of moisture glistened on his arms and throat. Still, his eyes flared like a child's at a carnival.

"Go." Virginia waved him on.

Isabel was thankful for the shade and a passing cloud while she caught her breath and sipped water. When they resumed the climb, Enid adjusted to a more leisurely pace, and Virginia lagged behind with them. After several more turns, Isabel's body began to acclimate. She found she liked the sensation of her muscles squeezing and releasing as she pumped her arms and legs. An occasional breeze floated through her sleeves. The leather grip shoes cushioned her feet, so she only needed to concentrate on one step at a time.

The older women walked in a companionable silence, interspersed with bursts of conversation. Enid asked after Virginia's baby, who Virginia said was delightfully easygoing, unless he was teething.

"Definitely doesn't take after me!" Her lips twisted with amusement. "At least he won't give Ansel's mother trouble while we're hiking."

When Enid gave an update on Mr. Michael and his heart problems, Virginia clicked her tongue. "A pity when he's such an elite climber." Gradually the talk turned to the wildflower garden and Enid's encounter with Mr. Harwell.

Virginia tsked in disgust as Enid recounted his latest demands. "How can he be so bullish? Surely Superintendent Thomson won't let him cancel your reappointment next summer. He's one of your staunchest allies."

"Mr. Harwell has lodged a dozen complaints against me. Says I've grown stale and oppose innovations like the auto caravans, bear feedings, and Indian demonstrations. And of course I won't stand for converting wildflower meadows into lawns."

"He calls those innovations?" Virginia scoffed.

"Also says I've collected material on government time and treated it as personal property, while piling up freak features in the garden. Oh, and evidently I don't know how to teach proper botany at the Field School."

"Really, did you ever! The man's a boor. He's jealous of you, that's what. He must not know what to make of a woman who knows so much more than he does."

"I suspect so, too. Charlie thinks I should send him a honeyed letter, full of compliments."

"You won't stoop to that, will you?"

"Virginia, you know this happens every year. I'll do what I have to. As long as he's my supervisor, he has the reins."

"Truly, all the commercialized gimmicks he says you oppose, like the caravans. Well, you're right to oppose them. It's the very things Ansel and I hate, too, since they're threatening these splendid wild spaces." Virginia threw her arms wide. "Anyhow, you shouldn't have to put up with that baloney."

"Some might say it's a small price to do what I love."

"Surely not. Surely there's some other way."

Enid turned toward her friend. "It's what I told Isabel the other day. A woman must do a man's job twice as well to get half the credit, without seeming opinionated, to boot."

"You're far stronger than I would be in your place."

Isabel examined Enid's penetrating blue eyes, straight nose, signature hat, scarf tied jauntily around her chin, and agreed; she had an amazing reserve of strength.

"If it will help, Ansel and I will write a letter to Superintendent Thomson on your behalf. We can organize a letter-writing campaign." Virginia gave a mischievous smile.

As they rounded a switchback, Isabel saw Ansel squatting beside his tripod, which was planted in the trail. He had angled his camera lens and bellows toward the immense crag of Half Dome.

"Keep going," he said. "I'll catch up after I get some exposures."

"He'll be a while," Virginia warned. "He says the perfect position means everything in a photo. That and capturing the sentiment of a place." After a long bare patch interspersed with chaparral, they emerged into a grove of rich green manzanitas and laurels. Behind it sprang a meadow of pink and white bells.

"What delightful buttercups," Virginia said, straightening her spectacles. "Do you suppose they'd grow in San Francisco?"

"Probably. My friend Alice Eastwood at the California Academy of Sciences said she picked buttercups and isopyrum along the Merced and planted them in her rock garden in the city, where they've done beautifully."

"I'd love to plant Yosemite natives in my garden. Something from the valley to hang onto during the cold and fog."

Isabel considered how lovely it would be to do that, too, but in the Tenderloin, she'd have nowhere to plant; the alley in back didn't carry enough light, let alone soil for flowers to flourish.

They arrived at a grotto, where silvery ribbons of water trickled down a moss-covered wall of rocks. After refilling the canteens, they took turns thrusting their heads into the flow.

The sensation of icy drops coursing down her throat revived Isabel, and she said, "This feels wonderful!"

Virginia trilled, "Doesn't it, though? Gives you a second wind."

Liquid notes rang and rippled through the air, each clear and distinct, like glass beads on a string. A warbling wrentit, Enid said. Isabel's leg muscles ached, but now that the pace had become more manageable, she was eager to continue climbing.

As they passed sand basins in the granite, she bent to examine a rosy, wax-like flower she recognized from the wildflower garden, wedged between the rocks. "Is this the Yosemite bitter root?"

Enid's face grew animated. "How well you remember, butterfly. Yes, the lewisia. They're hard to find since they hide close to the sand." Like ribs of a fan, she explained, the sepals opened and bent backward, and the wind carried the seeds to distant ridges. "Next spring, when the sand absorbs snow from the top of the dome, a new colony of children will be born." She looked perfectly serious, and Isabel stifled a smile. But then, part of Enid's charm was her anthropomorphic description of plants and animals. She saw them as purer, simpler versions of human beings.

Virginia pointed to a granite shelf on the side of the cliff, jutting out like a bench. "I'm famished! Let's eat lunch there while we wait for Ansel."

The three of them squeezed onto the shelf, and Isabel sagged with relief. Between bites, she swigged down water. The air, Enid had cautioned, was deceptively dry. Sometimes you didn't know you were dehydrated until your head pounded and your skin went clammy. Above them, the trail wound toward Mount

Watkins. Evergreens dotted the ridges on the opposite side of the valley.

When Ansel's head appeared at the switchback below, Virginia pushed up her spectacles and waved, and he imitated an owl's hoot and scrambled toward them.

"Got some gorgeous exposures. Reminds me of the trip we took with the Sierra Club to Kings River Country several years ago, before Michael was born. Virginia fell in love with the wildflower meadows, and I with the climbing." He turned to Isabel. "How you holding out?"

"A little tired, but the view is amazing. Before Yosemite, I hadn't made it more than a few miles out of San Francisco."

He nodded. "It's the beauty that brings me here. Yosemite's one of the few places the loggers haven't attacked. My grandfather owned a lumber company, which Papa now manages. Unfortunately, the company's cut down dozens of redwood forests. That's why I shoot in these remote places — so folks will know what's at stake." He jerked his chin at the tripod. "Ralph Waldo Emerson talked about living a modest, moral life guided by social responsibility to man and Nature. The two are interdependent."

"Then again, Ansel doesn't like to admit it, but some of his most famous photos have helped commercialize the park, since they bring in flocks of tourists." Virginia cast him a playful look.

"You take the good with the bad. This mountain is named after another Yosemite photographer, also from San Francisco. Carleton Watkins. His photos helped President Lincoln declare this area inviolable, which led the way to the foundation of the National Parks."

At least civilization hadn't yet reached the cliff and its pristine streams, sprays of wildflowers, wheeling birds. Isabel stared, enthralled, at the valley below. "It's like a painting. Still but vibrant."

"Hmmm. I've always imagined a mountain chorus singing in the High Sierras. When the river murmurs and the wind whips through the forest, it's like the swell of a hundred voices at eight thousand feet."

Virginia rested a hand on his arm. "Yosemite's part of him. He's been coming here since he was a boy. Claims it even cured him of Spanish flu."

"It's true. I'm not religious, but if I had to put my faith in something, I'd put it here." His face grew thoughtful as he peered at the valley.

Enid withdrew her hat and boots and stretched her legs toward the edge of the cliff. On a lark, Isabel unlaced her shoes, too, and wiggled her toes. Her feet had cramped, but the vista of the bluish-gray swell, including the mammoth spur of Half Dome, made up for the discomfort.

While Ansel climbed higher to take more photos, Isabel, Enid, and Virginia remained on the granite bench, watching swifts. The white-throated birds shot through the air at top speed, following the contour of the dome. Sometimes they flew so close to the surface Isabel feared they'd collide, but Enid assured her they were uncannily accurate.

"When they rush around like that, they remind me of humans," she joked.

After the swifts disappeared, Isabel gazed at a raven perched on an overhang below them. Her head rang with the dizzying beauty and solitude. Ansel rejoined them and asked, teasing, whether they were ready to scamper back down the mountain.

Virginia made a mock frown and turned to Enid. "You and Charles should build a cabin on the Diving Board." She pointed to the jutting shoulder of Half Dome. "Ansel and I would visit you often. I'd live here myself if only I could get Ansel to agree."

"Would you, my dear? Like a bird in an aerie?"

"Yes, but don't make fun. I love these high places."

He snagged her waist and pulled her close as she giggled.

151

It was after five by the time they returned to the Buick. Isabel was glad to stumble into the back seat and rest her feet. Ansel and Virginia rolled down their windows, and they rode in silence back to the New Village. Because of the toll from the sun and the physical exertion, Isabel allowed herself to relish the feat of having hiked partway to the top. She wondered whether the others felt something similar, even though the journey had been less strenuous for them.

As she climbed the stairs to the post office, she realized with a twinge she hadn't thought once of Audrey during the hike. Forgetting was a kind of sacrilege. All the same, a surprising calm settled over her, despite the sting in her back and legs.

"That was swell," she said to Enid.

"Hiking up mountains will become second nature before long, I promise."

Isabel felt her body lighten. Now that she was to stay the summer, she basked in the brief luxury of imagining a more permanent life at Yosemite: waking each morning to bird trills, leading tourists on hikes, pointing out flowers and wildlife, even climbing mountains. Ansel's observation about the moral responsibility to humans and Nature resonated. It occurred to her that Enid's goal for the national parks upheld that same belief. After all, she strove to preserve Yosemite while sharing its beauty with visitors, who left refreshed and inspired.

Dad's words drifted into her head: *Someday you'll blaze your own path.* She lifted her shoulders. *Why not?* Enid had blazed the trail to become the first female ranger-naturalist at the park. Why couldn't she become a ranger-naturalist, too?

CHAPTER TWENTY

It hadn't seemed possible, but after several weeks of morning hikes with Enid and afternoons in the wildflower garden, Isabel could identify dozens of plants and birds by sight. As they sat side by side on a boulder overlooking the Merced, Enid proudly pointed out that her favorite protégé – as she teasingly referred to Isabel—had learned to recognize Douglas firs, sugar, lodgepole, Jeffery, and white pines with tufted needles, bare on the windward side. She also knew white firs, flowering dogwood and azaleas, aspen, cliff buckwheat and buttercups, arnica, and larkspurs. And that was just the beginning.

Thanks to Enid, Isabel could also single out the song notes of canyon wrens, brown creepers, blue grouses, Brewer's blackbirds, belted kingfishers, band-tailed pigeons, robins, goldfinches, and American dippers who trilled like canaries. Earlier that morning, on the nature walk back to Camp Curry, she had gathered the tourists to watch a red-tailed hawk roosting beneath the branches of a Jeffery pine. To their astonishment, it had unfurled its enormous wings, then swooped down and snatched a field mouse.

Balancing her field notebook in her lap, Enid rapidly sketched a red-breasted nuthatch that perched on an oak by the river. Isabel watched, fascinated, as a creature with short tail, beady eyes, and stout legs emerged on the page. Beneath her drawing, Enid scrawled a few notes.

"See how his body's perfectly balanced between bill and tail? That's how he goes up and down trunks so quickly. A married pair of nuthatches just like this fellow have boarded at the feeding table for years."

Isabel winced. The feeding table again. Giving food to the birds, who had an endless supply of insects to eat at the park, still nagged at her, since she considered it an injustice to the thousands of hungry people. Last month, Enid said, she and Charles had uncovered a new nest of nuthatches, and two of the babies had descended from the treetop and bathed in a little pool by the table.

"The parents avoid the pool, though. They're more interested in their children's welfare than their own, and they've become horribly worn out... like most parents, I suppose. Working themselves to a frazzle to give their children every advantage."

She sounded relieved to be unburdened of human children, and Isabel was sure that if she herself had been a few years younger, the Michaels would never have agreed to take her in. And then she wouldn't have learned about this microcosm of strange, incredible beings. Wouldn't have known how to find it by simply staying still and observing.

Though the far reaches of San Francisco's parks had all manner of birds and plants, Isabel hadn't noticed them. But now that she'd learned so many of their names, she saw them everywhere: surprising, living delights, fluttering in trees, aloft in the air. She could do this: stay at Yosemite permanently, train with Enid to become a ranger-naturalist, hike, even climb the Sierras. She simply needed to craft a solid plan. And because Audrey had wanted to come and would have loved the park, Isabel felt her presence here more vividly than she had in San Francisco. All the same, the thought of her sister stirred up a deep ache in her chest.

•   •   •

On the way to the garden, Isabel spied James in front of the museum with his crew. He was crouching by the road, hacking brush with a scythe. They had managed to meet at least once or twice a week—brief strolls during his breaks. She raced toward him, breathless.

"James!"

He dropped the scythe and rose with a grin. "Fancy seeing *you*." His bare arms were bronzed and muscular, his face tanned. She flung her arms around his neck, and he kissed her cheek. "You're looking well, Izz. More so every week. The climate must suit you."

"*Yosemite* suits me." She waved at the garden and elbowed him. "Suits you, too. If I didn't know better, I'd say you'd found a girl." She had seen him chatting once or twice with a black-haired young woman by the Indian village, though she'd given it little thought. She'd been too far away to glimpse the girl's face.

To her surprise, a flush crept up his cheeks. "No time." He glanced at several boys from his crew, then bent toward her. "Say, have you heard yet from Mother?"

She shook her head. Enid had asked, too, though she would be the first to know as soon as a letter from Mother arrived; Mr. Michael would bring it from the post office.

"Don't worry, you will. Mail takes time, and even then, it's unpredictable. I got two letters from her yesterday, but she wrote them weeks apart."

"What did she say?" She tried to keep her voice calm.

"She asked after you."

"Did she receive my letter?"

"Don't think so. At least not when she wrote me. But listen, she misses you. And she's worried, besides. She wanted to know what you're doing, how long you'll be here, where you're staying."

"She'll learn all those answers as soon as she gets my note." By now, surely, it had arrived. Mr. Michael had mailed it over two weeks ago.

"It's hard on her, Izz. Being all alone." He waited for her to acknowledge this, but she remained silent. As far as she could tell, Mother had wanted to be alone. Surely it was better this way, all around. "You know, you don't have to wait till summer's over. You can go home anytime."

She hugged her arms, bristling with irritation. "No, I can't. I've made an arrangement with Mrs. Michael that I intend to keep." She didn't dare tell him about her half-formed idea to stay at Yosemite after summer and train with Enid. It was too soon, and she suspected James wouldn't understand.

He raised his chin, and she stiffened, expecting him to challenge her. After a strained silence, he said curtly, "Well. I'd best get back to work."

Isabel pressed her head against his shoulder, inhaling his familiar earthy scent, layered beneath sweat. His arms around her felt the same, but she could feel a barricade rising between them, like the blade of the scythe. As she picked her way toward Enid and the garden, a sharp, bright pain rose from her stomach up through her lungs and chest.

CHAPTER TWENTY-ONE

"It reads so much better now." Enid flourished the three pages that Isabel had typed and edited for *Yosemite Nature News*.

Isabel's cheeks went pink. She wasn't accustomed to receiving praise, and now she found she hungered for it, as if simple encouragement was nourishment her body craved. While she had typed Enid's article about ponderosa pines choking off the wildflowers in Sentinel Meadow, she had changed words, reorganized and shortened sentences. Mostly, Enid approved of her edits. Only once or twice she had refused to budge, arguing the revisions affected the gist of her story.

In the sitting room, Enid put on a record of Schumann's Fantasy piano pieces, which she said was a gift from Ansel Adams, who had played them himself as an aspiring pianist. The second song stunned Isabel. She sat motionless, gripping her sides, as the notes flew into passionate arpeggios, dipping and rising, frantic and fast, singing across octaves.

"What's the name of this piece? It's beautiful."

"*Aufschwung*. German for Soaring. It's one of my favorites, too. When I hear it, I imagine I'm swirling high over a summit."

Isabel gazed at a golden spray of sunlight stippling across the floor. It seemed that both melody and sunlight had melded in celebration.

When the piece ended, Enid mentioned a firefall program at Camp Curry. "It's my turn to lead it tonight. Tourists love it, and it's become a fun tradition. Every night from Glacier Point they push down burning embers, which fall to a ledge. Afterwards folks go to the Pits to watch the concessionaire feed the bears."

Isabel wasn't sure about watching bears up close, but since her outings with Enid were almost always interesting and informative, she asked to tag along to the firefall.

After supper, Enid pinned the ranger badge onto her breast and donned her white hat, and they hiked swiftly along the path to Camp Curry.

"Deer tracks?" Isabel pointed to fresh prints on the trail.

"Yes. Looks like half a dozen came this way not long ago. You're a quick study, Isabel! You'd ace the junior ranger school here. It's free to primary and secondary students."

"I practically have my own school with you."

"Yosemite's junior ranger school is the biggest in the country. The students receive certificates for every test they pass. Bet you'd pass most of them. For botany, you have to identify up to fifty species by their common and scientific names. Students go on hikes, too."

"Someday," Isabel said, voicing aloud a thought, "I'd like to do more than hike. I'd like to climb the Sierras."

Enid gave her a scrutinizing look. "Your legs are strong, and your endurance has improved, too. Tell you what. In a few weeks, if you're up for it, I'll take you on your first climb."

Isabel nodded, eyes shining. She was lucky to train under Enid's wing.

At the Curry campground, they veered onto a road gouged with tire ruts. Charcoal and ash lay scattered by the remains of campfires. Dented pots and pans were strewn outside tents, and wisps of smoke swirled overhead. Several yards ahead loomed a large wooden amphitheater. Families with young children, couples, and teenaged boys lounged on rows of benches that descended toward the stage. A handful of folks reclined on blankets on the lawn in front, eating picnic suppers.

"Let's see if the projector's been set up," Enid said. "We start with community singing and display the lyrics so everyone can join in."

An awning hung over the stage, whose only wall was a ten by twelve foot sheet of wood paneling in back. With Isabel at her heels, Enid mounted the stairs to the platform, and together they dragged a short podium and microphone into the center.

As Enid finished her inspection, a tall man in ranger uniform and hat climbed onto the stage. He had blond sideburns, a long aquiline nose, and severe grayish-blue eyes. Isabel recognized him as the man who had confronted Enid in the wildflower garden a few weeks ago.

"Hello, Mr. Harwell," Enid said, a smile plastered upon her face. "How good of you to be here."

The man didn't return her smile. "Mrs. Michael," he said with a curt nod and tip of his hat. "I trust you have what you need?"

"I believe so. I haven't gotten around to checking on the projector..."

"It's already been set up. I'm aware that ladies don't like to fret over gadgets."

"Why, thank you."

Isabel immediately disliked the man's smug, superior attitude. He sent Isabel a cold look.

"Is this a relative of yours?"

"This is Isabel Dickinson. She's staying with Charles and me for the summer and has been a big help in the garden, along with many other things. Isabel, meet Mr. Harwell, my supervisor."

At the mention of the garden, Mr. Harwell gave Isabel a thin-lipped nod. He didn't bother to extend his hand. "Why, that's fine. About the garden, Mrs. Michael."

A shadow flitted across Enid's face, and her lips tightened. "Yes, Mr. Harwell?"

He walked a few steps away from the podium, beckoning Enid with the crook of his finger, and she followed. Isabel frowned and remained where she was, but she could still hear the man's scolding voice.

"I've warned you not to clutter the garden with those... objects you find on your hikes. They're dreadful eyesores, the rusty tin buckets and old horseshoes and logging tools."

Enid flinched, and her face grew flustered.

"Please remove them immediately. I shouldn't like to remind you a third time."

"I hear you loud and clear, Mr. Harwell." She raised her chin.

"And one other thing. In tonight's presentation, please be as professional as you can manage. I know it's said you memorize your lectures, and that's fine, though folks take notice. But please try not to deliver your talk at a school-age level. When you use words like granddaddy bears and mama deer, it insults folks."

"If I may, Mr. Harwell, I think the young children and their families enjoy hearing animals spoken of in human terms they can understand..."

Mr. Harwell held up a large, callused hand. "I've given you my advice as your supervisor. All I ask is you give it careful consideration." His tone was scathing.

After a short silence, Enid said, "Of course."

"That's all, then. Best of luck with tonight's program. I may stick around in the back until the firefall, in case you need anything. Emmet will run the projector for you." Mr. Harwell clattered across the stage, climbed down from the platform, and mingled with visitors in the crowd.

The tension in Isabel's chest released. She took a step toward Enid.

"I guess you heard that."

"I'm sorry he treats you that way. You surely don't deserve it."

"It's like I said. Women must be on our best behavior."

"It's horribly unfair."

"Yes, but that's the lot of humans, same as animals. Survival of the fittest. Luck of the draw who's born a male, stronger or more powerful. Nature isn't fair."

Isabel's lips curled down.

"There he is by the projector," Enid said in an undertone. She jerked her head toward Mr. Harwell in his ranger jacket as he moved among the crowd. "Bet he'll stay through my program to make sure I don't deliver my talk in a sing-song voice."

Isabel was about to object, when Enid added, "Doesn't mean I'm going to change a thing. Not tonight, anyhow, since it's my turn as mistress of ceremonies." Her jaw hardened, even as she gave an enigmatic smile. "Find a seat on the benches. You'll have a better view of what's going on from there. After the firefall, come back onstage."

Isabel picked her way down the stairs and squeezed into a space on the closest bench, between a child of about ten on one side and a grandfatherly gentleman on the other. She estimated a hundred people now filled the benches.

Enid stepped onto the stage and tapped the microphone with an experimental, "Test, one, two, three." Her voice blasted out in a shriek. The crowd hushed, and heads pivoted toward her.

The child beside Isabel kicked his legs and demanded when the show would begin. The older gentleman to Isabel's left wore old-fashioned breeches and hiking boots and appeared to be with his grandchildren, who were sharing an ice cream cone. The night air, mingled with campfire smoke, crept around them. In the gloaming, folks twisted with anticipation. A glop of melted ice cream plopped onto Isabel's arm, and she shivered. Somewhere in the distance, a coyote howled. She imagined

161

Audrey sitting beside her with the stars peeking above, like a mirror of candles. Her sister would have loved it.

Pinned in a spotlight, Enid reappeared on stage. Behind her, the wooden panel projected the words, "Welcome to Yosemite!" She called out a greeting from the microphone.

"Hello," the crowd echoed.

"You're in for a treat." She described the program of sing-alongs, camper entertainment, and a wildlife talk, followed by the firefall from Glacier Point. At the mention of the firefall, the crowd cheered, and the teenaged boys behind Isabel whooped.

While lyrics projected onto the panel, they sang *Let Me Call You Sweetheart*, then ran through several other numbers, including *The End of a Perfect Day* and *Down at the Station*, which Enid organized into rounds of three groups. The children beside Isabel clapped and chorused: "See the little puffer-bellies all in a row. Toot, toot, puff, puff, off they go!"

When Enid led the group in singing, *There's a Long, Long Trail A'Winding*, Isabel's stomach tightened, and she laid a hand on her breast. "Seem to hear your footsteps falling, everywhere I go. Though the road between us stretches many a weary mile, I forget you're not with me yet, when I think I see you smile." Clapping, they ended with The *Big Yosemite Mountains*, sung to the tune of *In the Big Rock Candy Mountain*. Afterwards, a teenaged boy played *Red River Valley* on his harmonica as a young woman sang, and a man recited Robert Service's humorous poem, *The Cremation of Sam McGee*.

Enid took the microphone. "I'm going to tell you about a good friend of mine, a fellow known as the Birdman. Maybe your parents or grandparents remember him? He used to camp here at Curry and liked to feed cracked peanuts to the jays. In case you don't know, these birds are wild and very cautious about approaching humans. But they were his friends, and they trusted him." A photo of a pair of birds on a tree limb flashed onto the panel.

"I want to feed a bird!" shouted the little girl on her grandfather's lap.

Enid described the jay family: Sword, a male with a deformed bill, a female named Short-Stop, another named Buccaneer, and the old daddy, Scout, plus six children, had lived with the Birdman for two years. Just as one of the younger jays tried to dig a peanut from its shell, Enid said, Scout sailed in, grabbed the nut, and flew away.

A boy shouted, "Go, Scout!"

Enid swooped her hands up and down in imitation of the jays, then mimicked the birds with a series of whistles and clicks, chucks, whirrs, and whines. The crowd roared with laughter, and she launched into another story.

"My weasel friend, Snowy Toes, lived in the woodpile outside our tent when my husband and I camped on Roe Island. His body was twice as long as a meadow mouse's, and he had a white belly and feet, beady eyes, long neck, and a bushy black tail." Leaning into the mic, she confided, "Snowy Toes was the most acrobatic fellow I've ever known. He raced and flipped like a gymnast." A picture of a weasel on a log clicked onto the panel. "When I stood still, he stood still. His little face popped up to peer at me. When I moved, he moved, just like Simon says." The boy beside Isabel hooted, and the little girl struggled out of her grandfather's lap and stood on wobbly legs, straining to see.

"Twice Snowy Toes ate a mouse right from my hand. One morning after he finished his breakfast, he was feeling frisky. He peeked out from the woodpile and saw some jays eating. So just for fun, he started a game of tag. Do you like playing tag?"

"Yes!" shouted the girl.

"Snowy Toes leaped toward a jay, and the jay swooped into the air. Luckily, he never caught the jays. You can guess how disappointed he was." She imitated a weasel's short, sharp bark, followed by a deep hiss. Children squealed in delight, and the audience clapped.

The lights on the stage switched off, and they were engulfed in darkness. Low, excited murmurs rippled over the crowd. From the stage, Enid's voice crackled over the microphone. "Are you ready? Let's call up to the hotel on Glacier Point!"

"Hello, Glacier!" the crowd cried.

"Hello, Camp Curry!"

"Let the fire fall!"

"All right!" called the voice from the mountain. The campers fell silent and craned toward the cliff, which in the dark resembled the colossal head of a submerged dragon.

Urgent voices whooped, "Here it comes!" The teenaged boys behind Isabel guffawed, and a woman hissed, "Be quiet, will you!"

Incandescent ruby-red embers began cascading down the mountain. Almost simultaneously, a soprano belted out the crisp, ringing notes of *America the Beautiful*. As campers around her oohed and aahed, Isabel was reminded of watching fireworks on the Fourth of July. For several minutes, the embers flowed and zigzagged like a scarlet waterfall as a soloist sang *Indian Love Call*. Finally the glow faded, pitching the cliff into total darkness. Flashlights popped up as the crowd fumbled back to their tents. Isabel was awestruck by the thousands of stars glittering above the amphitheater. The night air swirled over her, sending goosebumps down her arms.

She joined Enid onstage. "That was splendid."

"Virginia and Ansel think it's contrived, but the children love it. Feeding the bears is even more gimmicky. Forty or more of them feast on garbage from the Ahwahnee Hotel."

Isabel made a face, and Enid said, "Supposedly they're less of a nuisance if they receive a nightly meal in the same place, but it doesn't always work that way. Occasionally they still roam the campgrounds, pawing through cans and tents."

Isabel shuddered. "I'd rather not go."

Enid sounded relieved. "I prefer Yosemite's remoter areas. Problem is, they're fewer and farther between. Let's go home."

At the mention of home, something inside Isabel loosened, and she felt her lungs expanding. Perhaps she was reading too much into the word, but she decided Enid had used it for her benefit, too: not a temporary lodging, but a place to which she could circle back after wandering away. It conjured up a memory of the house on Rainbow Lane, the five of them gathered around the table at night, joking and trading stories. The Michaels didn't care where they lived, whether in a tent or above the post office, but to Isabel, being in their presence felt surprisingly like home.

Alone in her room, she read a few pages from Muir's book on Yosemite, lingering over his descriptions of the mountains: "all these colors, from the blue sky to the yellow valley smoothly blending as they do in a rainbow, making a wall of light ineffably fine...the white beams of the morning streaming through the passes, the noonday radiance on the crystal rocks, the flush of the alpenglow, and the irised spray of countless waterfalls..."

Snapping the book shut, she pretended she was the Michaels' daughter, typing articles for Enid, leading the Yosemite Junior Rangers and tourists on hikes and nature walks, joining Enid on challenging climbs.

It wasn't terribly farfetched, after all. The more she thought about it, the more possible it seemed, like the approaching outline of a mountain from an automobile, growing larger and larger with each turn of the wheel. And eventually, she promised herself, it would come true.

CHAPTER TWENTY-TWO

Isabel led her young charges through thick groves of black oak, cedars, and ponderosa pines, climbing steadily to the footbridge above the Merced River. From there they would follow the Mist Trail, made famous by John Muir, to Vernal Falls. She and Enid had hiked the four and a half mile roundtrip circuit several days ago; and now Enid, heading up the rear, had allowed Isabel to guide the Yosemite Junior Nature School students on the same route.

The dawn air curled, delicious and cool, on Isabel's arms. Enid had loaned her a sturdy pair of grip shoes, along with a pair of khaki trousers, which she had rolled up at the ankles and cinched around her waist. She marveled at how much easier and swifter they made the ascent. Her legs had developed a little muscle over the last few weeks from the nature walks with Enid, and she felt surefooted and able, though she remembered to slow her gait to allow the children to catch up. She couldn't help picturing Audrey among them—her sister's eyes wide and curious, arms windmilling. But as she concentrated on the trail through the ancient forest, the remote knob of grief in her mind began to loosen.

From a vantage point on a switchback, Isabel pointed out laurel and ferns clinging to the damp sides of the cliff. She assured the children that before they arrived at the bridge, they could drink from a little spring. Not a lot of water, she warned, as they wanted to avoid bloated stomachs.

Most of the children were between the ages of eight and twelve, excited to be on their first hike without their parents. Two boys trailed closely at Isabel's heels, using walking sticks shaped from fallen branches to propel themselves faster.

"Don't go fast," Enid called from behind as they resumed their pace. "It gets slippery after the footbridge." Off in the distance, the falls surged, a thunderous roar over the granite boulders, though they couldn't yet see them.

At another switchback, Isabel paused, finger on her lips, as a northern goshawk with beetling brows perched on a branch of a hunchback ponderosa. Beneath the tree strutted a wild turkey. In excited whispers, the children watched as the bird crouched and leaned toward its prey. A little girl in the back squealed, and the turkey squawked and trotted into the woods while the hawk abandoned its pursuit and flew away.

"He must have decided discretion is the better part of valor," Enid told the children from the rear. They turned to her with confused faces.

The spring water tasted fresh and cool, like the grotto stream on Mount Watkins, better than anything Isabel remembered drinking in San Francisco. On the footbridge, they peered over the Merced crashing among the boulders. Above them, Vernal Falls foamed and emptied into the river. The children hopped and elbowed each other, struggling to get a better look through the treetops, and Isabel cautioned them to stand apart.

"Careful, don't jostle each other! It's dangerous to fall." She shuddered at the prospect of a small body tumbling and dashing against the rocks. Immediately afterwards trailed another thought: *What was she doing, overseeing young children?* If Enid or the children's parents had any inkling of her gross negligence in minding her own sister and the consequent disaster, they would snatch her from her charges in an instant. Her shoulders crumpled, but she forced herself to straighten and face the children.

As they resumed hiking, the trail climbed up a long, slippery granite staircase of cliff along the river. The children shrieked as clouds of mist from the waterfall drenched them, and Isabel was grateful they had made the hike in July, when the cool shower was welcome. Half a mile from the top of the falls, they stopped to view the brilliant rainbow hues against the sunshine of the cascading water sprays: rose-purple; iris-blue; golden-green.

At the crest of the waterfall, they stood at the guard rails, gazing down at the whitewater surge. As bits of driftwood careened against the boulders and vanished into the foam far below, a chill crept up Isabel's arms. A little girl about seven or eight, one of the youngest on the hike, touched her arm.

"Miss? Is this as far as we go?"

Isabel knelt. "Yes. Are you tired?"

"No! I'd like to go as high as the sky. To that waterfall." She pointed.

"Nevada Falls. We'll save that for another day, I promise."

Enid stepped beside her. "Well done for your first hike as a guide." She had plucked a tall flowery wand, spiked with whorls of purple buds, which Isabel recognized as Sierra lupine. As she waved the lupine toward Isabel's nose, Isabel caught a whiff of a sweet perfume. In her sing-song voice, Enid recited, "There is a flower that bees prefer and butterflies desire; to gain the purple democrat the hummingbirds aspire…Her face is rounder than the noon, and ruddier than the gown, of orchis in the pasture, or rhododendron worn. Before the world is green, her sturdy little countenance against the wind is seen, contending with the grass."

Isabel angled her head, knowing it was an Emily Dickinson poem she hadn't heard.

"The Sierra lupine is nearing her peak, and she reminds me of you. Hardy and resilient. Folks say the lupine symbolizes happiness and imagination."

"That's kind, but..." Isabel looked away, embarrassed. She wanted to add Enid was too generous in her praise. She hardly felt strong, and that type of exultant happiness was a distant memory. Besides, imagination had applied best to Dad and Audrey.

"You've led this hike. And you've learned the names of dozens of plants and animals." Enid paused. "That's Yosemite's magic. It brings out things people didn't know were inside them. Happened to me when I arrived, and I was more than twice your age."

A shard of sunlight spilled onto Isabel's cheek, as quick and gentle as Mr. Whiskers' tongue. A splash of warmth.

A couple of older boys, dripping from the soak of the spray, leaned against the railing, throwing stones into the wild descent of the falls. Isabel watched the stones' turbulent ride as they melded with the foam. A heavy rumble rose as the massive plate of water plunged over the brink.

"The falls are so deadly," she said without thinking. "And enormous. Next to them, we're ants."

Enid was quiet for a moment. "They put things in perspective when you consider everything they've outlasted and will outlast." *Including us,* Isabel finished silently.

"Whenever I'm here, I borrow a bit of their freedom." Enid swept her hands wide over the bridge, toward the falls and cliff. Isabel grasped what she meant. Away from civilization, you could push your problems aside with the knowledge they wouldn't last, that they paled in comparison to the centuries-old mountains, river and falls, trees.

Isabel arranged the children on rocks at a safe distance from the falls to eat the dried biscuits and raisins she'd packed. As she guided them back down the cliff, she thought about what Enid had said. She gave a start as Audrey's face floated in front of her. Her sister would have fit right in with these kids as they clambered down the slippery stone staircase, sashaying their hips, as Enid had recommended, to "avoid fatigue and wear and tear." Audrey would have delighted in the breathtaking beauty of the falls.

Enid's words merged with Mother's, and Isabel heard Mother rasp in her smoker's voice, *Life is senseless and short.* She felt a stabbing ache. It was humans' fleeting time to enjoy Nature that made its beauty so poignant.

CHAPTER TWENTY-THREE

Isabel and Enid had almost reached the post office when James' deep voice rang out behind them. Isabel spun around, smiling, as her brother jogged to her side. Enid told her to take her time, then mounted the stairs to the apartment.

He touched Isabel's arm. "Lucky I spotted you. I was looking for you in the garden."

With a prick of apprehension, she scanned his face. "Anything wrong?"

"No, everything's fine. Just wanted to let you know I've arranged time off this Saturday, so we can have the private memorial for Audrey."

Her eyes widened. "Where?"

"Wherever you like."

"The garden," she said without thinking.

"We can eat lunch together, too."

"Sure, I'll pack a picnic." The wind swallowed her words. They were silent.

"Oh, Izz. I know it's hard for you to remember..."

She didn't meet his eyes. "I want to do this for you. It's only fair." Even to her own ears, her voice sounded feeble, uncertain. What could she say about that day at Lafayette Square without going to pieces?

"Any word from Mother yet?"

171

"Still nothing." She steeled herself in case he repeated his suggestion that she return to the city before the end of summer. The other day he had mentioned again that Mother was alone and would welcome company.

"I thought surely by now... mail must have gotten delayed."

"Maybe. Mr. Michael said the same thing." She feigned a smile, but secretly she had decided Mother was relieved to be absolved of responsibility for her wayward daughter.

"Seems all news from the outside travels here slowly. We might as well be in a foreign land." He passed a hand across his forehead. "Just this morning, I heard there were riots in San Francisco after the Fourth of July. Ninety or more ships tied up at the piers. Shipowners lost a million dollars a day. When they tried to move cargo past the strikers, a brawl broke out. Turned into a battle all the way from Embarcadero up Rincon Hill and down Mission. Two longshoremen died, and over one hundred were injured. They had to call in the National Guard. Shoot, there were even tanks and machine guns in the streets." Her brother's face was grim.

Isabel's mouth fell open in shock. "That's awful. Is it still..."

"Nope. Apparently it ended after a couple days with a general strike. I think they've gone into arbitration. That's all I know."

A little sigh escaped her lips. "Thank God you weren't there!"

"Some ways, I wish I had been. It's what the fellows worked for. Dad, too. He wouldn't have wanted the violence, but in the end, it might get results. The longshoremen may finally get their hiring hall and wage raises."

Isabel considered the flip side: the longshoremen's livelihood compromised as they sat out; ports shut down and goods not reaching hungry people; the recalcitrance and threats, rapid turn to violence. "But was it worth it if they don't get what they want?"

"They'll have given it their best shot. At least they can hold their heads up and say they tried."

"Tried through violence, you mean. And for naught."

"They never meant for things to get brutal. If you want to blame someone, blame the shipowners and their finks! They're the ones who've refused to negotiate from the start."

She was surprised by the sudden fierceness in his voice and his cold, mistrustful stare, as though she were a stranger with opinions he didn't share. Maybe he thought she meant that if the longshoremen's actions amounted to nothing, Dad's own life would have been pointless. The stillness and untainted beauty around them made James' description of the San Francisco riots sound like something from another country—unreal, distant, improbable. She pitied the struggling city dwellers: longshoremen, clerks, factory workers, the unemployed.

"Do you want to come up for lunch?" she said to change the subject. "I'm sure Mrs. Michael won't mind."

The knot in his forehead unfurled. "Can't this time. Anyhow, I'll see you day after tomorrow. Whole afternoon."

Isabel squeezed his hand. But as he turned back toward the museum, her heart skipped a beat. What on earth would she tell him when they met on Saturday? She dared not upset him more by revealing her role in Audrey's accident. And besides, she had missed her chance; it was too late. A shadow of guilt slipped over her. Months ago, she hadn't kept secrets from James. But it was her penance, she understood, to suffer from the knowledge that her own carelessness and deception had caused her sister's death.

In the kitchen, she prepared a mushroom cheese casserole and fish soup for supper while Enid pored over notes for an article. Above the sink, a breeze drifted through the apartment, and a squirrel chittered in the tree outside.

As she sliced mushrooms, Isabel mulled over the longshoremen's abiding effort to correct the injustice they had suffered under the shipowners. Even if she didn't agree with their methods, she sympathized. There had to be something small she could do to help the struggling people outside the park. Recalling the quote Ansel had recited about man's responsibility to humans and Nature alike, she had a sudden inspiration. Maybe the feeding table could be used to benefit both birds and people.

She said to Enid, "I was thinking… we could take some of the leftover mess food to folks outside Yosemite, in nearby towns like El Portal. There would still be plenty for the birds."

Enid glanced up with a frown. "I'm not sure how we could transport it out of the park. Charles and I don't have an automobile."

Isabel continued slicing mushrooms. "A delivery truck brings supplies to Cascades every week. They could take extra food back with them to El Portal…"

"The logistics of it would be a nightmare. First we'd have to make sure the food doesn't spoil. Then we'd have to persuade Cascades to transport it, and they have all kinds of government regulations."

"President Roosevelt himself would surely approve of taking surplus food to the hungry!" Heat suffused her face.

"I expect so. But wishing it so and making it happen are two very different things."

Irritated that Enid couldn't or wouldn't understand, Isabel jerked her hand and accidentally nicked the corner of her index finger with the knife. She let out a yelp.

"Are you all right?" Enid hurried to her side as she stuffed her finger into her mouth.

"It's nothing. I was careless." She turned on the faucet and ran water over her hand.

"Let me…" Grasping her hand, Enid examined the tiny injured flap of skin on her finger. "You got lucky. I don't think it needs a bandage."

Peevishly, Isabel yanked her hand away. "There's got to be a way. I can talk with James about the camp rules ..."

"It's an awful lot of trouble."

"At least I can find out." Isabel's voice quivered with indignation. "It's immoral to feed birds when people are starving. Or do you prefer helping *animals*?" *There. She had said it.*

Enid stood stock still at the table, where she had been laying down utensils and napkins. Her face paled, and she looked taken aback. "Prefer it?" she repeated. Suddenly, defiance replaced the bewilderment on her face. Her mouth hardened, and her eyes grew flinty. "You won't change my mind about helping animals, Isabel. So don't bother trying."

Isabel was about to steer the conversation back to the logistics of transporting food, when the door opened, and Mr. Michael shuffled into the apartment. She chewed down on her lip, deciding she'd bring up the topic later.

As Enid turned toward the door, the hard look on her face slipped away. "You're home early, Charlie," she chirped.

He gave his signature bashful grin. "Got something for this young lady. Special delivery." He removed his cap, ran his fingers through his short dark hair, and handed an envelope to Isabel.

She immediately recognized her mother's spidery handwriting and tucked the letter into her skirt pocket to read later. Chances were whatever Mother had written would upset her.

"Your mother?" Enid asked, and she nodded.

After supper, the Michaels moved to the sitting room. But this time Enid gave a mischievous grin as she placed a record onto the turnstile. The lively notes of a polka rang through the apartment. Despite the cramped quarters, Enid did a gig of three short steps, a dip and a hop.

"Come on, Charlie! Give it a whirl."

He shuffled toward her and clasped her waist, his cheeks turning rosy. Beaming, she twirled under his arm. After two rotations, she skipped aside and tapped her feet to the music, then repeated her short steps and hop, followed by the twirl. From the kitchen, Isabel clapped.

"Join us, Isabel! It's easy. If I can do it, you surely can."

Before Isabel could protest, Enid grabbed her arm and swung her into a pirouette. Giggling, Isabel skipped to the wall and clapped in time, and Enid and Mr. Michael pivoted around the sitting room. Mr. Michael's eyes shone as he twirled his wife. Isabel worried he would stress his heart, but after watching more closely, she noticed that while he raised his arm, Enid was the one dancing. Later, in her room, she remembered the letter and withdrew it from her pocket. Rapidly she broke the seal and sank onto the couch to read Mother's note.

> *Dear Isabel,*
>
> *I received your letter yesterday and am relieved you're safe. I was terribly worried after you left. What a shock you gave me! It's a comfort to know you and James are near each other. But now I'm all alone, and thoughts of our family as we used to be pain me.*
>
> *My hours at the hotel are still spotty, but with the money James sends, I've enough to tide me over. My days are work and errands with precious little variety, save listening to programs. I hope you'll come home direct after your summer with this Mrs. Michael, in time for school. Also, I could use your help, probably a lot more than your Mrs. Michael, who seems to be doing well for herself and probably was managing just fine before you came. Mr. McGilligan asked after you, and I told him what you've done. I think you left him shorthanded.*
>
> *Love,*
> *Mother*

Slowly, Isabel tucked the letter inside the cover of *The Velveteen Rabbit*, then shoved it into her knapsack, which held the meager sum of her possessions. *I told him what you've done.* Her words seared like an accusation. Surely anyone who heard the story would conclude Isabel had been selfish and irresponsible. And although Mother hadn't mentioned the three dollars Isabel had taken, she wouldn't easily forgive, let alone forget. Isabel wasn't as worried about Mr. McGilligan. With all the folks out of work, he'd have an easy time filling her spot, though she missed his friendly conversation.

At the thought of obliging Mother, her chest constricted. Anyway, she'd already made up her mind not to return. The city's grime and crowds were foggy remnants of another life she'd shaken off. She was determined to become a ranger-naturalist—something Mother would never understand, since she couldn't see beyond the next paycheck or meal, certainly couldn't contemplate anything better. The next task was figuring out how to broach the topic with Enid. Isabel's tentative plan was to continue earning her keep with the Michaels, maybe through the fall, until she found her own lodging and a job that could sustain her as she trained. But this time, she needed to be careful about how she approached Enid with her proposal.

That night she dreamed of Audrey: glowing, lively, moving closer to a busy street with automobiles while beckoning Isabel to follow, a luminous smile on her lips.

"No, don't!" Isabel cried, but the words wedged in her throat, and she could only muster a squeak of terror as her sister stepped into traffic.

CHAPTER TWENTY-FOUR

From her perch on the granite bench, Isabel saw James striding toward her in his beige hat and trousers. She leaped up and rushed to embrace him.

"You were right, Izz. This is the perfect spot. Beautiful and peaceful." His eyes swept across the riot of blooms in the garden. "You know, I never thought of it till now, but all these colors remind me of Rainbow Lane."

"It's fitting today. Come, let's sit."

They watched visitors promenade down the flagstone paths, stooping to read the placards beside the flowers. Isabel felt a little swell of pride. Just days ago, she had deadheaded the geraniums and weeded the beds of lilies and paintbrushes. Meanwhile, Enid had worked with Arnold and two other CCC boys to complete the garden's irrigation system: a modern marvel that would nourish the plants far more efficiently than anyone could do by hand. Behind the bench, hummingbirds and jays flitted onto the feeding table.

James touched the worn copy of *The Velveteen Rabbit* in her lap. "You brought Audrey's favorite book..."

"I thought we might read some passages. But first, have you eaten? I brought berries and sandwiches."

"I can always eat." He rubbed his belly, and she managed a smile.

They chewed in silence, gazing into the garden. Isabel was thankful the bench was partly hidden by a stand of black oaks. Visitors strolled past it without lingering, perhaps assuming Isabel and James were sweethearts enjoying a private moment.

After they had finished the sandwiches and Isabel uncovered the tin of berries, James said, "How should we begin?"

"Can we wait… just a moment?"

His face softened. "I know this isn't easy, Izz."

She closed her eyes, longing to yank weeds, shovel dirt, let go of all thoughts and emotions, her mind gliding away as the physical pain of her muscles took over.

Her brother slid an arm around her shoulders, and she struggled not to cry. She couldn't tell him it was unbearable to speak of Audrey. But worse, if she didn't speak of her sister, would that amount to betraying her? Her eyes pooled.

"Are you all right?" James said.

The old pain sparked through her chest. "Yes," she managed, blotting at her eyes, "Let's read…"

"First, tell me more, Izz. About that day." When she felt his eyes on her, pleading, she involuntarily shuddered.

"I've told you almost everything." She bit the inside of her lip and tasted blood.

"What else?" His voice was sharp. When she didn't reply, he gripped her shoulder. "Tell me, Izz. What else?"

Her heart sank. It was there inside her, this terrible secret vying to get out, and she owed him the whole truth. But to her horror, her face crumpled, and a sob escaped from her mouth like a hiccup. She couldn't bear to tell him she had left Audrey alone while she and Claude necked beneath a grove of trees, couldn't bear his disappointment and judgment, the shock and hurt that she had kept this information from him for so long. As she dissolved into tears, he tightened his arm around her and stroked her hair. She admonished herself not to make a scene, to pull it together.

"I'm sorry. Truly, I am. But what happened that day to Audrey was so tragic and unfair. I can't bear to relive it."

"Shh, it's all right. She's with God now. Happy and young forever."

She wanted to shout that if there were a God, he was unjust and heartless and didn't deserve to keep their sister. But it would be cruel to rob James of his solace. And anyway, there was a chance he was right, though she felt Audrey's presence here instead, at Yosemite—a shadow behind a tree, a ripple in the river as if someone had thrown a stone, the soft crunch of shoes in the underbrush, a scampering of footsteps. Often she had the odd sense her sister had scurried by just as she turned her head, and they had narrowly missed each other. But if she waited long enough, kept her head down and eyes open, she would glimpse her again, she was certain.

After several minutes, her tears slowed. She clung to James as they talked about Audrey: her vivaciousness, imagination, love of outdoors.

"She wanted to visit you here," Isabel said, wiping her face with a napkin. "And really, that's why I came. She... inspired me. I wouldn't have thought to come if not for her. Though I didn't think through what to do once I got here."

"But you're here. I'm glad."

"She was so... free and energetic and full of life. Like Dad. Taken far too soon..." She pushed out the words, throwing him a wild look.

"Only God knows why. At least we had her, Izz, if only for that short time... and it was glorious while we did."

"She would have turned ten next month. August twenty-fourth." She felt a brew of bewilderment and anger that someone so innocent and young hadn't been allowed the chance to grow up. But then she silently berated herself. The answer to why wasn't a mystery, despite what her brother thought. *Her fault. Her carelessness, lust, self-centeredness.* She scraped her nails against her wrist. A few dozen yards away, two children knelt by the stream as their mother looked on, fanning herself.

"Shall we read now?" Isabel blinked and looked down at the book. James drew closer while she smoothed the yellowed page she had marked.

Slowly, she read, 'Real isn't how you are made,' said the Skin Horse. 'It's a thing that happens to you. When a child really loves you for a long, long time, not just to play with but REALLY loves you, then you become Real.'

'Does it hurt?' asked the Rabbit. 'Sometimes,' said the Skin Horse, for he was always truthful. 'When you are Real, you don't mind being hurt.'"

Isabel paused, her finger still marking her place, and tears sprang to her eyes. In a low voice, she said, "Does it happen all at once, like being wound up,' he asked, 'or bit by bit?'

'It doesn't happen all at once,' said the Skin Horse. 'You become. It takes a long time. That's why it doesn't often happen to people who break easily, or who have to be carefully kept. Generally, by the time you are Real, most of your hair has been loved off, and your eyes drop out, and you get loose in the joints and very shabby. But these things don't matter at all, because once you are Real, you can't be ugly, except to people who don't understand.'"

She stopped and sobbed, turning her face into James' shoulder. She couldn't help but think how Audrey had been hurt beyond repair, but she had been loved, without a doubt. As minutes unspooled, several passersby stopped, perhaps hearing her muffled sobs. Let them think what they wanted. She sensed her brother's shoulders shaking, and this hurt her the most.

"James," she whispered, grazing her fingers along his arm.

After a while, he gently took the book. "Let me read the last passage."

She drew away, swiping her eyes, while he arranged the book on his lap.

In a deep voice, he began, "Of what use was it to be loved and lose one's beauty and become Real if it all ended like this? And a tear, a real tear, trickled down his little shabby velvet nose and fell to the ground. And then a strange thing happened. For where the tear had fallen, a flower grew out of the ground, a mysterious flower, not at all like any that grew in the garden." He closed the book, his eyes clouding, and they both gazed at the stream and the rainbow shade of flowers.

"I'm glad we ended with that passage," Isabel said. "It's beautiful, like Audrey." As James returned the book, Mother's letter slipped from the cover. Isabel stooped to pick it from the ground, and her brother gave her a quizzical look.

"I meant to tell you Mother wrote." She handed him the letter, undeniable proof she had kept her promise to write. She held her breath as he scanned it.

"Izz, you know it's clear she wants you home."

Her stomach twisted. She wished he wouldn't speak of this. Not now.

"It's awfully kind of Mrs. Michael and her husband to keep you, but Mother's all alone and struggling. There's no point waiting till summer ends before going home. You've already been here well over a month."

"A month's nothing." She balled her fists in her lap.

"You see things from her point of view, don't you?"

She scooted away from him. "I don't see how I can help, except by doing chores."

"You're her daughter. Just having you nearby would comfort her."

"How do you know? I wasn't any comfort to her before. No reason why things will change. At least now she has one less person to worry about."

He shook his head. "She's been alone and grieving for weeks, going on months, and she misses us something awful. I can tell from the letters she sends me, too. We're her only family, and we're gone. You might not believe it, but she needs you."

"Why? Because I'm a girl? Easy for you to expect me to go home to cook and clean, when you've got all the freedom to come and go as you please." Her voice spiraled up, high and caustic. A couple who were strolling down the path by the Indian paintbrushes stared with disapproval.

"You know it's not like that. I have a commitment to the CCC. There are bills that won't get paid without my job. Besides, I didn't run away."

A squall of fury built inside her, and she shouted, "Stop saying that! I didn't run away either. I *chose* to come here."

When he turned to her, startled, she said more quietly, "I'd like to earn cash, too. And not just by sweeping floors." She squared her shoulders, determined not to let him stop her. "I want to find work as a ranger-naturalist, like Mrs. Michael."

Doubt flashed across his face, and he gave her a searching look. "A ranger? Sure, Mrs. Michael has an interesting job. But it's not the kind of thing you can just waltz in and do overnight."

"I never said I'd waltz in and do it! I'd train first. I'm already training." Let him challenge her; she would defy him with reason.

"It's not that easy, Izz. Don't get me wrong, a ranger sounds like a swell job. But it's next to impossible for a girl."

"Why, you don't think I can do it?" She jumped angrily from the bench and paced.

"No. I'm not saying that. I'm just saying it's mighty unusual for women. Mrs. Michael's the exception."

Isabel circled the bench in tighter and tighter turns, her hands wrapped around her waist. "She's already proven that women can be first-rate ranger-naturalists, so it will be easier for the next woman who applies."

"Maybe so." His brow furrowed. Isabel followed his gaze, where a young girl in a yellow frock knelt to sniff a long-stemmed iris, her face exultant. Nearby, her parents watched with smiles, then bent their heads together.

As Isabel passed him on her next circuit around the bench, he gripped her wrist, but she wrenched away. "Listen, Izz, if they ever let more women become rangers, then I'm sure you can do it. Only sometime later. Things are hard enough as it is. Now's the time for us to stick together and help each other out. Mother needs us."

"I *knew* I shouldn't have told you my plans."

"Don't say that." His voice was low, contrite. "We used to tell each other everything." She stopped pacing and bent her head, remembering the long months after Dad's death when James had been her confidant, and she had trusted and depended on him above anyone else.

Eyes glistening, he reached for her hand, and she let him draw her slowly back to the bench. For a long time they sat, arms touching. Convincing him would take time, but eventually he would see that Mother was doing fine and was better off without children underfoot. In time, too, he would understand that Isabel was serious about pursuing her dream of becoming a ranger. After they took a turn through the garden and hugged goodbye, she returned to sit on the bench. The intricate dance of butterflies and birds, accompanied by vivid buds, soothed her. She would need to talk soon with Enid about her plans, make it clear she wouldn't burden the Michaels if they couldn't keep her past August. If she had to, she would find another place to board, along with a job—whatever she could find. But she vowed not to return home. Come what may, she would stay at the park and forge her own path, step by step, to becoming a ranger-naturalist. As she walked back to the post office, Isabel sifted over the last line of *The Velveteen Rabbit* about the mysterious flower that had grown from the tear, unlike any other in the garden.

CHAPTER TWENTY-FIVE

A sudden tap on her shoulder, and Isabel sprang forward, her heart thundering. The mystery novel she had been reading slid from her lap with a thud, and she clapped a hand to her mouth.

"Sorry, it's only me," Enid whispered.

Isabel rose from the leather chair by the fireplace and managed a laugh. She had spent the afternoon in the Mariposa County library, which occupied the west side of the museum's ground floor, while Enid gave a botany lecture to the Field School students on the floor above.

"Must be a scary story," Enid said with a grin.

Isabel picked up the book and showed her the cover. "*The Murder of Roger Ackroyd*." Dad had told her once that he'd devoured the story in a single evening.

"Ah, I love a good whodunit! Have they found the killer?"

"No, Poirot's stumped. But with his amazing little gray cells, he's sure to solve it."

They shared a giggle, and from the front desk, the librarian shot them a disapproving glance and raised a finger to her lips.

"We'd better go," Enid whispered. "I'll check it out under my card so you can read it whenever you like."

When they stepped outside into the sunlight, Isabel traced her hand over the cross-section of a monarch sequoia tree, twenty-eight feet in diameter, on display in front of the museum.

She loved how the tree's rings told a story. The tacked-on placards showed major historical events during the tree's life, including the Battle of Hastings, Magna Carta, landing of Columbus, Declaration of Independence, Civil War, and the year Lincoln signed the Yosemite Grant.

Enid peered over her shoulder. "You might think this fellow's ancient, but Grizzly Giant in Mariposa Grove has him beat. By my estimate, Grizzly's four thousand years old." Isabel widened her eyes, struck by the same awe she had felt at the Falls—the knowledge that while humans scurried around on earth for a short time, Nature dwarfed them in size and years.

They turned to go, and she spotted several boys from James' crew repaving the road by the parking lot. She scanned for James but didn't see him. Odd, but she assumed he was working somewhere out of view.

"How was the lecture?" she asked Enid as they walked through the plaza.

"As well as I hoped. The students asked some good questions. I hear they've nicknamed themselves ninety-day wonders, since they'll be ranger-naturalists by the end of summer."

"The men, you mean." Isabel couldn't help but frown.

"You never know. Things might change now that the First Lady has visited Yosemite and met with Superintendent Thomson. Her position on women's rights and equal opportunities is well known." Enid had told Isabel about Mrs. Roosevelt's trip last week to Glacier Point and Tuolumne Meadows. She had even camped by Mount Conness and stocked a lake with rainbow trout. "That's reason to hope. Not to mention, Mr. Dixon has only been the Field School Director for a year, so he very well might do a better job of helping the women graduates find positions."

"No thanks to Mr. Harwell."

Enid tapped a finger to her chin. "Bert's no slouch when it comes to field training. After all, he founded the Junior Nature school. Though I suspect he did it as a way of keeping children from bothering the adults on their hikes."

"I'm sure he thinks their questions are beneath him. Same way he thinks of women."

Enid made an airy, tinkling laugh. "No matter. I dare not press my luck. Ever since he received my letter, he's called a truce. Albeit an uneasy one, and there's no telling how long it'll last. But I can't waste time fretting."

Curious, Isabel asked Enid what she had written.

"I sang his praises. Promised I'd work shoulder to shoulder with him in the garden, however he sees fit, for the sake of the visitors who find such hope there. And in just a few years the wildflowers will be naturalized, thanks to his excellent guidance." She grimaced, then said slyly, "The Adams have written letters of their own to Superintendent Thomson, advocating for my reappointment. And they've recruited others to do the same. We're using every trick in the book. For now, they seem to be working."

She cut onto the path through the woods. "Let's lunch somewhere cooler." They approached a boulder on the banks of the Merced. Enid withdrew a package of nuts, cookies, and berries from her sack, while Isabel filled a canteen at the edge of the river. Enid handed her a napkin with nuts and berries, and she sank onto the mossy rock. A minnow swam by the bank, then disappeared.

Enid said, "Hard to believe summer's almost over."

Ice slid down Isabel's spine. Today marked two and a half weeks from the start of the new school year. Though it was foolhardy, she had put off talking with Enid about staying beyond summer, hoping for the right opportunity. If she were honest, she was afraid deep down that Enid would reject her plan, citing similar objections to James.' But it was now or never.

187

Working up her courage, she plunged, "I'm not returning to San Francisco. If you can't keep me past August, I understand. I'll find another place to board." She paused. "I've decided to live at Yosemite year round and apply to the Field School."

Enid's face remained unruffled. Slowly, her lips curled into a thin smile. "I half expected you might. You're welcome to stay with us a tad longer and earn your keep while you firm up plans. That is, if your mother doesn't object."

A jolt burst through Isabel like the buzz of a drill. She beamed, her mind whirling. She could make it work. She could train with Enid as a ranger's assistant while finding part-time work at a hotel or gift shop or even an administrative office. Eventually get her own place. She croaked out, "Really, you mean it?"

"Somehow I can't picture you leaving Yosemite. You fit here so perfectly, and you have the makings of a young naturalist. You'll just need to work it out with your mother."

Isabel spluttered a hasty thanks. She was gratified, even a little flabbergasted that Enid regarded her as having possibility, a girl on her way to becoming someone else. It seemed too good to be true. But then, she should have known Enid would come through. On the children's hike to the falls, Enid had said Yosemite brought out the best in people. She was right, even though Isabel hardly deserved such good fortune. She and Enid were remarkably similar to each other, more so than she and Mother would ever be.

"I can't wait for our climb on Wednesday! And now, with this, I'm over the moon."

Enid stretched her arms high above her head and shook her hands in a mime of victory. "We'll celebrate when we reach the summit." She had offered to take Isabel on a day-long hike, two days from now, into Alpine Country, clear up the granite face of Half Dome. Isabel was ready, Enid had promised, especially since they would use ropes to climb, which she could surely manage. *Step by step. Bit by bit. Hand over hand.*

After lunch, they meandered into the plaza and cut toward the back of the museum. Isabel would weed while Enid oversaw the CCC boys as they hauled wheelbarrows of river rocks into the garden. As they approached the museum, Isabel marveled at how it was framed like one of Ansel Adams' photographs, with the Yosemite Falls sparkling in the distance.

They had almost reached the garden gate when a voice boomed from behind, "Izzie! Isabel!"

Swiveling, Isabel was startled to see her brother running toward her, clutching his hat. In another few seconds he was at her side, breathless and panting. "Thank God I found you."

She stepped back in alarm. His eyes were wild and unmoored. "What's wrong? What's happened?"

"I need to talk to you… in private."

Enid touched Isabel's shoulder. "Go on, take your time. I'll be here if you need me." Before Isabel could speak, she hurried into the garden.

"James, what is it?"

He shook his head. "Not here. This way."

In a daze, she followed him across the plaza, down the same trail she and Enid had just crossed. His strides were long and clipped, and she had to trot to keep up. She was overcome with a dark premonition. *What in the world had happened?* With a sinking feeling, she suspected it had to do with Mother.

In the thick of the forest, James slumped to the ground by a black oak. She knelt beside him and said urgently, "James, tell me."

"Here." He rummaged in his pocket and handed her a folded piece of paper. "This just came." Sinking onto her skirts, she unfolded it and read rapidly.

It was a note from Mother, dated two weeks ago. Her boss had fired her after criticizing her "slow and sloppy work." She sounded despondent. "My back's been flaring something awful. I'm all alone and at my wit's end," she had written. "I can't imagine how I'll find a new position when I can't even think straight, let alone stand properly."

Isabel took a jagged breath. Her insides had gone numb. The letter drifted into her lap.

James picked a twig off the ground and twisted it in his fist. "She needs help, Izz."

She tried to find her voice, but the words stuck in her throat.

James shredded the twig, tossed a piece of it aside. "Not only is she all alone, she's lost her job. And her back is making it worse."

Wordlessly, she folded the note and handed it to him, trying to sort through her thoughts. She knew she should feel sorry for Mother, but instead she wanted to cry for herself. Because it was clear what James expected her to do.

"Aren't you going to say something?" James said, pocketing the note.

"It's terribly unfair what happened to Mother."

"How soon can you get home?"

The ground tilted beneath her, and she dug her nails into the dirt to steady herself. "I... I don't know."

"I can talk to the delivery guy, help you catch a ride to Merced. From there you can take a train back to the city." He spoke of fares and train schedules, but she couldn't make sense of his words. "Isabel?" he said sharply. "Have you been listening? I'll arrange for you to get home, but you've got to speak with the Michaels and get ready. The sooner the better." He took her wrist and added more softly, "I know this is sudden."

Her mind snapped to attention, and she broke free of his grasp. An image of the fetid alley behind their flat flew into her mind, and she shuddered.

"More than that... it's not possible. I can't go."

His face clouded in disbelief, and she forced herself to meet his eyes. "I'm not going back to San Francisco. Mrs. Michael has said I can stay at her apartment until I find a job and a more permanent place at Yosemite. She's going to help me train to become a ranger-naturalist and apply to the Field School..."

He shook his head, his eyes tense and wary. "The *Field School?* That's... listen. Hardly anyone stays at the park for good. And nothing's even tying you down here."

She wanted to retort that people *did* live at Yosemite permanently—people who were different, adventurous, who believed deeply in the park. But that would send things off course. "This isn't an emergency. It's dreadful luck Mother lost her job, but thank goodness she isn't ill or badly injured."

"Think of what she's going through, will you? She's been fired, her back's ailing her, and she's utterly alone."

"I know, and I *am* sorry for her." She held his eyes, casting about for solutions. "Maybe in a few weeks, she'll have found something else..."

He shot her an incredulous look. "In this economy? Her chances of finding another position are damn low."

She suspected he was right; it was unrealistic to think Mother could get a job quickly when so many folks were out of work.

"Listen, Izz, she's awfully unhappy. It's too much bad news to take in such a short time."

She clutched her waist, her mind racing. "It's a setback, but it's only temporary. She'll pull through." She hadn't written back to Mother, had been waiting to firm up plans before explaining she would stay on at Yosemite.

James flicked a stone into the brush. "Not to hear her tell it. Every letter she sends sounds a little more desperate than the last, even before she was fired. She's struggling, and she's got no one to turn to. It's easy to read between the lines and figure out she's barely coping. She needs help."

And as a girl, I must be the one to offer it, she thought bitterly.

191

"You've got school starting in a few weeks, and Mother needs you more than ever." His eyes settled on her face. "It makes sense for you to go home now. This is the best for you, too."

Her voice reached a crescendo. "How on *earth* can you say it's the best for me?" She pictured herself crammed into the mildewy flat, unable to tear loose from its dark, depressing stranglehold.

"You can finish high school and get your diploma. Plus you and Mother need each other's company. You might not think so, but it would do you both a world of good."

Glaring at him, she shouted, "That's where you're wrong! What she needs is someone to keep house and do the chores. The same things I've done since January. As a girl, that's about all I'm good for." Her eyes brimmed. "You want to know what's done me good? Being *here*."

"You've been a trooper, Izz." He gave her arm a gentle squeeze. "More than anyone. You've kept things together while Mother worked. She knows that, too."

Isabel shook her head, doubtful. When was the last time Mother really saw her, since she couldn't even see beyond the next meal?

"But that's only a small reason why she needs you. Sure, she depends on you to keep things running, but she also cares about you more than you realize. I know you don't believe me, but she needs you because you're her *daughter*. She misses you."

Tears spilled down Isabel's cheeks. She strongly disagreed.

"I know you wanted to stay on and train to be a naturalist like Mrs. Michael," James was saying. "And maybe you can still make that happen sometime later. Just not now. You're needed at home far more than here."

His words smashed into her brain like a hammer. Springing away from him, she hurled, "Don't you dare tell me what's right for me! You don't know a damn thing about what I want.

Nothing at all!" She was panting, as if he had grabbed her throat in a chokehold.

He turned to her in confusion, his face crumpling in much the same way it had on the morning he'd left for Yosemite and she'd accused him of leaving them in the flat. But she didn't feel remorse, not this time. She had to get away; she didn't trust herself not to scream something truly damaging. Rising unsteadily, she brushed off her skirt and began walking briskly down the path. The tears were coming faster and faster. It occurred to her that she had left her knapsack behind, but it was too late to retrieve it. She needed desperately to increase the distance between herself and her brother.

"Isabel!" James shouted, but she didn't stop. A rustling movement came from behind. Suddenly fearful he was trailing her, she ran blindly, stumbling on roots and rocks, her face wet with tears. Branches tore at her skirts and scratched her arms. She didn't care; she wanted the rocks and tree limbs to wound her, knock her out cold. She hadn't the foggiest idea where she was headed.

CHAPTER TWENTY-SIX

After running so far her legs and chest ached, Isabel slumped onto a desolate outcrop of rocks in a thick aspen and pine grove, far off the well-worn trail. Tears surged down her cheeks. The Merced was nowhere in sight. In fact, she couldn't even hear its familiar burble. She didn't care if she were lost, didn't care if she never found her way back to roads and buildings and people. In her desperation to find a remote hiding place away from James and all the tourists, she had run for half an hour, probably longer. She'd even passed dusty horseshoe prints and clumps of fresh horse dung, which suggested she had crossed paths with the saddle and pack horses that visitors sometimes took on overnight hikes to the Tuolumne Meadows and points north. When she glimpsed the grand Ahwahnee Hotel in the distance with its spacious grounds and mashie golf course, she had run on, wanting to be far away from all signs of civilization.

Bending over, she sobbed freely, a ferocious, wrenching sound, as if her very core were being wrung from her. Her wails reverberated over and around her, the only noise in the forest except for the faint crackling of pine needles from squirrels. In an instant, as if the telltale symptoms of an illness had caught up with her, chills cascaded down her spine, and her stomach churned. On top of that, her temples throbbed — a fast, relentless beating. Meanwhile, her mind scrambled like a deer fleeing a predator.

She knew she should drink water, but she couldn't drag herself off the rocks and down to the river, wherever it might be. Her sobs reached a frenzy, siren-loud and herky-jerky. If there were any nearby animals besides the squirrels and birds, she was certain she had scared them off. She didn't care if she developed another migraine that took her out. Maybe that would be for the better—her body strewn here, immobile, for a day or more, so she could sleep her way through the next twenty-four hours and in her unconsciousness not remember.

She sprawled face down on the rocks, waiting for the migraine to overpower her. Her tears had begun to recede, but she twisted and bucked from the pain in her head and gut. At least she could open her eyes without the explosion of tiny lights. Turning her face to the side, she vomited her lunch onto the ground in a yellowish bile. After a moment, her stomach felt a little more settled.

The last few hours' topsy-turvy highs and lows looped through her mind. She had never dreamed she would run from James, yet she hadn't been able to listen to another word he said. The more he had spoken, the more bewildered she had grown, since clearly he no longer understood her. Perhaps he never truly had.

Convenient for him to order her to put her plans on hold and return to a litany of chores in cramped quarters, while he remained at Yosemite, free to roam like a rutting buck, providing he fulfilled his CCC duties. A few times she had spied him standing inappropriately close to a dark-haired girl near the teepees behind the wildflower garden. She wondered, for the first time, whether he had bedded her. If the girl bore his child, James wouldn't suffer the consequences. And Claude had behaved almost as recklessly—pinning her in a kiss at Lafayette

Square, certain his own actions would amount to nothing. Men always made the rules, and women followed.

She had been foolish to get her hopes up over Enid's offer to stay. Wouldn't wishes ultimately get batted down, like childish hands waving for attention? All the same, she wasn't ready to admit defeat and leave for good. Abandoning this place after the unlikelihood of finding it struck her as a kind of sacrilege, and worse, a betrayal of Audrey.

She raised her head, hoping to glimpse the familiar shape of Half Dome, but the surrounding forest was too dense, the trees closing around her like dark, menacing giants. Shivering, she shut her eyes. What had happened to Mother was truly unfortunate, and the timing couldn't be worse. It was as though a confluence of terrible events had conspired against them. But, she reminded herself, although Mother had lost her job, she wasn't laid up in the hospital. Surely her back would improve after she rested a bit. And with any luck, she would find another position, despite the scarcity of jobs.

It wasn't James' decision whether she made a trip back to San Francisco. Even then, on the slight chance she *did* go back, Isabel would make sure it was only a visit; she wouldn't stay more than a week or two. Long enough to tend to Mother, get her back on her feet, looking for work. James could do nothing about it. But then her stomach sank. This was by far the worst argument they had ever had; they had parted like bitter foes. At once, she wept anew. It was as if Dad and Audrey had died again, and she was doomed to suffer their loss over and over in her own private hell.

"James!" she screamed aloud, wishing against all hope he would materialize on the rocks. She blinked back tears and waited. Nothing. The stone beneath her arms and legs was cold and damp, and her stomach turned queasy again. Chances were when he learned she wasn't going home, he would refuse to see her again, let alone forgive her. But she had no choice except to thrust aside the thought; she had to contend with immediate danger.

A family of deer skirted through the brush, startling her. Isabel shifted onto her elbows and gazed after them. The shadows from the trees had sunk lower. Her tears had almost run dry; the length of her body was wrung out and bruised. Suddenly she felt exhausted. Enid would worry, as it must have been hours since Isabel had left her at the garden.

Gingerly, she stood and brushed dust off her skirt. Her hem was muddy and torn. Abandoning her knapsack when she fled from James had been foolish, too; now she had zero supplies. And though she knew far more about plants than she had when she first arrived at the park, she didn't trust herself to forage for edible ones in the woods.

Taking a breath so as not to panic, she picked her way toward what she thought was the direction of the Merced. From there it would be simple enough to follow the river back toward the path that led to the New Village.

She continued walking, but after fifteen or twenty minutes, as she entered a denser, darker part of the forest, she feared she was headed in the wrong direction. The familiar vast ocean rumbled between her ears, threatening to roar, and her eyes bulged wide. She paused, straining to hear the river, but the only sound was a goshawk's rapid-fire alarm call as it circled overhead, probably closing in on its prey. As it dawned on her she was utterly alone, a shiver skipped down her spine. Struggling to contain her tears, she commanded herself out loud to stay calm. The sound of her voice offered a tiny semblance of human comfort. But there was still no sight of Half Dome or any other landmark; trees encircled her in all directions, like a fortress.

Rooted in place, Isabel recalled something Enid advised tourists on nature walks: *Stop, observe, think.* She had explained: "If you're hiking and you get lost, moving around frantically will only make things worse." She had instructed the group to breathe from their bellies, since short, quick breaths only increased anxiety and confusion.

Sure enough, Isabel became aware that her limbs were aching; she was thirsty; and she was inhaling in shallow, rapid huffs. Placing a hand atop her diaphragm, she managed a few slow, deep breaths. Next, she needed to think. She must have first approached the outcrop of rocks from the opposite direction, since otherwise, she should have reached the river by now. She would have to turn around, retrace her steps, look for any familiar scenery — trees, plants, crushed pine needles and leaves from her own tracks.

She didn't have a timepiece, but the lengthening shadows indicated it was late afternoon. And if she thought hard, she remembered tearing uphill as she ran from James. Surely that meant she now needed to go in a downward direction. Enid had also explained that because the sun always set in the west, you could use a stick to cast a shadow, mark its tip and wait ten minutes until the shadow moved a few centimeters, then mark the second shadow's tip. The first mark would represent west, the second east.

After some consideration, Isabel decided to use that method as a last resort; she didn't want to fritter away precious minutes. Recalling that she had passed the Ahwahnee Hotel from the portion of the Merced by the New Village, she knew she would have to head west eventually, toward the museum and post office. Turning, she plodded back toward the outcrop of rocks.

When she spied a footprint pressed against the dirt, she paused and proceeded with caution. The light through the treetops was changing, dimming in pale hues of orange and yellow. Her shadow angled longer against the ground as the sun descended.

After arriving at the rocks where she had sprawled minutes before, she felt a smidgen of reassurance. Right back where she had started. Two steps forward, one step back, as Mother used to call slow progress. All of a sudden, she thought of a Saturday afternoon before Dad's death when she and Mother had sat side by side sewing, while Ethel Waters crooned *Stormy Weather* on the radio. As they worked, they had sipped iced tea and chatted like schoolgirls on holiday about the latest pictures, their favorite Hollywood starlets, local news. The garden's jasmine perfume had wafted into their rooms in the Victorian on Rainbow Lane. Shouts and cackles had floated inside, too, as the neighborhood children, Audrey among them, had played a game of tag.

"You make a fine stitch." Mother had nodded with approval at the pea coat lining Isabel had resewn. Isabel's face had grown hot with unexpected pleasure. "Those kids," Mother had added, "Thank God they're having a ball outside and not in here." They had shared a conspiratorial giggle.

Isabel blinked, snapping herself back to the danger she had waded into. From here she had to be even more careful, because if she made a wrong turn, she might still be wandering in the forest when it grew dark. She peered down at the ground around the rocks. In her haste, she hadn't paid attention to where she was going, hadn't noticed anything except her own despair. Brushing at her eyes, she looked closer.

There. A shoe print in the dirt. It was the only one she saw from the original path she had taken when fleeing from James, but it was enough to go on for now. She stepped onto it cautiously, then took another step and another, squinting, searching for any telltale signs. When she noticed a small bed of crumpled yellow violets with another print directly behind it, she knew she was on the right track, retracing her steps. She must have trampled on the flowers as she ran.

From somewhere ahead came the wild squawks of jays. Isabel kept going, then stopped short with a cry. Shoulders hunched, a great horned owl curled at the base of a pine, apparently asleep. A dozen jays had gathered around him, screeching in a cacophonous chorus.

Incredibly, though a jay occasionally zoomed by him, the owl never stirred or batted an eye. His feathers were speckled brown and black, and his body moved slightly. Isabel wondered whether he were ill, but decided he was simply a deep sleeper. A wonder that he had found his own repose on the ground, of all places, despite the chittering, shrill caws of the jays.

How many minutes had it been since she'd retraced her steps? She tried to count off seconds in her head, but it soon proved too distracting. At least she was going downhill, which surely meant she was orienting herself in the correct direction.

Hearing a conversational "chuk," she glanced up and saw a Brewer's blackbird nesting in a willow, mere yards from the river. She squealed. In the distance rose the prominent shelf of Half Dome. Trembling with relief, she ran to the Merced and hung over the bank, cupping water into her hand and lapping it into her mouth. She drank until her throat was cool and moist and her stomach tight. Wiping her mouth with the back of her hand, she stood and followed the river trail the few miles back to the New Village.

By the length of the shadows, she estimated it was well past four o'clock—around the time she and Enid usually finished up at the garden. In the plaza, Isabel scanned the front of the museum but didn't see the CCC boys. Swiftly she circled behind the museum and entered the garden. Few visitors were about. Near the stream, Enid was balancing Isabel's knapsack on her shoulders and chatting with Arnold. Neither of them noticed her, but in a minute, they finished their conversation and parted ways—Arnold to the wall by the Indian Canyon to collect his tools, Enid toward the entrance.

When Enid spotted her, she waved and sprinted over. "Oh, thank goodness! I was afraid we'd have to send a search party." Her eyes ran down Isabel's torso, lingering on the torn, muddy hem of her skirt and her soiled stockings. "I was terribly worried. So was your brother. He came looking for you, but he had to return to Cascades for supper crew." She glanced behind. "I'll ask Arnold to let him know you're safe and sound." Cupping her hands over her mouth, she called, "Arnold!"

Embarrassed, Isabel shifted her gaze to the ground. "I'm sorry for causing so much trouble. Truth is, I got lost."

Arnold loped over with his shovel and knapsack, and Enid instructed him to tell James that Isabel was safe.

"Thank you," Isabel murmured as he gave a thumbs up. Her cheeks flamed for the worry she had caused.

After he left, Enid put an arm around her shoulders. "Come on, let's go inside. I imagine you're tired and thirsty after wandering for so long."

"Not so much thirsty. I drank at the river." But she was grateful to let Enid guide her out of the garden, back to the plaza, up the stairs of the post office to the bright little apartment.

Enid made her sit at the table and sip mint and yarrow tea. "It'll soothe you," she promised. When Isabel tried to rise to fix supper, Enid shooed her back down. "That can wait. We can always whip up a salad after Charlie gets home."

As Isabel drank the tea, her stomach and chest warmed, and the tautness in her legs and back gradually relaxed. She let out a sigh. Enid slid into a chair across from her, cradling a chipped mug in both hands. Thankfully, she didn't ask what had happened.

Isabel lifted her gaze to Enid's. At the very least, she owed her an apology. "I'm sorry. It was frightening getting lost, and the last thing I wanted was to make you worry."

"There's no need to apologize."

"Your tips about what to do if you're lost sure came in handy. Stopping, observing, and thinking. That helped to keep me from panicking."

"I'm glad you remembered."

"I always remember what you say."

"Your brother was awfully worried about you, too. He darted into the garden three or four times, asking whether I'd seen you."

Isabel frowned at her lap. "Did he say anything else?"

"He let it slip that you'd run off." Enid paused. "I gathered you had a disagreement."

"Yes." Isabel's heart thudded. "We've had a bit of bad news. James received a letter from Mother. She was fired from her job." She took a breath. "And her back's been hurting, so it'll be more difficult for her to look for a new position."

"Oh dear." Enid's voice grew soft. "I'm sorry. Will you go home to help out and take care of your sister?"

At the reference to Audrey, Isabel did a double take and dropped her head. "I... I haven't decided. Mother might find a new job before we know it, and I won't be needed. Or I might go for a short visit to get her settled, then come right back to Yosemite."

Enid blew on her tea and sipped. "When my father was ailing near the end of his life, I made a trip to Pasadena to take care of him. It was terribly hard. I hated being in that town, even after teaching there for over ten years, because I never fit in." Isabel considered that she didn't belong in San Francisco, either; she despised the fog, the shabby buildings and streets, the grime and pollution, downturned faces in a hurry.

"Folks around town whispered I was off my rocker. Because what woman in her right mind lives in a tent and works as a ranger instead of baking bread and keeping house? Every day I thought about returning to Yosemite, but in the end I stayed. There was no one else to help my mother."

Isabel bunched her arms around her waist, wondering whether she meant it as a reproach.

"Course I was much older than you, and my situation was different."

"James takes for granted I'll go to San Francisco."

Enid said carefully, "I imagine he can't go if he wants to keep his job."

"Well, yes. It's just that I'm always the one who's expected to hold down the fort and manage the household. The girl who obeys the rules." She stared down at her mug. "Except for these last couple of months at Yosemite." *When I took matters into my own hands,* she finished silently.

Enid spread her fingers on the table. "You're young. It won't be this way forever. Someday you'll be able to choose where you live and work, even whether you marry and have children. By and by, you'll have more choices. And when you do, you can choose a path most women might not take."

"Like you've done."

"Not just me. There are plenty others who've made interesting choices. Take my friend Alice Eastwood at the California Academy of Sciences in the Golden Gate Park. She didn't go to college, either, but she's a botanist by training. We meet every year, and she helps identify the more extraordinary specimens I find on my climbs. She's even donated several plants from Yosemite to the academy's herbarium. Virginia Adams is also unusual; she climbs and has served on the Sierra Club's Board. Then there's Marjorie Montgomery Ward, the lady whose donation helped create the wildflower garden. And of course Mrs. Roosevelt. She created the New Deal program to help working women receive better wages."

Isabel nodded.

"Whatever happens, the invitation to stay with Charlie and me still stands. The choice is yours."

Isabel's chest and shoulders lightened, as if she'd set down a knapsack stuffed with rocks. She had desperately needed a choice that was entirely hers to make. Unlike James and Mother, Enid wouldn't judge her decision, would simply offer support.

While Enid poured her another cup of tea, she told herself she could figure things out; it wasn't the end of the world. She would begin by writing Mother to express her sympathy and inquire what she needed. Then she would gauge her next steps based on Mother's response: whether to postpone the trip or make a short visit to San Francisco. But for now she wouldn't speak to James. The rancor of their exchange was still too raw. What mattered most was that he would soon learn she was safe.

She said, "I won't make any decisions for a couple of days. Not until after our hike to Half Dome."

Enid smiled in response, and Isabel suffused with coziness. It was as though Enid had assured her that even this, waiting until she'd had time to collect her thoughts, was wise.

CHAPTER TWENTY-SEVEN

Isabel struggled for breath, a searing heat radiating through her calves and thighs. Thrusting a whittled-down stick onto the trail, she followed Enid, navigating around rocks and twisted tree roots. The morning air was thin and chilly, and her arms and legs quivered from the effort of hiking in higher altitude. But as she climbed up the Mist Trail toward Nevada Falls and the Little Yosemite Valley, her body thrummed with adrenaline. Her first climb to the summit of Half Dome would cover a staggering roundtrip distance of over seventeen miles.

"As climbs go, it's tamer than most," Enid had said as they finalized plans. "We'll have ropes to grab as we go up the cliff, and you're strong enough to make it without much trouble. But I dare not take you up anything sheer, since you don't have the advantage of experience. Even Virginia, who's gone on dozens of climbs, once fell from an old rope between the Acorn and Cathedral Rocks. Thank goodness we were there, and Charlie caught her!"

The trail ascended past Vernal Falls through a shady sequoia forest, where Isabel had led the children weeks ago. Gold rings of sunlight angled through the tips of the giant evergreens, and sparkles of dew had begun to dissipate. When Enid cast a look back, Isabel leaned down to catch her breath, palms bracing her thighs.

Enid peeled the canteen from her knapsack and thrust it toward her. "Go ahead, sit and rest a minute."

Isabel flopped onto the ground, planting her feet in front of her, knees bent. She took slow sips of water, though she yearned to guzzle it down. If given the chance, Enid would undoubtedly be much farther ahead. They hadn't yet hiked five miles and had already walked for over four hours since dawn. Lunch would have to wait until after Nevada Falls. They'd packed light snacks, since Enid had warned the scent of food would attract bears.

Isabel heard a rapid, ringing zeet-zeet and cocked her head. "American Dipper?" She was rewarded with Enid's delighted nod and smile. Her legs ached, but she rose and dusted off her trousers, and they resumed the winding trek through the forest. At a break in the trees, the monstrous shape of a cliff emerged, and Isabel was buoyed by a boost of energy. She longed to be on the summit.

"Bear tracks!" She pointed to the side of the trail at large paw prints that disappeared through the trees.

"You have a sharp eye," Enid said, then froze and gripped her arm. About a dozen yards into the woods, a great black bear with tufts of golden fur stood on its hind legs beside a sequoia. A black club dangled by its middle from one of the tree's limbs. Isabel's heart thumped as she and Enid took a step backward.

"Mama Bear with her cub," Enid whispered. "We need to stay quiet, or else she'll think we're after her baby."

When the animal turned toward them and grunted, Isabel gasped. For a terrifying moment, she met the bear's feral, dark eyes. A chill ratcheted up her backbone, piercing her to the core, and her knees went weak. Then without warning, the bear collapsed onto all fours and sniffed the air with its pointy snout.

Enid murmured, "Don't worry. We're not in danger."

Though she had spoken reassuringly and Isabel had seen other bears on nature and bird walks in the park's lower elevation, she swallowed down a bolt of panic. Here they were utterly alone, and the growling Mama was only a stone's throw away.

"Easy," Enid whispered and motioned for Isabel to follow her up the trail. Stabbing her hiking stick to quicken her pace, Isabel threw a look behind, fearful the bear would stalk them. She didn't see it, but she continued stumbling ahead as fast as she dared. Moments later, after she confirmed it wasn't in pursuit, she let out a breath, and her pulse slowed.

"Brown and black bears are harmless enough that I've danced with a few. They're more a nuisance when they steal food from under your nose. But way out here, we're in their territory. This is bear country," Enid said.

Isabel shuddered. "Danced with them? Truly?"

"I'll show you sometime if I hold another bear feeding program. It's the strangest jig I've done. The bear looked for all the world like he'd bow and offer me his paw."

They burst into giggles.

As they began a slow ascent up another rocky staircase, Isabel heard the deafening roar of Nevada Falls. Stopping, she gripped her hiking stick and lifted her eyes from the boulders to the powerful rapids churning and crashing over the cliff, indifferent to everything in its wake. Recalling what Enid had said about borrowing a bit of Nature's freedom, she drew herself taller, as if she could will something deep inside to break loose and merge with the whitewater.

A few feet ahead, Enid raised her eyebrows in a silent question: *Shall we go on?*

Isabel nodded and moved ahead, rejoicing in the mist beading onto her sweaty face and arms. High above the rapids, a hawk glided, nosediving into the trees.

Enid stopped by a pair of Douglas firs, which she claimed were two of the largest in the park. "Old grizzled granddads." Scars marred their bark, and their crowns were missing.

"They're veterans of hundreds of years of lightning storms and avalanches, but look." She gestured with a smile at the mass of fresh foliage that swirled around their trunks. "They're still hanging onto what's left of the green gowns they wore when they were young."

Near the crest of the falls, along the foaming Merced, they arrived at a fork in the road and went left, toward Half Dome. The Mist trail leveled out through the Little Yosemite Valley, and Isabel increased her pace, knowing they would eat their snacks above the campground. Enid had warned that the steepest leg of the climb came next. Her favorite hikes, she had explained, were on lonesome trails like this, near the timberline. A family of deer trotted across the trail and fled into the woods, their white tails winking.

When the magnificent granite face of Half Dome loomed above the timberline, Isabel sucked in her breath. Against the backdrop, in a clearing off the trail, a small knot of lavender flowers bloomed. She inhaled a mingled aroma of pine resin and florid perfume.

"Isn't this marvelous!" Enid said. "Let's break for lunch here. That's your flower, Isabel, the lupine. And that," she pointed at the cliff, "is what we'll climb."

Isabel sank onto a fallen branch in the clearing and gazed at the lupines and the stark shelf of Half Dome. It wasn't even noon, but the August sun was now punishing, blazing down in what she estimated were over eighty degree temperatures, a sharp contrast from when they began at dawn. Slipping a tiny box from her knapsack, Enid carefully plucked a lupine from its roots and tucked it into the box. A specimen, she said, that they might plant in the wildflower garden.

"You see, at this elevation, the lupine is a survivor out of necessity. Sweet smelling and beautiful, yet incredibly tough."

Isabel thought of Audrey, and something deep inside her chest tugged. It must have been hiking way out here, so close to the top of Half Dome, in a place her sister would have agreed was as close as they had ever physically come to the Isle of Castaways. A trip they rightly should have made together.

Enid withdrew a waxed paper of gingerbread cookies, chocolate, dried figs, and strawberries. They ate slowly and took turns sipping from the canteens, which they had refilled at the falls. Though her mouth was parched, Isabel drank sparingly, knowing they needed to conserve water for the trek to the summit and back. Besides, Enid had told her not to drink much on long hikes, warning it would make her feel sick. They reserved a few cookies and raisins for their return trip, but because the berries would spoil in the heat, they devoured them all. Isabel licked her fingers, savoring the sweet juice.

"Feeling all right?" Enid asked. "You seem to be."

Isabel stretched her legs and flexed her sore feet. "This is wonderful," she tried.

She couldn't articulate how hiking made her feel. A glorious mobile meditation in which you concentrated only on the present: the sun and wind on your cheeks, the contact of your feet against the trail, the ache in your legs, the hardening of your muscles, the steady progress toward a stunning view.

But now that they had stopped, and she was surrounded by lupines and the near-attainable precipice of Half Dome, a mental vision of Audrey—light, buoyant, alive—flooded her and left her weak.

"My sister would have..." She took a breath, sniffed the lupines.

"Your sister?" Enid said gently.

"Audrey..." The name died on her lips, as if the wind had snatched the word. "She would have fallen in love with Yosemite. It was her idea to come." Her voice cracked, and she blinked back tears.

Enid soothed, "There, my dear. It's all right." Her eyes were round with concern.

Struggling to compose herself, Isabel blew her nose and stared at the fortress-like granite of Half Dome.

"You can tell her all about it. Maybe someday she'll make it here, too." Enid looked confused, and Isabel remembered she didn't know about Audrey.

"Audrey's dead."

Shock and alarm streaked across Enid's face. "But you told me..."

"I know. I'm sorry. I couldn't bear to tell you the truth." Her voice caught again, and she gulped. "She was killed by an automobile in June, not long after school let out. The horrible thing is I could have prevented the accident, but I wasn't watching her. I was... with a boy in another part of the park when she wandered into the street." Tears dripped down her face and neck as she braced herself for the harsh judgment she knew she deserved.

For an awful moment, Enid said nothing, but then she took Isabel's hand. "You poor darling. I thought there might be something else you weren't telling, but I never knew what an ordeal you've been through."

"She was my responsibility." A hot lick of pain stole her breath.

"Your heart was in the right place. You had no way of knowing what would happen. It's clear you care for her very much." She caressed Isabel's arm and passed her a handkerchief.

Isabel had a sudden urge to tell Enid everything about Audrey—her bouncing curls, lively personality, how she had loved make-believe places and cats. "Even after the awful things that happened to our family, my sister was hopeful and imaginative. She wanted to travel here to visit James."

Referring to Audrey in the past tense jarred her, as it had when she and James had held the memorial. But Enid nodded, frowning in concentration, so she forged ahead. "After we moved to the Tenderloin, Audrey and I invented an island.

Whenever we were alone and feeling low, we sat beneath the table and pretended we were traveling there. It was kind of a cross between Shangri-La, where no one ages, and some idyllic place where the sun always shines and we could eat as much food as we wanted. Nothing like San Francisco."

Enid gave her hand a gentle squeeze.

"When we talked about the Isle of Castaways, I had no idea I might actually go to a place like it someday." Isabel dabbed her eyes. "Sure, Yosemite isn't an island. But it's sunny, and there are more plants and wild animals here than people. The air's fresh. You can hike past flowers up gorgeous mountains. It's almost not real." She gestured with her free hand. "You'd never know there's a Depression or that people are trying to find work and wondering how they'll get their next meal. Even the birds here eat better." Enid flinched, and Isabel went silent. She hadn't meant to accuse; she had merely wanted to explain who her sister had been. "It's strange, but out here I feel close to Audrey, almost as though she's just out of view. Maybe because this would have been the perfect place for her. So wild and beautiful." She glanced at Enid. "I know I sound nutty."

"No, you're not nutty. I truly believe this park has a magical effect on people. It helps us try on new versions of ourselves that we didn't think were possible." She paused. "I never imagined a woman forty, fifty years old could climb mountains. And I didn't dream I'd be a ranger-naturalist. So it's not surprising you'd feel close to your sister here."

"Audrey loved adventures."

"Yosemite's the place to try the things you could never do in an average town." Enid added softly, "I know Charles and I are lucky to live here, tucked away in a pristine little corner of the world. Sometimes it's easy to forget that my problems on the job are mainly annoyances. No doubt there will always be arrogant men like Mr. Harwell. But the truth is, I have more freedom here than I would anywhere else. Like I said, folks in Pasadena called me an odd duck." She tilted her face toward the breeze. "Besides all the unconventional things I did that women weren't supposed to do, I took more to animals than people, and the town resented me for it. And you've learned this about me, too, since you reminded me again just now that I prefer to feed the birds."

"No, no, it's true, Isabel," Enid said as Isabel's mouth fluttered open in protest. "You told me as only a genuine friend would. And you're right. If I'm honest with myself, it's because I understand birds better than I understand people. At least, people outside Yosemite." She glanced down at the valley. "You see, animals are driven by basic instincts and needs. They're not conniving or cruel. Some would say they're not loving or kind, either, but I've observed them up close with their families, and I disagree. I think they share humans' best traits but none of their worst."

"Most people aren't scheming and cruel. They're just trying to get by. My father wanted to help folks like the longshoremen who are struggling. At least tip the scales a little in their favor."

"He must have been a good man." They let this sit between them for a moment. Enid leaned closer to Isabel. "You remind me of myself when I first arrived here. Not being an odd duck, but having the chance to blossom." Her eyes grew veiled as she studied the face of Half Dome. "People can change at any age. If they decide to."

Isabel considered how different Enid was from Mother in her energy and willingness to try extraordinary things, take advantage of her good health, find clever ways around problems. Probably it helped that her only children were her beloved plants and animals. Unlike human offspring, they wouldn't burden her with obligations, couldn't make her suffer. "It's not right that I'm here now and not Audrey."

"Sometimes horrible things happen that don't make sense. Nothing anyone could have prevented. Your family's had its share. But it doesn't mean you should punish yourself for enjoying any little good thing that comes your way."

They fell silent. Isabel's eyes wandered to the lupines. She touched one of the purple petals. When she withdrew her fingers, it sprang back in place. It was the resilience that reminded her of Audrey, here in the high mountains, a spot she would have loved.

"Do you want to keep going to the summit, or do you want to turn back? If we keep going, we should go soon, before it gets too late."

"Let's go! I want to climb Half Dome." Isabel felt curiously revived, as if she had woken from a deep slumber and fortified herself with a hearty meal. *Enid had called her a genuine friend.* She had never imagined that a woman a decade older than Mother would understand her well enough to become a close confidant. She was determined to reach the pinnacle, even if every muscle in her body throbbed with pain.

Enid said, "When we arrive at the summit, we'll say a little prayer for your sister. On to the High Sierras!"

CHAPTER TWENTY-EIGHT

Isabel wet her lips, plotting how to negotiate up the gigantic staircase of rocks and boulders above her. Enid had said the steep incline of Sub Dome would be one of the most grueling parts of the hike to Half Dome, since they had now reached an elevation of around eight thousand feet. "Take your time," she advised, "Rest and save your breath."

Enid began the precipitous ascent, and Isabel climbed slowly after her, grasping the hiking stick for balance. To her dismay, she was soon huffing. As it was, she found she could only walk for twenty to thirty seconds without stopping. Her legs and feet ached, but the grip shoes made it easier to find purchase on the rocks. She used the stick to propel her forward, a few inches at a time. Before each stair, she caught her breath and waited, calculating where to place her feet before scrambling up the next stair.

Yards above, Enid craned her neck behind and waved. "Half Dome is just ahead!"

Isabel stopped, gasping for oxygen, and wiped sweat from her brows and eyes. She didn't have room to consider anything but the climb, one foot in front of another, guided by the pain in her legs and chest.

When she cleared the last Sub Dome step, she sank to the ground and gazed at the massive shelf of Half Dome itself, sweeping into the sky. Two strands of steel cables, about two and a half feet apart, ran from a series of poles on either side of the shelf. The poles were spaced at rough intervals. Isabel saw pits where James' crew must have tried to install new stakes back in May. She remembered he had said a different crew had come here to finish the job one or two weeks ago. Just in time.

"Here," Enid dug into her knapsack and handed her a pair of leather gloves. "You'll need these to protect your hands."

Way above, a tiny black speck inched up the vertical cliff. "It's a hundred eighty degree angle," Isabel said in alarm.

"It's not as steep as that. You have the strength to do it. I wouldn't have taken you here otherwise, you know. Besides, this is a cakewalk compared to the climbs Charles and I have done with only crevices to grab hold of."

Isabel swallowed.

"One foot forward. That's all we need to do." Enid slipped her hands into a pair of gloves. "It shouldn't take us long now. Another four or five hundred feet up."

Isabel slid her hands into the garden gloves. They were heavy and awkward, but as she edged after Enid onto the worn granite between the cables, gripping the steel for dear life, she was grateful for their protection. Without them, she suspected her palms would be ripped and bloody. Every ten feet, when Enid encountered a wooden slat, she paused until Isabel caught up, and they rested for a few minutes.

Isabel made the mistake of glancing up and gasped at the precipice awaiting them. To her horror, she felt a touch of vertigo and swayed before hastily righting herself.

"Don't look at anything but your feet," Enid warned.

Her upper arms burned with the strain of pulling herself up the cables. Because of the steep incline, this had become a necessity, and her feet dragged helplessly behind like hauled cargo, several inches at a time. After a foolhardy attempt to keep pace with Enid's slim limbs maneuvering up the cliff, she felt her arms shake violently. Exhausted, she stopped on a slat, trying to catch her breath and wanting desperately to cry. She bowed her head, her eyes welling.

Enid's voice was jubilant. "We're here, butterfly! One more step, and we're on the summit of Half Dome!"

Isabel raised her face toward Enid, whom she could barely make out, then lowered it, suddenly dizzy. Marshaling up the last of her energy, she hoisted herself up two more slats, then stumbled and collapsed onto the flat granite surface. She lay spread-eagled, panting.

"Congratulations!" Enid cheered. "You've made it! See, you had the pluck and strength all along." She bent to wipe Isabel's brow and handed her the water canteen. "Easy does it. Just a sip. You're flushed. But when you're able, look at the view. It's absolutely astounding!"

The air was thin, deliciously brisk and gusty. Cautiously, Isabel rose and took a few wobbly steps toward the edge of the gigantic shelf of boulders. The Yosemite Valley, thousands of feet below, was a doll's island of green and silvery blue. Awestruck, Isabel dropped to her knees. Across the valley, a ridge of cliffs peaked into the sky, and below was a smattering of tiny waterfalls, which Enid indicated were the Nevada and Vernal Falls. Humbling to think they had climbed all this way in the space of a day.

"So this is how it feels to be an eagle," Isabel whispered.

Enid nodded. "I always feel like a bird in her highest perch when I climb. At peace."

The Mist Trail, Merced, Yosemite Valley, and swirls of evergreens crystallized into miniature perspective. Two small figures stood on a sheer ledge on the other side of the granite shelf of Half Dome.

"That's the Diving Board," Enid said, crouching beside her. "It's a granite blade on Half Dome's south shoulder, about five hundred feet long, and overhangs Mirror Lake. Charles and I climbed there once from Mirror Lake."

"Without the cables?"

Enid lifted her chin, and her eyes flashed with defiance. "Just our bare hands. Remember, we're crazy daredevils." She gave Isabel a conspiratorial wink. "As Emily Dickinson said: Much madness is divinest sense to a discerning eye; much sense the starkest madness… assent, and you are sane; demur, you're straightway dangerous and handled with a chain." She swooped her hands toward the valley. "It's near impossible to find views like this, or anything truly special, without going against the grain."

"I'd like to climb without ropes someday."

Enid didn't look surprised. "When you're ready, I'll give you a hand."

Isabel bowed her head and whispered, "Audrey, I've made it here for you. God bless you and keep you safe."

She screwed her eyelids shut, even as tears squeezed down the sides of her face. But she had cried enough, and she willed herself to stop. She couldn't see her sister, but she could sense a wisp of her presence in the afternoon sunlight dancing on the cliff in the grand, aerial view of the Yosemite Valley. Up here was as close as she had ever felt to heaven, her heart soaring like a wild thing, pure and holy. Beside her, Enid was silent, head also bowed.

Twining her fingers together, Isabel whispered a prayer for Mother. *Dear God, let her find peace and comfort. Let her find a new job quickly.*

In another two weeks, school would start. Now, thanks to Enid, she didn't have to return home, at least not for good. Of course, she would make sure Mother was all right, and if necessary, she would travel to San Francisco for a brief trip. So long as she had a place at the park to sleep and enough food to fill her belly, she'd gladly seize the chance to guide visitors on nature walks and tend the garden. *Please, God, let me make a home at Yosemite.*

She concentrated on the sensation of her muscles strengthening, growing; the flesh of her legs and torso firming; even her carriage and gait becoming sure and steady. She owed Enid for this and more: guiding her up mountains, teaching her about hundreds of plants and birds, letting her assist with nature and bird walks, preparing primrose tea that eased her eczema.

Isabel peered at the older woman's inquisitive blue eyes, encircled by tiny crows' feet; sun-weathered face; sinewy arms and legs; strong, determined mouth. She had climbed cliffs with her bare hands, stood up for herself against sneering supervisors, developed a garden to inspire tourists, created a plan to preserve the National Parks, and had the quaint habit of naming her favorite plants and animals. Sheltered here, she did the things she loved best, using her body and mind equally.

But as kind, admirable, and accomplished as she was, she chose to forget the suffering folks outside, considered her untainted animal friends to be more deserving of help. And though she was a dear friend, and Isabel finally understood her reasons for helping animals instead of humans, she couldn't, didn't, agree.

Enid sat cross-legged, hands resting on her thighs. More climbers had appeared on the Diving Board, little dolls with uplifted arms. Tourists who came and went, enjoying the beauty of the place before returning to their real lives.

Wind whipped against Isabel's back, and she shuddered. As she drew her knees against her chest and tucked her head, a sudden, sharp comprehension flashed through her. *Yosemite is a rest stop.* She drew a quick breath. She had imagined she was making a life here, but in the end, she had behaved no differently from the tourists passing through, hoping for a brief escape. The fact was, Audrey wasn't here anymore than she was in San Francisco. Isabel's eyes dimmed. Her sister was nowhere.

The thought of this was so painful her chest and belly ached, and she hunched with the weight of it, her heart thudding. All along, she had imagined she was running to their special isle, where she would find evidence of her sister in signs left by Nature, and they would revel in the glory of a wild, achingly beautiful place. But James was right. She had simply run away. She let out a soft mewl, carried swiftly away by the wind.

Another dark thought wormed into her head. As much as she dreaded to admit it, she would have to put her plans on hold. Even if Mother didn't need her help, they needed to talk about Audrey. More than that, they needed to find a way back to each other, if that was still possible. Each of them had suffered since Dad's and Audrey's deaths, but maybe... Isabel felt something hard lodge in her throat. Things might never get fixed between them, but she had to find out. After that, she would decide her next steps.

From the other side of the cliff echoed faint voices, and riding over them, the wind's eerie howl. Isabel blinked back tears. She wasn't sure how much time passed—five, ten, even twenty minutes? A throbbing began in her temples, and she straightened her head and inhaled slowly, determined not to let a migraine overtake her. Her gaze rested on the cliffs and valley below as she thought about the hike down the mountain.

"Are you all right?" Enid's voice sounded far away.

"Yes. It's just being way up here... it's made me think of something."

Enid must have known not to press her, because she didn't reply. Isabel pinched her cheeks, then thumped a fist against her chest. Enid touched her arm and handed her the canteen. As she took a quick swig, she made a vow: She would return to Yosemite when the time was right. She must. It was her decision. Until then, she would preserve it, gloriously boundless and wild, in her mind.

She locked eyes with Enid. Way below, the miniature waterfalls tumbled, and Isabel felt a vast, timeless essence enveloping her on the summit, as if for a moment, she had merged with Nature, and was one of the grand old sentinels of rocks, silent observer to the tragic and magnificent happenings thousands of feet down there. A breeze stirred, and she lifted her chin. Against the clouds, a hawk winged over the rocks, dipping and wheeling as sunlight illuminated its dark feathers.

CHAPTER TWENTY-NINE

James marched through the garden in long strides, Isabel at his elbow. They had been tramping down a circuit of twisting paths for fifteen minutes, unwilling to slow. She circled after him around the stream, past the beds of strawberries and geraniums. The tourists had thinned, since California schools were slated to start in a week, and instead of families, a handful of couples strolled the grounds, bending to sniff flowers.

Isabel stopped in front of the bed of Sierra lupines in the back of the garden and tugged on James' sleeve so he would stop, too.

"I can't help it," she said. "Every time I see a lupine now, I think of Audrey."

He turned a quizzical gaze on her, and she explained what Enid had told her: that the flowers were hardy and resilient, drawing nitrogen from the air and tunneling it into the soil, making the earth more fertile. They could thrive in even the harshest of climates, and most bloomed by spring.

"Enid said they symbolize imagination, happiness, and opportunity."

"That suits Audrey."

"Apparently the Indians brewed the leaves into teas, and they made poultices with the flower to treat nausea and boils." She sighed, stooping to sniff the sweet perfume from the spires of bright purple petals. Just as Enid liked to name her favorite flowers, Isabel had already named the special bunch at her feet after Audrey, though she didn't tell James; he might think she'd gone cuckoo.

But there was something else she had to tell him; she couldn't clear her conscience otherwise. Even if he broke down or yelled at her, it was her only hope of salvaging the friendship they'd once shared.

"James," she began, "I couldn't bring myself to tell you before. But I see how wrong I was."

He looked at her, his face becoming still.

In a quaking voice, she explained how she and Claude had been in a different part of the park when Audrey ran into traffic and was hit by the car. Her words petered out, and she waited, half yearning for him to yell, chastise her, stalk off. Bile rose up her throat.

His mouth crumpled. "Why didn't you tell me earlier?" he said in a pained tone. "*Hell!*"

"I'm sorry... I was scared of how you'd take it." She clasped her waist. "You see, it really is my fault. I understand if you don't forgive me." She stepped away and bent her head.

Tears clotted beneath her lids. She was preparing to go, give him some space. But then she felt his hand on her arm, a gentle pressure. "This doesn't change things. It's not your fault, Izz. You had a right to some privacy with your... sweetheart."

She flinched.

"You didn't know Audrey would wander into the road."

"Her head was always in the clouds. I should have known something like this might happen. She was only nine. I didn't watch her like I should have." *Proof that horrific things happen when girls don't follow the rules.* She felt herself go limp.

He slung an arm around her. "Shh. Don't blame yourself."

"I'm sorry for not telling you sooner."

He was quiet a moment. "Yeah, I thought... we used to tell each other everything."

"At first I was afraid to say it out loud, even to myself. Then by and by, when it seemed too much time had passed, I decided I'd missed my chance. And I was sure you'd disapprove, since we haven't seen eye to eye lately." She looked up at him. "I know that's not an excuse."

He sputtered and coughed. When he finally found his voice, he sounded agitated. "All that arguing has bothered me, too. An awful lot. Listen, I know it's hard to go home when you had your heart set on staying here. But you'll come back someday, Izz."

The midday sunlight beaded onto their arms and faces, blinding in its intensity. But Isabel hardly noticed; this was her last day at Yosemite, the last day with her brother, at least for a little while. She was prepared to stay with Mother anywhere from a week to several months.

"Sooner than you think," she said. "I've got to save up money, though."

She hadn't thought through the logistics of how she'd find a ride back to Yosemite, since asking Claude a second time was out of the question. Truthfully, she had no idea how soon she could scare up enough cash to return by train, or even where she would stay once she returned, though she hoped Enid's offer would remain open. For now, her only plan was to apply to the Field School next summer. The trip to the city was for Mother's sake, to help her get on her feet and try to set things right between them. She walked several paces to a bench overlooking the stream and sat.

James slumped beside her. "I thought about what you said right after you learned Mother's news." He rubbed a palm over his chin.

"What about it?"

"You said I don't know anything about what you want."

She eyed him. "Things are different for girls than men. They always have been."

"After you ran into the woods, I was beside myself with worry. Couldn't for the life of me understand why you were so upset." He sighed. "I went over and over what you said, trying to figure out where you could've gone. Then I pictured myself in your shoes. And if I was told to sink my plans and go back to the city, it would be hard. Real hard."

Isabel put her hand on his, grateful he saw her point of view.

"I think it's swell you want to be a naturalist." James poked her in the ribs. "Who would've guessed the family bookworm would become an outdoorsman? Er, outdoorswoman?"

"Dad was a bookworm, too, and he worked outdoors every day."

"Because he needed the money. But yeah, I think he preferred being outside."

"You prefer it, too."

"Being at this park is like getting a second wind up a hill."

"Yes, exactly!"

James gave her hand a gentle squeeze and let it go.

"I wish we could talk like this every day," Isabel said. It seemed her timing was terrible; just when they'd found their old familiar groove again—the easy back-and-forth conversation—she was leaving. "Dad always helped the underdogs. And... I wanted to talk with you about something I've been thinking of doing to help folks who are down on their luck. It would be a small way of honoring his memory." She recited the Ralph Waldo Emerson quote about serving man and Nature alike. "Before we got Mother's news, I meant to ask you about the Cascades delivery truck and how to take leftover food from the mess hall to hungry people nearby."

"That's a noble idea, Izz." Neither of them said the obvious: It wouldn't happen anytime soon, especially since she hadn't the foggiest idea of what awaited her at home—didn't know how long she'd stay or when she'd be back. Before them, the stream meandered like a magical path to a wondrous land of flowers guarded by mountains. Isabel didn't have a camera, so she would have to imprint it inside her mind, like a photograph to be studied later for its fine detail and mood.

"I should get back and help Enid. You're still coming to supper, aren't you?"

"You kidding? Wouldn't miss it for the world."

•

Since it would be Isabel's last meal at the Michaels' apartment, Enid had insisted on helping with supper—even, she joked, if Isabel relegated her to the role of sous-chef. The other day, Mr. Michael had caught two more fabulous speckled trout, which Isabel now battered and fried, to be accompanied by new potatoes and rolls, while Enid made a fresh spinach, berry, and nut salad.

"We'll sure miss eating like this after you've gone," Enid said with a sigh. "Charlie will hate going back to our boring soups."

"You'll have to convince him to go fishing more often."

"If only it were that simple. I don't have your knack for adding the right ingredients. Never liked cooking, either, truth be known."

"I think food cooked on a campfire would taste even better." Isabel had already decided that after she returned to Yosemite, she would go on an overnight camping trip.

"It does indeed! One year after the mad summer rush, we rode burros into the high country with friends. The grasses in the meadows had gone to seed, but there were some late-blooming asters and goldenrod. We made our base camp past Merced Lake." Enid leaned toward Isabel. "And because Charlie and I weren't alone, and the others wanted hearty meals, we ate unusually well. Beef steak roasted on a willow stick, bread and butter, rice and dried figs with tea and coffee. Plus a pair of trout." She smiled at the memory.

Since the kitchen table was tiny, they arranged the dishes of fried trout, potatoes, rolls, and salad on the counter, cafeteria-style. Fifteen minutes later, Mr. Michael and James arrived together. It was the first time the four of them had sat down and shared a meal. Bittersweet.

"This beats the food at Cascades," James said, forking a bite of trout. "Hands down."

Enid nodded at Isabel. "Thanks to your sister."

"Aw, was this your doing, Izz? I can't believe it." He laid a hand on his heart in mock disbelief, and she gave his arm a playful punch.

Enid asked him about the goings-on at Cascades camp.

"Did Izz tell you? The crew finished up the work on the stairway at Half Dome a week or two before your hike."

"Oh my. Come to think, the wooden steps looked new. What lucky timing. Were you with that crew, by chance?"

"No, ma'am, not in August. But I was with the company that started the work in May until a bad storm blew in and we had to postpone it."

"Yes, I remember! Rain, hail, and snow. May's unpredictable. That's why Charlie and I prefer the fall." She described how one October, they had explored the ice cone at the foot of the Upper Yosemite Falls, which had dried out. To reach the base of Pulpit Rock, they had followed a deer trail, where they saw the perfect round tracks of a mountain lion.

Isabel and James listened, astonished, as Enid described how Charles had scrambled up the ledge from Pulpit Rock and traversed back across the upper fall's sheer wall. Against all odds, he had arrived at the waterfall's central course.

Despite his usual reticence, Mr. Michael said, "I called it the blue balcony, since it was so sheer and shiny. But it had plumb dried up. Not a lick of water. It gave me the strangest feeling, because from the valley floor, it didn't look like it was possible to stand in the middle of the falls."

Enid relayed how he had dropped the end of a string to where she waited on a granite slab below. After he cut the string, they measured it at four hundred feet above the pool at the base of the falls—a true marvel. "When we looked up one last time, we wondered how on earth a human being could ever have made it all the way up there."

Isabel's eyes went wide, and she saw that her brother was equally impressed.

"Fact, I started wondering whether I had dreamed the whole thing up," Mr. Michael said, and they broke into chuckles.

James said, "Fellow at camp says you two are the best climbers at Yosemite, bar none. I can sure see why."

Isabel told him, "And they don't use fancy techniques or ropes. Just their bare hands." Her brother looked suitably awed. *See what I told you*, she wanted to crow. *Mrs. Michael is amazing in her own right, never mind being the park's first female ranger-naturalist.*

"But unfortunately, Mr. Michael can't climb any longer," Enid was saying, and Isabel understood she was referring to his heart troubles. "In fact, his doctor has advised him to retire from the post office."

Isabel looked at Mr. Michael in surprise, uncertain what to say. This, surely, was recent news. "Does this mean you'll leave the park?" she asked.

"We've talked it over, and in the winter we'll return to Pasadena."

"Oh no!" Isabel burst out before she could stop herself. Enid would dread returning to a town that didn't understand her. And with a sudden sinking feeling, Isabel realized this also meant she couldn't stay with the Michaels if and when she returned to Yosemite.

Noticing her crestfallen expression, Enid said, "But providing Chief Thomson agrees, and Mr. Harwell doesn't prevent me, I plan to come back every summer as a ranger-naturalist."

"I'm glad of that."

"Course we can't stay in this apartment after Charlie leaves the post office. But I'm certain we'll be assigned a cabin. That's what they've done for the other naturalists." She turned to Mr. Michael with an impish look. "What fun it'll be to live simply again, won't it, Charlie?" He grinned back. Isabel suspected the cabin wouldn't have room for more than two, then chastised herself for her selfish concern.

After supper, Enid put the polka record on the phonograph, and she and Mr. Michael danced a small, careful jig as James and Isabel watched, clapping. When Mr. Michael sat down, James stepped forward, grabbed Enid's hands, then galloped her across the room, breaking only to twirl her. She chirped with laughter. She must have told him to dance with Isabel next, because before Isabel knew it, James was spinning her in a circle while the Michaels clapped. When he released her, she joined Enid against the wall, breathless and giggling.

After a dessert of berries and honey, James thanked the Michaels for a wonderful evening and wished them well. Isabel walked with him to the landing by the post office stairs. Behind the fringe of trees, the moon cast a silvery sheen on the stone façade of the building.

"I'll miss you something awful," she said, clinging to him.

He stroked her hair. "Me, too. But you're a trooper, Izz, and anyhow, it won't be long before I get leave to come home. Just another couple of months."

"I'll probably be back at Yosemite by then."

He angled his head, skeptical.

"Or…" she seized his hands, "If I'm not, we can return to Yosemite together after your visit home." The perfect solution. She waited for her brother to agree, but he looked away, and she felt a smidgen of resentment. "You don't want me to come back."

"That's not it. It's just that you might decide it's too soon. I thought you were going to wait and see, get Mother settled. Could be a while before she finds another position."

The prospect of returning to the mildewy flat and cold city overflowing with desperate people sent a shudder down the length of her spine. But she suppressed the urge to argue. She dared not part from him on bad terms, not after all this, after they'd come together and made a truce.

James said, "Listen, write me, let me know how you and Mother are getting on. Tell me right away if you need more cash."

"Yes, all right, though we'll be frugal." *Until Mother finds a new job.* Briefly her mind wandered to Mr. McGilligan and whether he felt sore that she'd left him high and dry. Would he let her work part time again for a few weeks? But by now, surely, he had found a replacement.

"Here, I almost forgot." James dug into his pocket and handed her a small envelope with the fare he'd promised for her return to the city.

She took it dully, and he hugged her again. Her eyes prickled.

He kissed her forehead, then drew back slowly. Isabel tried to keep her face impassive, but she couldn't help it; her lips wobbled. She dreaded saying goodbye. He must have felt the same, because he pivoted and descended the stairs.

She watched him, stung and adrift, but then his voice echoed up to the landing. "When I see you next, have a big feast ready for me. Food, music, balloons, the works. I'll expect nothing less, sis."

"You bet!" she called back. She tittered until her sides ached, and then, to her dismay, tears flooded down her cheeks.

CHAPTER THIRTY

As the delivery truck wound its way out of Yosemite Valley through the spirals of the Sierra Nevadas, Isabel mashed a fist against her eyes, determined not to cry. In her lap, she held a bag of cheese sandwiches, nuts, and berries that Enid had packed. James had scraped together a little over four dollars for her passage: fifty cents for the driver to drop her at the Atchison Topeka Santa Fe depot in Merced and three dollars and change for a train ticket to San Francisco. Along with the lone dollar she still had from when she first arrived, she would have enough cash to catch a streetcar from the train station to the Tenderloin.

Earlier that morning, as Isabel bid the Michaels farewell, Enid had given her the Muir book on Yosemite she had borrowed, along with a small packet of lupine seeds.

"Plant them so they'll remind you of Yosemite," she had said, closing Isabel's fingers around the packet.

Isabel had promised she would, though she wondered where and when. As she hugged Enid, her chin trembled. She'd never dreamed this woman would become her closest friend. More than that, she regarded Enid as family—someone who symbolized comfort and home, who would unconditionally support her, root for her to achieve her dreams, welcome her back after long absences.

"I've been meaning to tell you," Enid had said, "I did some digging into the Field School admissions requirements. Turns out they expect applicants to graduate from high school and finish at least two years of college classes or the equivalent." She must have noticed Isabel's distress, because she had touched her arm and murmured, "For now, don't worry about anything besides your mother. You'll be back here before you know it."

Acid had seared up Isabel's throat. The chances for a woman to gain admission to the Field School were low to begin with; she'd never buck the odds without meeting the school's requirements. Two more years before finishing high school. And two years of college? The prospect of waiting another four years and scaring up cash for college courses made her weary. In the end, it was too disheartening to contemplate, so she had thrust it from her mind.

At the Merced depot, she took a window seat in the late morning train bound for San Francisco. While the Pullman cars chugged out of the station, she glued her face to the glass. Despite her complicated emotions about returning to the city, she thrilled as the train streaked through open country between towns, slashing past farms, cattle and crops in a whir of green, gold, and brown patterns. After several hours, she dozed, then started awake when the conductor boomed their arrival in San Francisco.

It was after dusk, past eight o'clock. A band of hoboes huddled on boxes and blankets in the rail yard, on the outskirts of the Embarcadero. Salt air and the stink of beached sea creatures wafted from the wharf, and a fog horn howled. Amidst the shouts from the docks, Isabel trudged to the stop she and Audrey used to take from school. An old man in a slouch hat and a pair of ragged suspenders and stained trousers shuffled down the street. He cradled a paper bag against his chest and drew it to his lips. Another drunkard, down on his luck. As Isabel passed him, he disappeared into an alley. This is what she'd longed to escape—the squalid, crowded city, folks wretched with hunger and despair.

A column of automobiles and two trolleys piled onto the loop. It wasn't until she was on the streetcar, hurtling past saloons and storefronts, that she let herself wonder how Mother would receive her. Her chest wilted; her throat felt thick and raw. There hadn't been time to let Mother know she was coming.

At the cracked stoop of their building, Isabel waited a few beats, then rapped on the door. The paint was peeling, something she hadn't noticed before. For several moments, she stood with her fist pressed against the corrugated tin. The curtains were drawn, the window dark. Maybe Mother was abed, and she would have to hunker overnight with a neighbor. She tapped her knuckles against the door again, and a light flicked on.

"Just a minute," Mother's voice called. "Who is it?"

Isabel straightened, swallowed hard. "It's me, Mother."

Plodding, jerky footsteps and a thumping sound, then the door flew open. "Isabel?" Mother's pink bathrobe hung open around her waist, and she grasped a wooden cane. Her face registered a mixture of shock and elation.

Isabel swayed, suddenly exhausted.

The cane clattered to the floor, and Mother seized Isabel by the shoulders. "Thank God you're home!"

"Careful, Mother, let me help so you don't trip." She stepped into the flat and held Mother's arm, guiding her to the couch. The cane alarmed her; she'd had no inkling that Mother's back was this bad. After settling Mother against the cushion, she retrieved the cane and stood it on the end of the couch, then sat beside her. The familiar moldy scent rushed up her nostrils, and she peered at the mildewed water stains on the ceiling.

"Darned back doesn't let me get around the way I want to, but at least I can do this." Mother reached for Isabel, gathering her against her chest. After a few minutes, she held her away, running her gaze from Isabel's head to the hem of her dress. "You look different somehow. I can't put my finger on it."

"Tanner?" Isabel forced a small smile.

"That, and also stronger. Like you've built up muscle."

"I have."

"I suppose traipsing around parks will do that," Mother clucked, quirking her lips.

Cigarette smoke lingered, but the flat was tidy: counters and table wiped clean; no dirty dishes in the sink; Mother's coat hanging by the door; her brogans lined against the wall. Isabel sank her head against the sofa, her eyelids drooping. It had only been two months since she'd left, but the apartment no longer felt familiar, certainly not inviting. She longed to listen to a soothing record on the phonograph, pick up a book, watch a bird flit onto the sill, blanket herself with the comforting hum of the Michaels' voices.

"Let me fix you tea and something to eat," Mother said with a hint of eagerness, as though she had an important guest.

"Stay put. I'll make us some tea." Isabel heaved herself off the sofa and pulled down mugs and the tea canister from the cupboard.

"There's bread and a tad of butter in the icebox you can set out, too."

The kettle perked and whistled on the stove. Isabel handed Mother a steaming mug, then placed a plate of bread on the floor and sat beside her with her own cup.

"You must be bone tired," Mother said.

"More hungry than tired." She reached into her knapsack to remove the remaining sandwich Enid had packed.

"Eat up."

Isabel took a bite of the sandwich. "I'm awfully sorry about what happened. I can't understand why they fired you. You're a hard worker."

"It was one thing after another." Mother sighed. "Over the summer, my boss accused me of being slow and leaving rooms untidy. Claimed the teenagers cleaned up faster and better. He picked on me for little things—leaving dust motes on the baseboards or not making perfect hospital corners with the bed sheets. Early August, he told me not to bother coming in the next day. Said I'd been canned."

"Oh, Mother. I'm sorry. And your back..."

"Even before they fired me, it hurt like the devil. Probably from stooping around so much. Now it flares and goes stiff. Super saw me limping and loaned me this cane." She shifted against the sofa, as if the reminder had triggered shooting pain. "One good thing about being out a job is maybe it'll have time to heal." Her lips drew down into her familiar grimace. "But enough about me and that godawful hotel."

She scrutinized Isabel's face. "We don't have to talk tonight if you're too tired and want to go to bed. But when you feel up for it, I want to hear all about Yosemite and the ranger woman who took you in. Also everything about James."

Isabel met Mother's eyes. The sandwich hovered in her hand. She detected in Mother a barely restrained eagerness. Her lips twitched; her eyes glinted; yet she sat still, hands tucked in her lap, watching Isabel with a solicitousness normally reserved for special visitors.

Isabel laid down the sandwich and took a breath. She began with her arrival at the Cascades camp, meeting the Michaels, the garden and nature hikes, typing Enid's articles, and finally the climb up Half Dome. Then she talked about James and his work with the CCC, their meetings in the garden, how he had helped her travel home.

Mother waited until she finished speaking. "You're sure lucky this woman and her husband let you stay with them."

"She's truly remarkable. She's the first and only female ranger-naturalist at Yosemite, and you wouldn't believe what she has to put up with to do her job. Her supervisor treats her terribly unfairly, yet she takes it in stride and does so many incredible things, like climbing up mountains and writing and illustrating her own articles..." Isabel stopped short when Mother's jaw tightened. Maybe she had overdone her praise. After all, instead of taking her own supervisor's nonsense in stride, Mother had raged at having her hours at the hotel cut and hadn't managed to hold onto her job.

"You say she doesn't have children. That's likely her secret for doing so much."

Isabel drew back. Something caught in her throat like a caked-over clump of dough, and she broke into a spurt of jagged coughs. Mother had confirmed what she herself had long suspected. Corralling her voice, she said, "So was it easier without us underfoot?"

A stricken look slithered across Mother's face, and she pressed a fist against her mouth. Isabel's heart raced, but she resisted the urge to pace away.

"No!" Mother's fingers curled around Isabel's wrist. "God, no!" Then she was weeping into her hands—loud, bleating sobs, her shoulders heaving. Slowly, tentatively, Isabel laid a hand on her back.

It took several minutes for Mother's sobs to subside. Between sniffles, she said, "That came out wrong. I never meant you children tied me down—just the opposite. It's been much harder with no one here to help me out."

It was precisely this—her mother's neediness, her dependence on Isabel as a helpmeet, and above all her inability to change her routine or picture how things might be different, that made her Enid's polar opposite. Isabel swallowed and swept a pointed glance around the flat, which looked neater than it had in months.

As if reading her thoughts, Mother said, "I cleaned to keep busy. Otherwise, that would have been the end." She snapped her fingers.

Isabel winced, and Mother daubed at her eyes. "It's just... when I heard all the things that woman does and how *remarkable* she is, something inside me cracked."

Isabel scanned Mother's face, struggling for the right words. Clearly she felt jealous. "Listen, Mother, the only reason she can do those things is because she lives in a special place. She'd never have the opportunities outside Yosemite. She's lucky, is all." *Tucked away, in her own beautiful, private isle.* She touched Mother's wrist. "I'd like you to meet her someday."

"Well. I'm glad you got to spend the summer with her. It was awful kind of her to take you in." Mother's voice grew hoarse. "But I wish..." Her head drooped.

"What is it you wish?"

"Nothing. Just... I needed you far more than she did."

"To help with chores, you mean," Isabel said tightly.

"Not just chores... your company. "I wish you'd been *here*." Isabel lowered her face, unable to think of a response. Mother sought her eyes. "I know it's my fault you left. I let my temper get the better of me these last few months. Not surprising you turned to this Mrs. Michael."

"I didn't turn to her."

"It's all right. I'm glad she was there for you. If I was in your shoes, I'd have done the same."

"I only wanted to see James. I met Mrs. Michael by coincidence."

In a small voice, Mother said, "It wasn't any easier being alone, even before I lost my job." She hooked her gaze into Isabel's. "I've had a lot of time to think. And I've realized I was awful hard on you. All the cooking and cleaning you did. And on top of that you watched Audrey and went to school and worked at McGilligan's. It was too much for a teenage girl."

"Yes," Isabel said. It was a relief to have it out between them, Mother's acknowledgment of the burden she had shouldered.

"And that was my fault." Mother blew her nose on a napkin. "With so much time on my hands, I see I've made mistakes. When I think back on how things were just nine months ago, back in December..." From down the street drifted barks of laughter and the screech of tires.

Isabel's head sagged against the couch. "I miss Dad and Audrey so."

"I do, too." Mother stifled a cry. She said something more, but Isabel's eyes misted over, and before she could stop, she was weeping silently.

She felt Mother's arms around her, stroking her hair, her neck. "I've missed you and James, too. More than you know."

Bit by bit, Isabel leaned into Mother's chest, sank her head against Mother's shoulder. It was the first time Mother had held or comforted her since Dad's death. She was struck by a distant memory of running home in tears from the playground after falling from a tree and banging her forehead. Mother had gathered her onto her lap and rocked her. As the minutes had ticked by, the discomfort of her bruises and scrapes had melted away, and she had imagined herself snuggling in a warm, safe cocoon.

Mother whispered, "I hope you'll forgive me."

Isabel gulped, burrowing herself in the sensation of Mother's fingers brushing her hair. She had wanted to hear those words for months, yet now that she had, they stung, since she was the one who should ask forgiveness.

"There's nothing to forgive."

"Like I said, it was unfair of me to expect so much of you. I'm sorry."

"Oh, Mother." Now was the time to make her own confession and reveal her poor judgment on that terrible day. It would give her a bit of breathing space, like the loosening of a rope round her neck. But it would undo Mother. After all, even a scant reference to Enid had upset her. How would she react if she knew Isabel was responsible for Audrey's death? Too much to lose. And just when Mother had given signs of returning to her old self.

Mother spoke into Isabel's ear, her voice soft and low. "I thought you'd left for good, and if you never returned, I'd deserve it."

Isabel snuggled closer. She started to apologize for taking three dollars from the jam jar, not saying goodbye, going away. But now that she was here with Mother in the flesh, those transgressions seemed less important.

"I'm awful glad you came back." *Would Mother still be if she knew the truth?*

"So am I." Isabel stuffed the ugly secret down into a deep recess of mind, where she willed it to lie inert.

CHAPTER THIRTY-ONE

Mother rose and limped heavily to the dresser, like a woman well over sixty. Isabel was shocked by how swiftly her back had worsened during these last few months, effectively reducing her to a hobble. At the bureau, Mother selected a plain brown dress and removed her nightgown. Without a brassiere, her breasts sagged like deflated balloons. The folds of her waist hung in flabs, and her legs were thick and swollen.

At least the room was the same: trundle mattress on the floor with faded cotton sheet and blanket, bureau with rickety drawers, tiny closet. Last night, when Isabel had pulled the sheet to her chin, she had detected no trace of Audrey—just the flat's mildewy odor. An undeniable disappointment.

She sat up. "Morning."

Mother turned with a smile and echoed the greeting, her voice floating out in the same gentle lilt she had used years ago. "I'll put on a kettle for tea," she said, then grabbed her cane and hobbled into the kitchen.

Isabel stood still for a moment, letting the weight of all the things that needed to be done sink in. She would have to sit down with Mother, figure out what help she needed and what kind of work she might reasonably find. And then she would have to plan her own next steps. Based on Enid's findings about the Field School admission requirements, she had no choice but to finish high school.

But completing two years of college classes or the equivalent... the thought sucked her breath away. She might as well have climbed to the top of a peak, only to discover it was an optical illusion; the real summit was still miles up. With rising anxiety, she cast about for solutions. Maybe Enid would vouch that her training at Yosemite satisfied the requirement. After all, Enid herself didn't have a college degree. Or if Isabel passed the Field School botany and zoology exams, perhaps the school would waive the college requirement. But if not... she had no cash for classes, and it seemed unlikely she'd have enough savings in two years, either.

As a wave of panic surged over her, she sat down heavily on Mother's bed and closed her eyes. *Stop, observe, think.* With effort, she took a steadying breath. *One step at a time.* Next week, she would resume classes at her old school. Whether she transferred later to a high school near Yosemite—maybe Mariposa or Merced—depended on Mother. Anything could happen, she reasoned; there was plenty of time. A tiny kernel stirred inside her.

Mother bent over the stove, frying eggs. She pointed her chin at the counter. "There's a little more bread for toast."

"Sit down, Mother. I'll finish." Isabel took the spatula from her. Within minutes, she had flipped the eggs, fried the bread, poured coffee, and carried the platter of food to the table.

At first, neither spoke as they dug into their breakfast. Isabel considered broaching the question of the help Mother would need, but before she had a chance, Mother leaned toward her.

"How long are you staying... are you home for good?" She sounded nervous, as though she were afraid of Isabel's answer. Her fork hovered over her mouth.

Isabel hesitated. "As long as you need me."

"I wasn't sure if you'd want to go back. You kept saying it's a lovely park, and you seemed to like it plenty." She stuttered on the last syllable.

"Yes, it *is* lovely. And someday... I do want to return and train as a ranger." The words flew out before she considered them.

"A *ranger*?"

"Yes, a ranger-naturalist, like Mrs. Michael."

From somewhere in the building, a pipe whined. Mother pushed her plate away, her brow puckering, and Isabel regretted spilling it out, not thinking through the right way to say it. Worse, she shouldn't have revealed her plans so soon, just when she and Mother were finding their footing.

"You can't be serious! What is it about this Mrs. Michael?" A dark flame flashed behind Mother's eyes.

Isabel fought an urge to answer. If Mother were more open-minded, she could explain how she intended to choose a completely different life from the pinched-faced people in this cold, dirty city. Funny how she wanted desperately for Mother to understand.

"It's not about her," she began, but stopped at the suspicious look on Mother's face. Now wasn't the time; everything between them was too tenuous, the bindings unsecured. "Anyhow, it's nothing more than a pipe dream," she said instead, and tugged her hands, which were shaking slightly, into her lap. But as she spoke, she knew she hadn't told a white lie to appease Mother; it was the truth. She had no concrete plans, and the tentative ones she'd made at Yosemite were slipping away. To change the subject, she said, "Mother, have you thought about looking for another position?"

A sigh. "With this sore back, I won't be much use at any job that makes me stoop and kneel."

Isabel swallowed a piece of toast and glanced out the window. Mother's bad back ruled out most domestic jobs. But surely there were other possibilities—clerical work, factories.

"Puts me right back where I started."

"Maybe... what about applying to a textile shop? At least you could sit, and you're a dream at sewing." Isabel drilled her eyes into Mother's. "I think it could work if we can find a way in for you."

Mother gave a little snort. "That'll be the day."

Isabel wished she would muster a little optimism. "Can't hurt to try. I'll look through the classifieds ..."

Mother waved a hand toward a pile of yellowed papers in the corner. "Have at it."

"And I'll take care of things around here so you don't have to worry about taking time out for interviews."

"School starts in a week."

"I know."

"Your father always wanted you kids to finish high school, since he never had the chance. You've got to go to class."

"I will." It didn't mean she had to *finish* school in San Francisco. "Meanwhile, I'll talk with Mr. McGilligan to see if I might get my old job back."

"I saw him once or twice after you left. To his credit, he never said one bad thing against you, even after you skipped town without a word."

"I didn't say goodbye to you, either. I'm sorry."

Mother waved a hand. "Water under the bridge."

Isabel chewed her lower lip, uneasy. That she and Mother had agreed to give it a go should have been enough. But the threads between them were gossamer-thin, strung together on false pretenses. She couldn't shake her fear that if Mother learned the truth about Audrey's death, those loose ends would unravel for good.

• • •

Hands stuffed in her old cardigan, Isabel hurried down Turk toward Market. The morning fog had dissipated, but the air remained cold and clammy. At the stoplight, a streetcar with cowcatcher clanged its bell. On the loop behind it, a row of automobiles and two other trolleys had piled up. Isabel had left the flat too late, during rush hour. A crowd of dockworkers and shop clerks swarmed around her, their shoulders hunched with impatience, faces downcast. City folks didn't have time to linger, let alone observe; they barreled from one point to the next.

As she entered the neighborhood of shops by the Embarcadero, a stray cat slunk past her into an alley, its tail tucked between its legs. It vanished into the debris of rusted cans and broken glass. Earlier that day, she had asked Mother whether Mr. Whiskers had ever returned, already knowing the answer.

At the door to the grocery, she paused for a moment, then pushed through the door. Mr. McGilligan was ringing up a woman at the register. A cloche hat sat lopsided on her head. Isabel glanced around the store but didn't see any helpers. As Mr. McGilligan cracked a joke about fog and pea soup, the woman brayed with laughter. She took her package and turned, noticing Isabel, and fixed her with a look of disdain.

Isabel's hands floated to the weeping eczema pocks on her cheeks and throat, which had begun to flare again, now that she no longer had the benefit of Enid's primrose tea. She held the woman's gaze, not flinching. The woman's painted red mouth fell open, revealing a maw of stained, crooked teeth.

Mr. McGilligan said smoothly, "Will that be all, Mrs. Donovan?"

Nostrils flaring, she turned to the grocer. "Indeed, for now. But I'll be back for flour on Thursday. So make sure you've got at least a pound for me, hear?"

"Yes, yes, up to here till we're drowning in it." He flashed a finger across his neck.

She tittered. "Aren't you a card, Mr. McGilligan?" She exited the shop, heels clicking.

Mr. McGilligan hooked a finger through his suspenders, his eyes brightening. "Isabel! Didn't think you'd darken the door again."

"I'm sorry for leaving without letting you know."

"Your mother said you went to Yosemite."

"Yes, but that wasn't an excuse for not telling you first." She didn't elaborate, and he didn't pry. He simply stood against the register, hands folded over the apron around his waist. Isabel met his eyes. "I'll understand if you don't want to hire me again. But I thought I'd ask. In case you haven't already found a replacement, I'm willing to work any hours you need..."

Mr. McGilligan cleared his throat. "I've got another helper. Didn't know if or when you were coming back..."

Isabel nodded. "I understand." It had been a long shot.

After an awkward silence, he asked her what she had done at Yosemite, and she described the park, the garden, Enid, James. Her voice sounded like someone else's—steady and brisk, as though she were recounting a tale secondhand. Mr. McGilligan looked interested and expressed surprise that Yosemite had a female ranger-naturalist.

When a woman and her young son entered the shop, Isabel turned to go.

"Come back in another few weeks," Mr. McGilligan said. "I can't promise anything, but there's a chance Billy will work fewer hours once the school year gets underway. Can't hurt to check in if you haven't found anything else by then."

Isabel thanked him and left. He was simply being polite by not shutting down her hopes completely. She and Mother could get by without a few extra dimes a week. What worried her more was that her chances of returning to Yosemite were rapidly dissolving; she had no savings and no income to squirrel away. Her plans were good as sunk. Anyhow, it was no use; she didn't deserve to live anywhere pretty, outside San Francisco. A raw, soggy wind swished through her lungs. Lowering her eyes, she tramped down the street.

At the corner, a man was selling roasted sweet potatoes, two for a nickel. Behind him slouched a line of men at a soup kitchen. Their heads were bowed, as though they were ashamed of being spotted by anyone they knew. At the back of the line, a slip of a woman in a man's overcoat gripped the hands of two frail-looking children. All three were barefoot and dirty. Something in Isabel's chest squeezed hard, and she broke into a cough. When she finally stopped and looked up again, she could no longer see the family. She hoped with all her might the food wouldn't run out by the time they reached the front of the line.

•   •   •

"Look, Mother." Isabel pointed to an advertisement she had found in the *San Francisco Chronicle* for a textile worker. "You should apply. You could do this in your sleep."

Mother lifted her head from a sock she was darning and scanned the page.

"What do you think?" Isabel pressed.

A one-shouldered shrug. "Why not?"

Isabel allowed herself a tiny bubble of hope. At least Mother had applied to half a dozen positions in the last three days, an improvement over her record of zero before Isabel's arrival, even though she had yet to receive an invitation to interview.

"See, just by being here you've done me a world of good. I didn't have the energy to hunt for a job on my own. Too overwhelming." Mother squinted as she rethreaded the needle.

"No doubt something's bound to work out." Even to her own ears, Isabel sounded formal. She and Mother had begun addressing each other with polite caution, like guests at a party, as though the other would bolt at the slightest hint of conflict. By mutual, tacit agreement, they didn't speak of Audrey. If Isabel's secret wriggled out, it would undoubtedly upend the shaky seesaw between them.

Mother had taken Isabel's news of Mr. McGilligan's rejection stoically, had urged her to concentrate on school, which began tomorrow. Besides, she'd said, they could get by on what James sent home for a few months if they had to. Isabel had forced a reassuring smile.

But now, as she sat at the table, poring through the classifieds, she knew something wasn't right. Though she was helping Mother get back on her feet and find a job, she herself was back to where she'd started months before. *Adrift. Helpless.* Further than ever from having a plan or the means to return to Yosemite, not that she deserved to. In dismay, she felt the walls of the flat closing around her again, one day stacked upon another, shapeless and gray.

CHAPTER THIRTY-TWO

To Isabel's surprise, the dingy yellow hallways and musty classrooms with their chalkboards and scratched-up desks were an odd comfort. Classmates who had heard the news about Audrey hugged her and clasped her hands between classes, whispered their condolences, extended invitations to their homes.

In history, as she took a seat, Isabel spied Claude on the other side of the room, talking with another boy. Her heart gave a little stutter, and she looked down at her notebook. When she glanced up again, he was watching her, and she gave him a quick, furtive wave. He raised a hand in reply, concern rippling over his face. After class, she considered catching up with him so she could thank him for driving her to Yosemite, but he was chatting with a group of boys. And after everything she had put him through, she suspected he wasn't overly eager to talk with her.

When school let out, she trudged down the sidewalk. Taking the trolley was a luxury she couldn't afford as long as she and Mother remained unemployed. Besides, the hour and a half walk back to the Tenderloin amounted to another penance to pay.

A heaviness crept up her chest. She couldn't help but think she'd gone backward to that awful space between Audrey's death and her escape to Yosemite. Sure, it wasn't as bad as that, now that she and Mother had rekindled relations. But she had begun to suspect they were playing a game of charades, imitating warmth that had once come naturally.

Just that morning, Mother had inquired delicately, as though Isabel were a guest at the Sir Francis Drake, "When will you want supper? Right when you get home?" Isabel had assured her not to worry; she would fix it herself. At first Mother had looked ready to protest, but then she had compressed her lips and nodded slowly. "Whatever you like." Isabel was starting to doubt they'd ever recover the ease they'd had months ago. Worse, any reference to Audrey had become taboo. They didn't talk about her at all. And somehow that amounted to the most egregious of betrayals.

As she slogged past blocks of secondhand stores, diners, and bars, it occurred to her she shouldn't have been walking this route alone. Audrey should have been with her, returning home on the first day of school. Her sister would have chattered about her teacher and friends and volleyed questions, her eyes lively and glowing, hands fluttering. At the corner, automobiles stalled, and someone blasted a horn.

When Isabel neared the flat, the remaining vestige of her energy siphoned away, and a sludge-like lethargy oozed into her veins. Head spinning, she stumbled up the stairs to their stoop.

Mother looked up from the table, where she had spread the classifieds. "How was the first day of school?" When Isabel didn't immediately respond, she said, "I found a couple other openings that might work." A smile ghosted across her lips.

Isabel dropped her knapsack by the door and crossed to the table. "I'm glad." But even to herself, her voice sounded flat, unconvincing. She planted a kiss on Mother's cheek and slid into a chair.

"Got so carried away looking at ads that I haven't started on supper."

"That's all right. There's no rush."

Mother peered at her. "Anything wrong?"

"No, everything's fine. School was fine..." She crossed to the sink and poured herself a glass, sensing Mother watching her. Standing, she gulped down the water.

"Bet you got real thirsty walking home and felt faint?"

Isabel ran her tongue over her teeth, wiped the back of her hand against her mouth. A dim ache had entered her temples. "Yes." She looked away. "I guess that must've been it."

"Why don't you sit down. You look a tad peaked."

She slumped next to Mother.

"Are you hungry? I'll warm up the chowder soup." Mother made to rise.

"No, no. Please don't."

Mother looked baffled. "What's wrong?"

Something sharp and stinging clawed against her skull, trying to escape. "It's nothing. It's just... I'm not hungry." She looked down, despising herself for the white lie. "Anyhow, there's no need for you to go to trouble. I'll make supper by and by."

"Not if you're sick, you can't."

"I'm not sick. I'm... tired." Isabel pressed a palm against her forehead. How much longer could she continue hiding behind a spaghetti pie of fibs? Before she could stop herself, she blurted, "Audrey should have been with me on the way home."

Mother flinched, her eyes registering a cocktail of surprise and pain. "I was thinking about that, too," she said in a low voice.

Isabel wheezed, and her fingers flew instinctively to her throat. In that instant, the rope around her neck was so palpable she imagined prying it off. She couldn't go on like this; it was too painful. More than that, it was impossible. If there was any hope for a real relationship with Mother, she had to lay bare the truth. She recalled the clarity of her resolve on the summit of Half Dome. *Now or never.*

Clearing her throat, she met Mother's eyes. "There's something I have to tell you. About Audrey."

A flash of fear in Mother's face. "What do you mean?"

Isabel cast about for the right words. "I did a bad job looking after her."

"You did a fine job. The best you could. Better than I did." Mother's eyes softened. She reached over and patted Isabel's shoulder.

Isabel choked out, "No, Mother. It's my fault she ran into the street."

"No one could stop Audrey when she was daydreaming. Not a soul could have prevented her from running headlong into that godawful automobile."

Isabel's voice grew louder. "No. You don't understand." She closed her eyes. "I was with a boy. Claude. On the other side of the park. I left Audrey by herself near the swings. I told her to… to look for rocks."

Mother's grip on Isabel's shoulders loosened, but Isabel plunged ahead. "I don't know how long I left her. Maybe forty-five minutes or an hour. Remember how it was raining and foggy that day? And then… and then…" she stopped, unable to continue. Mother knew the rest, anyhow.

Mother let go of her shoulder. "Oh, Isabel!" She sounded horrified.

A shock of cold blasted through her limbs. Let Mother scream, send her away. It was fair punishment. She would endure it. But something worse happened. Mother scraped back the chair and hobbled into the bedroom, shutting the door. Behind the wall came a broken, sputtering sound, like a moan strangled beneath a pillow.

"Oh God," Isabel cried. This was it, then. She had destroyed the fragile binding, launched them both back to that unbearable time before she'd fled San Francisco. Placed her bets and lost. The familiar black ocean engulfed her. Waves crashed through her skull and crowded the edges of her vision, and a gasp stuck in her throat. It wouldn't, couldn't release. She buried her face on the table.

Suddenly, tiny dots of light swarmed before her eyes, and a sharp, suffocating nausea surged up her stomach. Her temples throbbed as if a leaden fist had slugged her head, hard. Gradually, she grew aware of a sickening drumbeat between her ears. *A migraine*. The thought was dim, unformed.

·   ·   ·

"Isabel, Isabel?" A hand pressed the back of her head.

She moaned.

"Stay there, don't move."

Somehow, in fits and starts, she was guided, stumbling, to the sofa, a hand bracing her back. Maybe she vomited, or maybe she lay, spent and sweaty; she wasn't sure. The giant black ocean seized her and spit her out like foam. When she woke — minutes or hours later? — it was pitch black, but something — someone — stirred on the floor beside her.

"Mother?" Her voice emerged in a high, childlike quaver.

"I'm here, honey."

"Mother, you can't sleep on the floor like that. Your back...."

"Don't worry about me. You're the one who took sick. God only knows what you've come down with. I hope to Jesus it isn't scarlet fever..."

"It's a migraine. I had one when I first arrived at Yosemite."

"Wait a minute." A drawer slid open and closed, followed by bangs and taps as Mother riffled through the medicine cabinet in the bathroom.

Before Isabel could protest, Mother flicked on the lamp by the couch and thrust a glass of water and a pill into her hands. "Here. It's an aspirin tablet." Isabel swallowed obediently.

Mother knelt by the sofa. "How do you feel?"

"I think it's passing."

Mother put a cool hand on Isabel's cheek, then smoothed sweaty tendrils of hair away from her forehead. "You scared me something awful. Can't say I ever had a migraine, but my oldest sister used to get them." Her voice was slow, soothing. "Drink more water."

Isabel rose to a sitting position to sip, then let her head sink back against the sofa cushion.

"Is your stomach queasy? You threw up a couple times overnight."

"A little. It just takes time."

Mother touched her cheek. "Try to go back to sleep."

Isabel's eyes filled, and tears streamed down her cheeks. "Mother, I'm ever so sorry about what happened the day Audrey..." She stifled a sob, but the tears ran faster.

"Don't talk about that now. You need to rest."

"I can't." Inside her head, she said many other things—all variations of an apology. But in the end, she must have fallen back to sleep.

"No school for you today. The only thing I want you to do is rest." Mother handed Isabel another aspirin tablet and a cup of ginger ale. A chalky light trickled through the front curtains.

"Yes, all right. But I'm feeling better."

"You're not out of the woods yet. Can't be too careful." Mother sat down heavily on the chair beside the sofa. Her pink bathrobe, frayed at the hem, bunched around her waist and thighs. Dark spots shadowed her eyes, and her face was haggard. She must have been up half the night.

Last night was a jumbled haze, like a blurry photograph. Tilting her head to the side, Isabel discovered that in the main, the throbbing pain in her temples had receded. But similar to how she'd felt after the migraine at Yosemite, her head was foggy, her stomach a touch upset. She reached for Mother's hand and held fast. Years ago, when she had caught the flu or woken from a nightmare, Mother had done this, too—kept vigil at her bedside, offered steady comfort.

"Do you want a bite to eat?" Mother said.

Isabel struggled to sit. "Maybe a piece of bread. I'll get it..." But as soon as she tried to rise from the sofa, the floor spun, and she groaned.

"Lie down. You're not well enough to get around." Mother plumped a pillow for Isabel, then limped into the kitchen and returned with a plate and a mug of lukewarm tea. Isabel ate slowly, letting the tea coat her throat.

She had to try again. "Mother, I'm sorry about that day in the park..." A sob caught in her throat, but she forced herself to continue. "When I was supposed to be watching Audrey."

In the strained silence that followed, Isabel's heart stalled. She wasn't sure whether Mother had heard, or perhaps she had refused to acknowledge her apology.

"Mother, did you hear..."

Mother's face had frozen. At last she drew a labored breath. "I'll admit you gave me a shock." She sounded weary. "But it wasn't your fault. When all's said and done, Audrey was my responsibility. And if you made a few bad choices, it's because I wasn't there to set you straight."

When Mother began stroking her hair, Isabel exploded into a round of tears. She felt something like blank relief, of a pup being licked by its mom after wandering lost for days in the cold. As her body slackened, she began to drift back to sleep.

Mother murmured, "The only thing that matters is we have each other. Let's get through this the way we should have months ago. It's a chance at a fresh start."

A sudden lightness flowed through her. *Step by step.* She reached for Mother's hand.

CHAPTER THIRTY-THREE

After fourth period, Isabel caught up with Claude in the hallway. In a low voice, he asked how she had been.

She shrugged. "Mother and I are managing as best we can."

"How was Yosemite? I was terribly worried when you took ill, but I knew you were in good hands."

She fidgeted with the hem of her blouse. "I should have said something sooner, but I guess there's no time like the present. Thank you for driving me all the way out there. It was a lot to ask, and I'm grateful."

"Of course. It was the least I could do."

"And I want to apologize for how I treated you after the... accident."

He shook his head. "You don't need to say another word, Izz. You don't owe me any..."

"Yes, I do. I'm truly sorry. My behavior was uncalled for."

"It's understandable. You were in bad shock."

"But that wasn't an excuse. I shouldn't have implied you were somehow to blame."

He watched her with solicitude, his pale blue eyes flickering. "Don't blame yourself, either."

Isabel released a sigh and recalled something she'd been contemplating over the last few days. It was an observation Enid had made before they climbed the last leg to Half Dome—how some tragedies were beyond anyone's control, just terrible bad luck, though you could choose how to go on. She had refused to ease her conscience by chalking the events of that day up to fate. But it struck her that she was the only one who hadn't forgiven herself. She met Claude's gaze. "I wondered if after everything… you'd still want to be friends?"

He broke into a smile. "Fact is, I never stopped being your friend."

· · ·

The sky rumbled, and a mesh of clouds unleashed a cold, driving rain. Isabel tucked her head into her hood and hurried down the street. Puddles gathered at her feet, sloshing with bits of oakum, cigarettes, and shreds of newspaper. She stopped at the corner, debating whether to catch a trolley. *No. A waste of money.* Rain splattering her coat, she navigated around puddles. At least she was outdoors instead of stuck in the flat, but boy, how her expectations had plunged.

When she cut through a back alley in the Tenderloin, she whiffed the unmistakable reek of urine and spied the makings of a cardboard shelter by a trash bin. A hobo in a tattered shirt crouched behind it, watching her, his eyes dark and flat. With a frisson of fright, she ran on. This, then, was what she'd exchanged for Yosemite. Unbidden, Dad's words floated back to her: *Someday you'll blaze your own path. You have a strong will and a sharp mind.*

Heat rose from the pit of her stomach through her lungs as the horror of what she'd settled for took hold. No denying, she'd reversed course from a beautiful park back to a squalid neighborhood where people had few choices and little hope for anything better. Here they were trapped in body and mind alike.

The sky released an explosive crack of thunder. She jumped, heart pounding, and struggled to catch her breath. A dark thought funneled into her head. Who was she kidding? She was every bit as stuck. She had stopped thinking about how to meet the Field School requirements, fearing her chances were hopeless. No, *believing* her chances were hopeless. How could she return to Yosemite, let alone blaze a new path, when she had as good as buried the kernel of her plans? Lifting her face, she received a rapid-fire pummeling of raindrops. *Nothing to do but push through.* She tightened her hood and splashed ahead.

At the stove, Mother was frying cod. The window sash was pushed up, but the pungent, fishy odor permeated the flat. Grease splattered onto the countertop, and a small bowl of sticky flour sat by the sink.

"Letter came for you today." Mother nodded her chin at the table.

Isabel removed her sodden coat and shoes at the door, then seized the envelope. When she saw Enid's return address, she stared at it for a moment, struggling to contain a brazen gush of hope. At last she broke the seal.

After inquiring about her trip back to the city and Mother's health, Enid had written: *By the time you receive this, you'll have started school. If you decide to return to Yosemite next summer, I want you to know you're very welcome to stay again with Charlie and me. I should warn you we'll be in a tiny cabin, but at least you could continue your training for a few months. And if you return every summer until graduation, you'll meet most of the Field School admission requirements before you know it.*

Clutching the letter to her chest, Isabel pictured herself in bracing mountain air, winding her way through woods. Spending the summers in Yosemite could be just the thing to buoy her through the next few years, assuming she could find a ride to the park and back. Enid hadn't mentioned the school's requirement of completing two years of college or the equivalent, but maybe her summer training would satisfy the admissions committee. Isabel would have to investigate; she dared not leave anything to chance. Her heart clipped faster. It might have been nothing more than coincidence, but receiving Enid's letter now was like a serendipitous, gentle rain, helping a seedling unfurl.

"What did Mrs. Michael write?" Mother asked.

"She asked after you. Wanted to know how we're getting on..."

"Right kind of her." Mother flipped a piece of cod, and the pan made a sharp hiss.

Isabel hesitated. The kernel inside her stirred, desperate to free itself, no matter the cost. Surely coming clean to Mother about Audrey was the worst thing she could have shared, yet they had gotten through it and resurrected something genuine and solid. She owed Mother the truth about her plans to become a ranger. Still, recalling her bewilderment when she had last brought it up, Isabel worried it would trigger a setback to their goodwill. She stared at Mother hunching over the stove, willing her to listen without judgment.

"Mother, I want to become a ranger-naturalist. At least, I want to try."

Mother turned from the stove. "*What?*"

"I told you before it was only a pipe dream, but that's not so. I've got a plan."

Surprise streaked across Mother's face. "What does this mean? You're leaving again?"

Isabel glanced at Mother's brogans by the door, the peeling linoleum in the kitchen, the stained oilcloth, threadbare carpet in the parlor. "No, not for a while. I'll stay and finish high school."

Mother's face relaxed imperceptibly. She turned off the gas, laid the plate of cod on the table, and sank into a chair across from Isabel.

"Mrs. Michael has invited me to stay with her next summer."

"Already? You just got here!" Mother's voice climbed in indignation.

"June is months away. I'm just planning ahead."

"For what?"

Drawing a breath, Isabel described her plan to apply to the Yosemite Field School for Rangers after she had finished high school and possibly two years of college classes. "It'll take plenty of time, and I'll have to save up." She added that the chances for women to gain admission, let alone ranger-naturalist positions, were low. "But that's where Mrs. Michael might help, since she's been employed at Yosemite for so many years." *Against all odds*.

"Why on earth do you want to be a ranger?" Mother frowned. "Mrs. Michael talked you into it, didn't she? You were at that park for barely over two months, and all of a sudden you want to do what she's doing. Monkey see, monkey do."

Isabel gazed at the ceiling and clenched her hands in her lap. "She didn't talk me into anything. I decided by myself."

"How is that even a job for a woman? Traipsing through woods and running up cliffs! It's unseemly."

Isabel hid a scowl, then forced herself to say calmly, "Before I made it to Yosemite, I hadn't the faintest idea it was possible. But Mrs. Michael has proven that women can be just as good ranger-naturalists as men." *If not better*.

Mother shot her a skeptical look, and Isabel wrestled over how to help her understand. Dad would have instantly grasped what she wanted to do. But with Mother, she would have to lay things out plainly. Slowly, she recounted how she had learned the names of hundreds of plants and animals, described how hiking, gardening, and guiding nature walks gave her a thrill — a freedom she had never experienced in the city.

"And that's not all. Ranger-naturalists publish articles about the plants and animals. So I can write and edit, too." A park naturalist's job, she explained, was to observe, guide, and capture their findings, all while conserving wild spaces and inspiring visitors.

As Mother listened, a thin glimmer of pride, even grudging admiration, stood in her eyes.

"But like I said, the whole thing will take time and money. And there aren't any guarantees."

"When I learned Mrs. Michael was a ranger, it surprised me to no end. First I heard of a woman ranger."

"I'd never heard of it, either. Not until I met her. But it's sure not easy. Every year she has to reapply for her position. Plus her supervisor is a horribly conceited man who constantly criticizes her, even though she's more knowledgeable about all manner of plants and birds and the back country than any male ranger." As far as Isabel was concerned, this was the truth—and that didn't even count the climbs Enid had done up cliffs, with only her bare hands.

"Imagine. Is she really?"

"Yes, but the male naturalists refuse to give her credit." Isabel was sure she'd mentioned these details about Enid before, but for the first time, Mother was really listening.

"Then why does she put up with it? Why not find something else?"

"She loves her job. At least when she climbs and gardens and helps visitors. It's hard to explain how it feels, Mother. When I went hiking in the mountains, it was almost as though a little piece of me was soaring over the trees. Out there, it seems like time slows down. You notice all sorts of birds and plants and animals. It's like a wide space inside you opens up."

"Hmm." Mother pressed her lips together as she considered. "Mighty different from what you'd find around here, that's for sure."

"That's why I want to return to Yosemite next summer, to continue my training. Assuming I can get there." She waited a beat. "Only if you can spare me."

"This sure means an awful lot to you."

"Yes. And how."

"It's the most unusual thing I've ever heard. For a girl or woman."

Isabel went still, waiting for Mother to object.

"Don't look so terrified. I won't stop you."

Isabel released a breath and gripped Mother's hands. "You really *do* see?" She thought it unlikely she would ever fully understand. After all, Mother's world was shrunken down to hard, desperate facts. And for those struggling to get by, it was difficult to envision anything beyond the next crummy meal or paycheck. Mere months ago, that had been her own situation.

"Sounds finer than any job you'd find in San Francisco." Mother inclined her chin. "I just hope you'll get to live somewhere nicer than this. You're still young. You've got time."

A bud of joy sprang up inside her. "You're not old, either, Mother."

Mother gave a short, sarcastic bark. "The time for me to try new things has passed."

"It's never too late," she protested. She hadn't told Mother that Enid was in her fifties and age didn't matter; taking advantage of the time you had was what counted. But for now she had said enough. She might convince her another day. "Becoming a ranger-naturalist isn't a sure thing. Especially since the Field School female grads hardly ever get hired. It's only a possibility. But I've got to give it a shot."

That, she realized, was the crux of what she wanted: the freedom to make her own decisions and forge her way forward, even as a girl. The next time she returned to Yosemite, it would be to make a life there—not to escape the things she hoped to forget.

CHAPTER THIRTY-FOUR

Isabel considered it one of San Francisco's oddest facts that the city temperature peaked in September. Today, near the end of the month, she didn't even need her cardigan. When she entered the grocery, a jazz number was playing low on the radio. She walked behind the register, where Mr. McGilligan was stooping to adjust the dial.

He straightened with a grin. "Remember that big shipment of canned spinach we got in last week that we thought wouldn't move?"

She nodded.

"Well, it's plumb gone."

"Already? Gee, that's good news."

"Not surprising, considering how popular those Popeye shorts have gotten. Now all the mothers have a reason to serve green vegetables."

"Clever way to convince kids to eat spinach."

"Aye, that it is," Mr. McGilligan imitated Popeye's rough twang, then shoved his pipe into the corner of his mouth and winked.

Isabel laughed. "What do you want me to do today?"

"You have such a good eye that I thought you could arrange the store window. Spruce it up with something new."

"Really? You mean it?"

"Go to town. Try whatever you see fit."

She thanked her lucky stars Mr. McGilligan had let her have her old job back. When she returned to the store in late August to inquire again about openings, he had informed her that Billy, the kid he'd hired over the summer, was indeed working fewer hours; and with business picking up ever so slightly, Mr. McGilligan could take them both on alternating afternoons of the week. He had never rebuked Isabel for her sudden, inexplicable departure to Yosemite. Instead, he had remained steadfast in his wry humor, had let her try out her ideas for improving the store, then complimented her aesthetic touches.

For the next hour, she cut colorful flour bags from the stockroom into letters that spelled McGilligan's and pasted them onto a large sheet of cardboard. At the base she arranged a can of pumpkin, a bag of sugar, and canisters of cinnamon, ginger, and nutmeg. Later in the week, she would drape yellow and orange mums and sunflowers from the school garden around the corners of the display.

"Halloween and Thanksgiving are just around the corner," she said as Mr. McGilligan admired her work. "We might as well get people thinking now about what they'll need for their menus."

He nodded, looking thoughtful. "Early advertising. You're onto something there." He tapped a finger against his chin. "I forgot to tell you, I've saved some dented cans in the back for your soup kitchen. Take them whenever you like."

She thanked him and packed the canned peas and corn into her satchel. When she had first described her idea of supplying a nearby soup kitchen with damaged items every couple of weeks, Mr. McGilligan had agreed to give it a try. So far, he had donated a dozen cans. The neighborhood baker had also given Isabel several loaves of stale bread. It was a good start, and she was planning to donate more items to a second soup kitchen in the Mission.

As editor of the paper, she had written an opinion piece, encouraging her classmates to bring tomato, corn and onion seeds to school, which they could plant and grow in the school garden. The fresh vegetables, she explained, would be a welcome addition to the local soup kitchens. In this small way, she was honoring Dad's memory by helping the disadvantaged. The garden had been beneficial in other ways, too. She had convinced the school to let her plant primrose, which she used in a replica of Enid's tea to help diminish her eczema rashes.

And now Isabel had another reason to be grateful: James was coming home for five days in mid-October—just three weeks away. She sprang around the corner and headed toward the flat, sifting through plans for what they would do while he was on leave.

On a sunny Saturday in October, Isabel, Mother, and James stood at the edge of De Laveaga Dell in Golden Gate Park. It was a secluded glen with a stream, twenty foot tree ferns, and moss-covered rocks, mottled with shadows. On either side of the stream ran footpaths, flanked by gullies. On the eastern end, closest to the Children's Playground, grew pink and purple dappled rhododendrons and azaleas. It was the only part of the dell that received a little sunlight. An unexpected oasis in San Francisco.

Over the last month, Mother's back had improved, but she moved cautiously to avoid flares or reinjuries. Though the textile factory job hadn't panned out, she had been invited to a second interview for a sewing position at a tailor shop. During the first interview, she had met the man who would be her boss, and next she was scheduled to meet the shop's owner. They were hopeful her luck would hold, and it would be the perfect break, allowing her to sew and stay off her feet while keeping her spine upright.

Isabel withdrew the packet of lupine seeds, a twist of soil, and a spade from her knapsack. Per Enid's instructions months ago, she had scratched the seeds and soaked them overnight in lukewarm water. According to Enid, fall was the best time to plant.

"Lupines are beautiful and hardy," Isabel said. Enid had explained they were perennials; the dead could be replaced each year by fresh progeny, grown from their ancestors' seeds. Mother and James watched as she dug three holes opposite the rhododendrons and filled each with soil. She handed seeds to Mother and James. "In memory of Dad and Audrey." Kneeling, they dropped a seed into each of the three holes, which Isabel covered with soil.

"Now they'll bloom in a place they both liked." She recalled the day years before when they had all picnicked at the Golden Gate Park, played tag and tossed rings, then walked through the grounds, admiring the trees and flowers. She was hopeful the lupine would thrive here.

"This is a perfect spot, Izz," James said, nodding at the stream and trees.

Mother said, "We'll come back every summer to watch them bloom."

At the mention of summer, Isabel flushed with anticipation. In June, she would return to Yosemite to continue her training with Enid. By then, James would have another short leave; and if all went well, they could travel to the park together. In the meantime, to be sure she satisfied every last Field School requirement, Isabel had visited the library and discovered that San Francisco State Teacher's College offered classes at a tuition of forty dollars a year. It was an awful lot of money, but she hoped that by working longer hours at Mr. McGilligan's or elsewhere, she could save up enough cash to attend one or two years of college classes after high school. Perhaps, if she were lucky, she might earn a scholarship to further reduce her tuition.

Her mind fluttered with the possibilities. But that was far in the future, and she returned her attention to the dell. Sunlight skimmed and danced along the shadows of the trees.

Like the stunning view from the summit of Half Dome, these massive, old-growth redwood and sequoia trees soothed Isabel, with their reminder that her life was part of something larger, wilder, longer lasting. Even here, in this small grove within the city, she could immerse herself in Nature, admire its timelessness and wild beauty and feel the disconsonant pieces of herself snapping into place, growing and stretching.

They ate their picnic lunch beneath a grove of cypress and live oak on the banks of Alvord Lake, near the park's Haight Street entrance. On the opposite side of the lake, a peacock strutted across the lawn, and a squirrel chittered at them in the tree overhead.

James pointed at the squirrel. "That fellow seems to think we've stolen his spot. He sounds downright angry."

"Maybe it's a she," Isabel teased. "Think of that?"

"Sure. Her spot. Aiming every ounce of her energy at us to show her displeasure."

Mother tipped her head to watch. "That's how I think of Audrey. How did you put it? Aiming her energy. But in a good way. She was excited, looking forward to things. Must have gotten it from your father. He was like that, too."

"They were like hummingbirds. Always in motion," Isabel said.

James nodded. "Imaginative, optimistic, energetic, one of a kind."

Isabel glanced at her brother. "A precious flower, not at all like any that grew in the garden." He locked his gaze with hers, and she knew he remembered the last line of *The Velveteen Rabbit*, too.

After lunch, they strolled past the Children's Playground, toward Bowling Green and the tennis courts. The afternoon spread before them, expansive and rare, like a holiday.

Mother said, "I can't remember the last time we had a vacation."

Isabel tucked her hand in James' left arm, and Mother took his right, and they promenaded down the path. Sunshine glinted across Isabel's face. She closed her eyes briefly and drank in the fresh air. Somewhere near the lake, a songbird twittered.

CHAPTER THIRTY-FIVE

June 1938

From the cupboard, Mother withdrew a jug of homemade cherry wine and poured it into two small mason jars. "Been saving this for a special occasion, and what better time than now?"

Isabel clinked her jar against Mother's, and they savored the sweet tang. An electric charge zipped through her. "I can't believe it's finally happening." Four months ago, she had been stunned to receive a formal admission to the Yosemite Field School. Competition had been fierce, with only fourteen men and six women selected from hundreds of applicants.

"You worked hard for this. You deserve it."

"A woman has to work twice as hard as a man..."

"To get half the credit," Mother finished.

For the last two years after high school, Isabel had taken classes at San Francisco State Teacher's College while working as a stenographer in the school's administrative offices. The small salary she earned paid her tuition. Over the last four summers, she had continued training with Enid, shoring up her knowledge of Yosemite's botany and geology. She had even accompanied Enid on a week-long hike into the high country. Enid had written her a stellar recommendation, vouching personally for Isabel's detailed knowledge of the plant's flora and fauna and her ability to complete rigorous hikes.

"You've got a big day tomorrow," Mother said. "You should get to bed early."

"I will. Listen, I have an idea. When you visit, we'll plant some of the lupine seeds from the Golden Gate Park in Mrs. Michael's wildflower garden. Continue the tradition there."

"Hmm. Full circle," Mother said. Every summer, they visited the Golden Gate Park to watch the lupines bloom and replace the dead flowers with offspring born from their seeds. Mother's eyes clouded. "It'll be strange being all by myself after you go."

"But you're visiting in August, and James is only a train ride away." Her brother had found a job near Santa Cruz, where he had a steady girl. "And I'll come back to see you whenever I'm able."

"Don't worry about me. It's only right that you two move on with your lives. That's what young people do."

"Not just young people."

"When you get to be my age, you simply don't have the energy."

"Mother, that's not true. You have plenty of energy." A year after Mother landed the job at the tailor's, her back had improved enough that she started joining Isabel on excursions to the park and wharf. Last May, when the Golden Gate Bridge was finally completed, Isabel and Mother had crossed it together, wind cupping their cheeks. They had marveled at the shimmering bay below with its white sailboats, had thrilled at being suspended high above the water while automobiles rushed past them.

Isabel had a sudden thought. "You should find yourself a new place. Something bigger and newer, maybe near Russian Hill."

Mother's head dipped up, and for an instant, Isabel glimpsed a young girl's anticipation in her eyes.

"It's high time you did. You can afford something better. You've saved up a nice little nest egg over the last few years."

"Well. I don't think... moving's an awful big hassle."

"James and I can help. You'd enjoy a nicer place. You can do it, Mother."

"Hmm. Do you really think..." She frowned. "Maybe... I could, couldn't I?" Her voice held a tinge of wonder.

Isabel grabbed her hands. "Yes, Mother, of course you can!" On a lark, she pulled her to her feet and whirled her around the flat, imitating Enid's polka steps.

"What on earth?" Mother cried in mock reproach, bright splotches blooming on her cheeks. After a couple of rounds they collapsed, tittering, onto the sofa.

When Mother went to bed, Isabel had a sudden craving for a gust of cold air. On the front stoop, she gripped the corrugated metal rail and stared down at the street. Automobiles whizzed by, and neon lights flashed at the bar. Years ago, when they had moved to the Tenderloin, she had loathed their downgraded quarters, had assumed that recovering what they'd lost would be next to impossible. But now that Mother had agreed to consider finding a new place, Isabel saw that the flat wasn't an end-of-the-line tenement, after all. It was a way station to something else, something better.

The Field School was another way station. Isabel assured herself that if she didn't find a ranger-naturalist position after the program ended, she would try another avenue: apply to be a park secretary, stenographer, even an assistant editor for *Yosemite Nature Notes*. She had beaten the odds once by getting admitted. Why shouldn't she beat them again, no matter if it took time? And that alone, having a plan, gave her a small thrill.

She closed her eyes, enjoying the sensation of the wind battering her arms and legs. For a fleeting moment, as she let herself go still, the din from the bar and the traffic receded, and she saw a lush valley surrounded by steep cliffs.

"We made it, Audrey," she whispered. It had been months, even years since she had thought long and hard about the Isle of

Castaways. But when she examined it now in her mind's eye, she saw that it had changed. It wasn't so much a place as a conscious choice. An attempt to forge a path that matched the hope inside her. She wasn't running to forget or escape; she was traveling deliberately.

The San Francisco sky didn't come close to the Yosemite big top of stars, where constellations winked back like thousands of fireflies spilling from a glass jar, unrestrained. From the stoop, Isabel could barely see beyond the city lights. But in under two days, she would stand at the rim of the majestic Sierra Nevada Mountains and drink in the crisp fragrance of pines. She concentrated on this moment—the feel of her hand on the railing, the wind kiting through her hair, her excitement about returning to Yosemite, attending the Field School. A beginning, but also the culmination of the many moments that had led her here. She took a last look at the street, then turned and went inside.

ACKNOWLEDGMENTS

I am deeply indebted to the following people for their support, encouragement, and willingness to read passages and early drafts, sometimes multiple times!

A big thanks to Melissa Hurley, Heather Bell Adams, Caleb Rocke, Janice Horner, and Louise Jensen for their feedback on early versions!

I am also extremely grateful to my critique partners—Linda Ulleseit, Jen Olson, and Laura Beeby, who read large passages multiple times and provided me with excellent food for thought.

I would like to thank the Women's Fiction Writers' Association (WFWA) and fellow members Maria Daversa, Kerry Chaput, Jen Craven, and Kim O'Brien for reading sample chapters and offering input. Thanks also to Jean Roberts, Samie Facciolo, and Joane Luesse for their comments.

A special thanks to Reagan Rothe and the Black Rose Writing Team for bringing this book into the world!

Last but not least, I am eternally grateful for the support of my husband, Dan, and our daughter, Lara.

AUTHOR'S NOTE

While *The View from Half Dome* is a work of fiction, Enid Michael, her husband Charles, her supervisor Bert Harwell, and Ansel and Virginia Adams were real people; and the Cascades Civilian Conservation Corps (CCC) camp at Yosemite operated from 1933 to 1942. For accuracy, I drew information about these people and places from historical archives and papers.

Enid Michael was born Enid Reeve on May 27, 1883 in Gilroy, California. She moved to Los Angeles with her family in 1897 and worked as a third grade teacher in Pasadena from 1907 to 1918 before marrying Charles Michael, Assistant Postmaster of Yosemite. Both Enid and Charles were elite climbers who prided themselves on not using ropes.

Though not a university graduate, Enid was an astute field observer of birds, mammals, and plants. Because of her persistence and extensive knowledge of botany and ornithology, she served from 1921 to 1942 as a seasonal park ranger — Yosemite's first female naturalist. In this position, she conducted bird and nature walks, taught at the Yosemite School of Field History, and authored over five hundred articles — the largest body of writing on Yosemite.

By 1929, she had collected and mounted 1,000 plant specimens and recorded 120 different species of birds. Her biggest accomplishment was the creation and management of a wildflower garden behind the Yosemite Museum, which she hoped would inspire visitors to cherish and ultimately preserve the national parks. Annually Enid had to reapply for her appointment as ranger-naturalist. In particular, she faced opposition from her supervisor, Chief Naturalist Bert Harwell, who disagreed with how she had organized plants in the wildflower garden. He also criticized her "slovenly" appearance and the way she delivered talks "in a high-pitched sing-song voice." Moreover, he argued that the Civilian Conservation Corps boys who helped with the garden would be better directed by a male naturalist.

In 1935, Enid's husband retired because of heart problems, and the couple moved to Pasadena, though they continued to spend their summers at Yosemite. In 1943, Enid's position, along with all seasonal ranger-naturalist positions, was eliminated because of World War II. She died in Pasadena on February 11, 1966, at the age of eighty-two.

Enid and Charles Michael were close friends with Ansel and Virginia Adams, the famous Yosemite photographer and his wife. The Adams were outspoken advocates for environmental conservation. Ansel first visited Yosemite in 1916, when he began photographing its stunning beauty. Virginia grew up in Yosemite, where her father owned an art studio. Both Ansel and Virginia were active members of the Sierra Club and served on its Board of Directors.

The following books and articles were extremely helpful in my research for *The View from Half Dome:*

Federal Writers Project of the Works Progress Administration, Introduction by David Kipen. *San Francisco in the 1930s: The WPA Guide to the City by the Bay.* Berkeley and Los Angeles, California: University of California Press, 2011. (original publication date 1940).

Knoss, Trent. *"The Story of Enid Michael, Yosemite's First Female Naturalist."* backpacker.com, July 12, 2016.

Muir, John. *The Yosemite.* New York: The Century Company, 1912.

Orr, Lois. *"The Civilian Conservation Corps (CCCC) in Yosemite."* Yosemite: A Journal for Members of the Yosemite Association, Volume 67, Number 4, Fall 2005.

Penalosa, Fernando, Editor. *The Joy of Yosemite: Selected Writings of Enid Michael, Pioneer Ranger Naturalist.* Rancho Palos Verdes, California: Quaking Aspen Books, 2004.

Penalosa, Fernando. *Yosemite in the 1930s, A Remembrance.* Rancho Palos Verdes, California: Quaking Aspen Books, 2002.

Rhudy, Lisa. *"Enid Michael."* Yosemite Nature Notes 46(2), 1977.

Selters, Andy. *"Enid Michael, Yosemite's First Woman Naturalist, Was a Badass Climber Too."* adventure-journal.com, February 13, 2020.

United States Department of the Interior, National Park Service. *Yosemite National Park Brochure.* Washington: United States Government Printing Office, 1935.

"Virginia Best Adams: The Woman Behind the Legend," The Ansel Adams Gallery: December 31, 2020.

Additionally, credit for cited snippets from the public domain goes to Margery Williams, author of *The Velveteen Rabbit* (original publication date of 1922), and Emily Dickinson, collected poems (first published in 1890).

ABOUT THE AUTHOR

Jill Caugherty is the author of the debut historical novel *Waltz in Swing Time*, set in Depression-era Utah. Her short stories have been published in *805Lit*, *Oyster River Pages*, *The Potato Soup Journal*, *The Prospectus Blog*, and *The Magazine of History and Fiction*. After holding software development, product management, and marketing positions in the high tech industry for nearly thirty years, she now writes full time. Jill is a member of the Women's Fiction Writers' Association and the North Carolina Writers' Network. She lives in Raleigh, North Carolina with her husband and daughter.

Please visit
https://www.jillcaugherty.com
for more information.

NOTE FROM THE AUTHOR

Word-of-mouth is crucial for any author to succeed. If you enjoyed *The View from Half Dome*, please leave a review online — anywhere you are able, even if it's just a sentence or two. It would make all the difference and would be very much appreciated.

Thanks!
Jill Caugherty

We hope you enjoyed reading this title from:

BLACK ROSE
writing™

www.blackrosewriting.com

Subscribe to our mailing list – *The Rosevine* – and receive **FREE** books, daily deals, and stay current with news about upcoming releases and our hottest authors.
Scan the QR code below to sign up.

Already a subscriber? Please accept a sincere thank you for being a fan of Black Rose Writing authors.

View other Black Rose Writing titles at www.blackrosewriting.com/books and use promo code **PRINT** to receive a **20% discount** when purchasing.

CPSIA information can be obtained
at www.ICGtesting.com
Printed in the USA
LVHW031130160523
747047LV00005B/630